TRUB

RED

RUBY REDFORT

LAUREN CHILD

TAKE YOUR LAST BREATH

CANDLEWICK PRESS

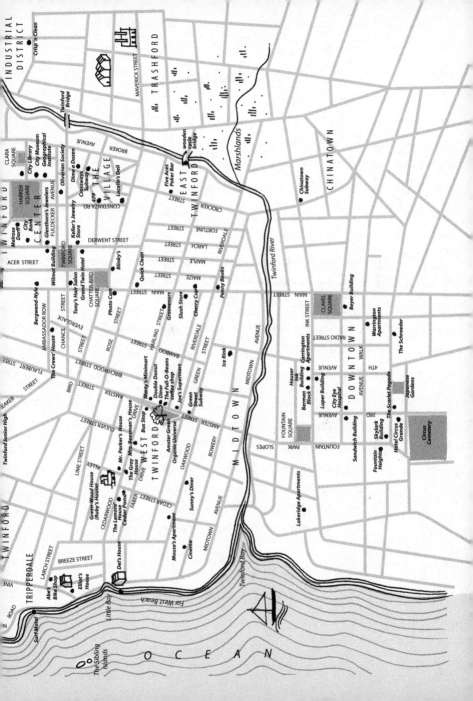

For **Helena**

Copyright © 2012 by Lauren Child
Series design by David Mackintosh

First published in Great Britain by HarperCollins Children's Books, a division of HarperCollinsPublishers Ltd

First U.S. paperback edition in this format 2018

Library of Congress Catalog Card Number 2012955155
ISBN 978-0-7636-5468-9 (hardcover)
ISBN 978-0-7636-6932-4 (paperback)
ISBN 978-1-5362-0048-5 (reformatted paperback)

18 19 20 21 22 23 BVG 10 9 8 7 6 5 4 3 2 1

Printed in Berryville, VA, U.S.A.

This book was typeset in Eames Century Modern.

Candlewick Press
99 Dover Street
Somerville, Massachusetts 02144

visit us at www.candlewick.com

The Old Seafarers' Legend

They say it can lure a child to a watery grave, that it can strangle the breath from the strongest man. Some say it can persuade a stranger to tell his darkest secret.

Coming Up for Air

THE SUN FLICKERED ON THE OCEAN, cutting bright diamonds of light into the surface of the indigo water. A three-year-old girl was peering over the side of a sailboat, staring down into the deep. The only sounds came from her parents' laughter, the singsong hum of a man's voice, and the clapping of the waves against the yacht.

Gradually the sounds became less and less distinct until the girl was quite alone with the ocean. It seemed to be pulling her, drawing her to it ... confiding a secret, almost whispering to her.

She barely felt herself fall as she tipped forward and slipped into the soft ink of the sea.

Down she twisted, her arms, her legs above her like tendrils. The water felt smooth and perfectly cold; fish darted and silver things whisked by — her breath bubbled up as transparent pearls.

Then suddenly, like a snap of the fingers, all the fish were gone: it was just the girl in the big wide ocean.

But she wasn't quite alone.

There *was* something else.

Something calling to her, but she couldn't see what. *It* saw *her* though, with ancient eyes, unblinking as it steadily pulsed its way through the blue. Something with long, long snaking arms hovering between her and nothing.

And then, vine-like, the thing coiled a limb around her ankle and tugged her firmly in the direction of infinity. Down to who knew where.

Oops, thought the child. And on she spun. Bubbles fizzed about her, and her head began to throb, her breath almost gone.

And then *yank*! Something grabbed her arm, some*one* grabbed her arm. The strangling-thing released her — suddenly she was coming up for air, breaking through the surface of the ocean.

She found herself slapped mackerel-like onto the hot deck of the boat, coughing saltwater from her lungs. Her green eyes blinked open and she smiled up at two troubled faces. She felt the water dribble from her ears, and heard the sound of the gulls screaming in the sky above.

An Ordinary Kid

WHEN RUBY REDFORT WAS FOUR, she noticed something unnoticeable while reading the back of the Choco Puffles box. What looked like a word-search game to every other breakfast-eating kid, she could see at a glance was in fact some kind of message — a code.

It took Ruby five days and seven helpings of Choco Puffles to puzzle it out, and when she had, this is what she read.

Fill in this coupon and win a lifetime supply of Choco Puffles. Entry address can be found somewhere on this package. WARNING: you will have to search long and hard to find it.

Ruby found the address in thirty-two seconds, cut out the coupon on the side of the box, filled in her name and address, popped it in an envelope, and asked her father to mail it.

He forgot.

Ruby discovered this thirteen and three-quarter months later when she was searching her dad's pockets for confiscated Hubble-Yum bubble gum. There, in his gray suit jacket, was the slightly battered envelope, addressed in her handwriting, stamp in the top right-hand corner. The deadline had long passed.

Ruby took the letter up to her room and slipped it into the secret hiding place she had made within the door frame of her bedroom. It was a shame about the lifetime supply of Choco Puffles; they were, after all, her favorite breakfast cereal.

Some several years later . . .

CHAPTER 1
Don't Back Away or They Will See You as Prey

IT'S PERFECT WEATHER CONDITIONS FOR SHARKS," announced the dive instructor. "So don't be surprised if you run into one or two. Don't go panicking or anything."

Ruby Redfort spat in her diving mask and rubbed at the lenses, rinsing them with seawater. Her fellow students were checking their gear, zipping up their wet suits, and snapping on fins.

Ruby, a newly recruited Spectrum agent, was attending a dive camp at a secluded location on one of Hawaii's many islands. The dive master was an affable sort; he had tutored so many agents during his years as an instructor that they all sort of merged into one, with the exception of Ruby.

Agent Redfort kind of stood out from the crowd.

A thirteen-year-old schoolgirl not even five feet in fins, sleek dark hair parted to one side, neatly secured with a barrette above her right eye, it was hard to ignore *her*. Aside from anything else, she was the only dive student here still attending junior high.

Everyone else had long since graduated school; everyone else was in full-time Spectrum employment. Ruby hadn't even heard of Spectrum six weeks ago.

This, in itself, wasn't surprising. Not many people had heard of Spectrum. It was an organization so secret that access to its headquarters could change from day to day, hour to hour. Once you exited, you could never be quite sure you would ever find your way back: which was just the way Spectrum liked it.

Spectrum — a spy agency set up to foil the plots and plans of evil geniuses capable of grand theft, extortion, fraud, and murder — did not employ agents who were less than a hundred percent smart and a hundred percent discreet. As far as LB was concerned, "You mess up, you leave forever."

LB — the big cheese, the top dog, the head honcho in charge of Spectrum 8 — was not big on second chances, so the odds of getting kicked out were high, and Ruby would have lost her agent status almost before she'd begun if it hadn't been for one thing: she was brilliant.

Actually, brilliant was an understatement. Ruby Redfort was a genius: her specialty lay in puzzles and codes. In fact, she had won the Junior Code-Cracker Championships when she was just seven, and the following year was offered a place at Harvard

University, though she had turned it down flat. She didn't want to be regarded as some kind of geek freak.

It was because of this phenomenal skill at cracking codes that LB had recruited Ruby. The Spectrum 8 boss had no desire to employ a kid. Kids could be trouble, LB knew that — but what choice did she have? Her ace code breaker, Lopez, had been murdered at the hand of Count von Viscount, a villain so dreaded that one shivered to speak his name.

When one dared to speak his name at all.

Ruby had first encountered LB about a month ago, on her first visit to the Spectrum offices. The spy boss had been dressed entirely in white and sitting behind a huge desk that dominated an entirely white office; the red polish on her toenails being the only flash of color in the room. At fifty-something she looked both beautiful and intimidating: one tough cookie. Ruby was a confident, somewhat fearless kid, but she instinctively knew that in LB she had met her match: an intelligent woman who did not suffer fools gladly. In fact did not suffer them at all.

It was fair to say Ruby hadn't exactly followed orders during the weeks spent working on her first Spectrum assignment, but she had foiled the Fool's Gold Gang and prevented Count von Viscount from stealing the priceless Jade Buddha of Khotan.

It was for this reason that LB had granted Ruby Redfort a second chance, and for this reason that she was now being trained at the Spectrum dive camp.

"If you do come face-to-face with one of our ocean friends," continued the dive instructor, "then just stay where you are. Don't back away. If it comes toward you, then swim toward it. He'll probably get the message."

"Oh, yeah," said Ruby. "And what message is that?"

"That you aren't lunch. Lunch usually swims in the other direction," said the dive instructor with a wink.

"And what if this shark ain't so smart?" asked Ruby. "What then?"

"Then," said the dive master, "it will probably try to explore you with its teeth. That's how they check things out. Only you don't really want them to do so as it could mean waving bye-bye to an arm or a leg."

"Well, I kinda need my arms for waving — my legs sorta tend to come in handy too," said Ruby.

"So that's why I suggest you swim with this stick." The instructor picked up a retractable aluminum pole. "If said shark gets too near, just prod him and he'll most likely back off."

"And if he doesn't?" asked one of the other divers — a guy

named Bosco. He was trying to sound casual, but you could tell the whole mentioning of sharks thing had him worried.

The dive master smiled. "Then try to look unappetizing."

Ruby rolled her eyes.

"Don't worry, Redfort," said the dive instructor, chuckling. "It's highly unlikely the sharks will want to snack on you — far too small."

"On the other hand," said Kip Holbrook, another of Ruby's fellow trainees, "maybe the kid's the perfect bite-size portion."

"Funny, really funny," said Ruby. She pulled down her mask and fell backward off the boat.

Ruby Redfort was not scared of sharks — not yet anyway.

CHAPTER 2
One Drop Could Save Your Life

NOW, THERE ARE A FEW LOGISTICAL PROBLEMS involved in being a schoolkid secret agent, the most obvious one being: how to get enough time off class to carry out your secret-agenting missions.

Not easy. But Ruby Redfort was a good persuader: she could convince most people of most things. She avoided "complete" untruths if at all possible, preferring to steer clear of certain topics. Her tactic was to leave out various details, keep the picture blurry; this wasn't so much lying as being economical with the facts. As far as this particular trip went, Ruby's friends believed her to be on a family vacation over spring break. She hadn't told them that she was with her family; she hadn't told them she was on vacation; they had just put two and two together and come to this conclusion.

As far as Ruby's parents were concerned, Ruby was on a school dive trip: "An opportunity not to be missed," was how Ruby had sold it to them. She had not actually told them that it was a school dive trip, but they had naturally made this assumption.

RULE 65: PEOPLE BELIEVE WHAT THEY WANNA BELIEVE.

In other words, if they expect you to be on a school dive trip, then they'll assume that that's where you are.

Ruby's personal dive instructor was Agent Kekoa. Ruby had never seen Kekoa in anything but swim gear or dive suits, and her hair — black, long, and sleek — was always tied neatly back from her face in a practical way.

Kekoa was the strong, silent type, not what you would on the whole call blabby; she only spoke if there was something she really needed to say. Perhaps this was a habit developed in the ocean, where talking was not an option. Or perhaps she had found the career that perfectly suited a person who didn't particularly need to share.

Ruby, on the other hand, was indeed a talker. She often found it hard to keep her mouth shut, and so to her, Agent Kekoa was a conundrum.

"But what if I need to tell you something — urgently I mean?" said Ruby.

"Signal," replied Kekoa.

"Yeah, but I mean, how many signals are there?"

"Enough," said Kekoa.

"But I mean, what if I need to say something that there isn't a signal *for*?"

"Then keep it for later."

"So you're saying there's no gadget for underwater talking?"

"There is," replied Kekoa. "But I don't use it. Much better to listen with your ears, your eyes, your hands; use all your senses and keep your mouth shut. Just . . ." Kekoa drew her fingers across her lips. Her meaning couldn't have been clearer: *keep it to yourself, zip it,* or *shut your cake hole,* depending on how polite you thought she was being.

Ruby shrugged, put her regulator in her mouth, and sank beneath the waves. Of course, Kekoa was right. Signals did the job fine. There was no need for words down here, and Ruby, despite her talkative nature, enjoyed this watery universe full of sounds rather than voices.

As they swam deeper into the ocean, they saw some incredible marine life, passed cities of coral, met creatures that were beautiful, a few that were lethal, and several that were both. Useful to know the difference, but the general rule seemed to be, don't touch! A lot of these things could sting, and some of these stings could kill.

If you *were* unfortunate enough to brush tentacles with something unfriendly, then there was still hope. Each Spectrum agent was equipped with a tiny vial of anti-sting Miracle antidote, just enough to save a life if administered at once. It came in a little fluorescent orange envelope bearing a tiny logo of a fly, with a picture showing the canister attached to the zipper of a dive suit. It was very discreet and looked like it was just part of the design, a tag or something.

The label said:

ANTIDOTE SERUM FOR SEVERE UNDERWATER STINGS
Administer fast for successful results.
CONTAINS ONE DOSE.

Followed by the caution:

Attach canister to wet-suit zipper and
DO NOT REMOVE.

Kekoa repeated this particular instruction more than once. "Keep it attached to the zipper on your dive suit and never be without it. These few drops could be the most important liquid you ever tasted. You understand?"

Ruby had nodded. She had no intention of letting go of the tiny life-saving tincture. Why would she? Only a total bozo would deliberately part company with a piece of gear that could prevent his or her death.

Once the dive basics had been mastered, Ruby picked up other skills. She learned how to navigate underwater in daylight and in moonlight and, finally, in pitch-dark swimming through underwater caves. It was here that Ruby came up against the one thing she was *truly* afraid of.

Small confined spaces. Spaces that might be short on air. Spaces where you might find yourself gasping for breath. Spaces where you were highly likely to die.

They brought on her deepest fear: her claustrophobia.

As Ruby discovered, claustrophobia made cave navigation *particularly* challenging. A large part of underwater caving was about discovering ways in: fissures in rocks that led to secret caves, to spaces inhabited only by sea life. Sometimes the rock entrance would appear impossibly small, but with a certain amount of contortion and expertise one could make it in and hopefully out. How to look for telltale signs of ways *out* was a key part of the training, for obvious reasons. Ruby had rarely been so grateful to learn anything before.

The less time she had to spend in underwater caves, the better — in fact, she wished quite fervently never to have to go in one again.

It was a wish that wasn't going to be granted.

CHAPTER 3
Plankton and Sea Cucumbers

DURING DIVE TRAINING, Ruby was also given instruction in unarmed underwater combat. This was even harder than it might sound. Punching underwater was a little like running in space. The trick seemed to be to disable your opponent by cutting off their air supply, or releasing their dive weights. Kekoa was an expert: she was slight and she was fast, and Ruby mastered dodges and grips and tackles.

Agent Kip Holbrook was Ruby's in-training dive partner, and the two of them spent a whole lot of time winding each other up.

"Redfort, you call that a punch? I coulda sworn I just got patted on the nose by a plankton."

"Holbrook, you call that a nose? I coulda sworn I just spotted a rare and ugly sea cucumber."

They got along like a house on fire.

Ruby particularly looked forward to mealtimes. Ruby Redfort might be shrimp-size compared to the other trainee agents, but she'd always had a big appetite, and Spectrum camp food was surprisingly good. On the whole, she was having a pretty good time; her fellow trainees were a friendly bunch, and hanging out on a Hawaiian island was no huge chore. Everything was swell.

Well, except for Sergeant Cooper.

"Redfort! Get your sorry behind out of that bunk before I inhale my next breath or tonight you and your bed ain't even gonna make contact."

This order — given every daybreak by Sergeant Cooper, the drill sergeant employed by Spectrum to "motivate" — was beginning to wear.

Oh, brother, thought Ruby. She was not a natural early bird, and so would reluctantly and with some effort drag herself from her uncomfortable bunk. More than once she had found herself scrubbing the bathroom floor with an orange toothbrush (her own) — punishment detail.

If Sergeant Cooper wasn't impressed by Ruby's time-keeping, then her flouting of the camp dress code really got him marching up and down. His least favorite item was a T-shirt printed with the words: ***could you repeat that? I wasn't actually listening.***

"Redfort, how many times have I told you about that T-shirt of yours?"

"I'm sorry Sergeant Cooper, I haven't been counting, but I can take a wild guess if it's important to you."

Sergeant Cooper was keen to put Ruby "back in her box" whenever he got the chance. He was under the misguided impression that this hard-nut approach would instill respect in the kid.

He was wrong about that.

One such time was when Ruby had done particularly badly in her free-dive training, free diving being the art of swimming underwater unaided by any breathing apparatus. Ruby's parents were big fans of free diving; indeed, her father, Brant, had gone to Stanton University on a free-dive scholarship.

In fact, free diving was how Ruby's parents had met. Brant had been working with a famous Italian marine biologist, free-diving from his yacht off the coast of Italy. Sabina had been sailing single-handed around the Mediterranean and had bumped into Brant underwater. She was pretty good at holding her breath too, championship good.

As a result, there wasn't a lot that Ruby didn't know about breath-hold diving, but for the life of her she just couldn't begin to contemplate holding her breath for a whole lot longer than seemed entirely sensible. It went against everything that was natural and sane. Dive down 220 feet without oxygen? No thank you. It was a claustrophobic's nightmare. The free-dive training involved a lot of slow, rigorous preparation — years of it, in fact. It was a difficult and dangerous technique to master, and Ruby wasn't about to risk her life for something that seemed so wrong. Diving to great depths with scuba gear: no problem. Diving with a snorkel and fins: a breeze. But ask her to hold her breath for more than one minute and one second? No way was she gonna do that. She didn't have the lung capacity, which, combined with the darkness at great depths, made her feel claustrophobic.

On Thursday she resurfaced just as Sergeant Cooper walked by. This chance encounter was not a good one.

COOPER: *Well, well, well, look who it is. Agent Redfort coming up for air.*

REDFORT: *Jeepers, I should have stayed down a few minutes longer.*

COOPER: *I doubt that you are capable of that, Redfort. I hear you can only make one minute, hardly a record.*

REDFORT: *If I'd known I was going to be coming face-to-face with a giant sea cucumber when I next took a lungful, I might have put some effort in.*

COOPER: *You don't know what effort is, Redfort. Now, Bradley Baker, he really could hold his breath. Seven minutes, I heard. Years and years of hard work and training.*

REDFORT: *No kidding. Were you standing there holding the towel?*

COOPER: *It would have been a privilege to hand that young man his towel. You should take note: Baker also started his Spectrum duty as a kid — younger'n you an' smarter'n you too.*

REDFORT: *What? That's meant to bug me?*

But of course, it did bug her. This Bradley Baker guy bugged the life out of her. Of course, he had long since grown up, become the most versatile agent Spectrum ever trained, loved and admired by all — the youngest, smartest agent Spectrum had ever hired, and no one was going to let her forget it. To make matters worse, Bradley Baker had tragically met his end, dying in a plane crash in the line of duty, and so had died a hero's death. If Bradley Baker's ghost didn't haunt Ruby, then his legendary status certainly did.

Of course, no one got away with speaking to Sergeant Cooper this way, and Ruby found herself scrubbing all the latrines in the camp for the following three days. Kip Holbrook, who despite all the constant metaphorical hair-pulling was actually a nice guy, was kind enough to wade in and help her out. He didn't exactly know why but he found himself liking this kid from Twinford.

"Can I give you some advice, Redfort?" he asked in the middle of day three's latrine scrubbing. "You might wanna learn to keep that mouth of yours shut. It gets you in some unsanitary situations."

"I can't help saying what's on my mind," replied Ruby. "It's the way I am."

"Then buy yourself a pair of good rubber gloves, because it looks like you're going to be scrubbing latrines for many years to come," said Holbrook.

Having endured a week of what she saw as drill sergeant Cooper's poor attitude, Ruby wasn't exactly grief-stricken when one day she swam up through the clear ocean water to see a sign.

Well, to Ruby Redfort it was a sign: to the mere mortal it was just a donut on a plate sprinkled with candy numbers. The numbers she recognized without rearranging them: they were all digits that together and in the right order made up one long familiar number. Without any hesitation she crammed the donut into her mouth and made her way hurriedly to the bank of telephones outside the canteen.

One of the phone booths had a half-drunk milk shake

balanced on top of the phone and next to it a stack of coins. Ruby picked up the receiver and dialed the number. The phone was answered on the third ring.

"Double Donut, Marla speaking."

"Hey, Marla, it's Ruby."

"Hang on, I'll get him — he's right here."

One minute and twenty seconds later a man's voice came on the line.

"Hello."

"What took you?" Ruby said.

"Kid, can't a person eat a donut in his favorite diner without getting harassed?"

"I believe you wanted me to contact you," said Ruby.

"Glad you can still read the signs," he said. "So how are the plankton?"

"Oh, the plankton are OK — it's the sea cucumbers I'm having trouble with."

"Sergeant Cooper?"

"Uh-huh."

"I gather he isn't your biggest fan."

"I'm not too fond of him either."

"Well, this is your lucky day, Redfort. Dive school is done with you and Twinford Junior High would like you back Monday at eight a.m. pronto. So slip out of your fins. You're on a plane back to Twinford in . . . oh, seventeen minutes."

Ruby Redfort smiled, but before she hung up, she asked, "So, Hitch, why didn't you just leave a message with the camp coordinator, like a normal person? It's not like you've gotta be covert about it; everyone knows you're my sidekick."

"Kid, you can fool yourself that you have a sidekick, but you've got a long way to go before you're going to fool me, LB, or anyone else in Spectrum."

"OK man, I'm just kidding with you. I haven't forgotten that you are Spectrum's number one *numero uno* action agent — I was only asking. Why all the secrecy?"

"Just keeping you sharp, kid. Don't want you getting sloppy."

Ruby smiled. Yep, that was Hitch all right — one royal pain in the behind.

CHAPTER 4
The Recurring Dream

THE DREAM HAD BEGUN IN THE USUAL WAY: Ruby alone, treading water in a bottomless ocean, an ethereal voice whispering to her, almost singing. She would turn this way and that, but she could never see "the thing" until it was too late.

Suddenly she would feel something grab her leg, and she would spin down, down, down into the indigo depths. And the miniature man who appeared in the water just couldn't save her. And all the while the calling, like someone whispering a song to the ocean.

The vision was so real that whenever she awoke, she felt sure it had happened, the whispering so familiar that she could believe that she must have heard it once before, a long, long time ago, perhaps in a past life.

Ruby sat up in bed. She was covered in perspiration, freezing cold, and her head was thudding. She put out her hand and blindly felt around for her flashlight. But somehow the beam it shone just made things worse, more dramatic. She fumbled for the switch on the lamp beside her bed.

Click.

The room was bathed in light, and Ruby could breathe again. Through the blur of her less-than-perfect vision she was reassured: there was the comic she was working on, spread out on her desk; there were the floor-to-ceiling shelves crammed with books, hundreds of them — fiction, nonfiction, graphic novels, codebooks, puzzle books. Her record player, her records, her telephone collection — eccentric designs, from a squirrel in a tuxedo to a conch shell — all perched haphazardly on shelves and furniture. There was the jumble of clothes on the floor. She was definitely in her room and not miles beneath the heavy ocean, sinking through indigo.

Ruby lay back on her pillow, sighed a deep sigh, and drifted back into sleep, this time dreamless, her glasses still perched on the end of her nose. She was only wrenched from her slumber when her subconscious tuned in to the sound of screaming, coming from the backyard.

Ruby scrambled to get out of bed, tripped over the tangle of discarded clothes, and limped to the window. There she saw clouds of seagulls swooping and diving around the house, filling the air with their wings, legs trailing, ready to land. Seagulls are sizeable birds, and as they dodged and swooped, their gray and white feathers almost made contact with the glass, and Ruby found herself instinctively backing away.

The noise they made was enough to drown out most other noises, but not the screaming — this was coming from a small elderly woman who was darting around the yard waving a broom.

It was Mrs. Digby.

Mrs. Digby was the Redforts' housekeeper and she had been with the family forever, which is to say longer than Ruby had existed, longer, even, than Sabina had existed. No one could do without her, and no one wanted to do without her: she was the family treasure.

Ruby stood transfixed, watching the tiny woman attacking the birds, shouting abuse at them and generally telling them where to go. It seemed that they had made the mistake of settling on her freshly laundered sheets, and this had got her hopping mad.

"I didn't get up before six in the a.m. and work my fingers to the bone only to have you feathered vipers do your business all over my clean linen!"

It was fair to say Mrs. Digby was furious.

Just then a well-groomed man came into view. He was wearing a beautifully cut suit and appeared entirely unruffled as he calmly strolled out into the yard, a tiny device in his hand. He held this up to the sky, depressed a button, and suddenly, in a deafening screech, the birds all rose as one and squawked their way back in the direction of the ocean.

Ruby pushed open the large square picture window that made up most of the wall beside her desk (the Redfort house was a miracle of modern architecture) and leaned out.

"Wow!" she said, somewhat sarcastically. "I didn't know you could talk to the animals."

The man looked up and winked.

"Hey, kid. Surprised to see you up before noon."

"Oh, you should know, Hitch. Early bird catches the worm and all that."

"Too late for worms," said Hitch. "Gulls got 'em, but I can rustle up some pancakes, kid."

Ruby pulled on her clothes: jeans, sneakers, and a T-shirt printed with the words *honk if you're happy, hoot if you're not, toot if you couldn't care less* and scooted down the stairs two at a time. Mrs. Digby and Hitch were already in the kitchen and discussing the avian invasion.

"So what is that?" asked Ruby, sliding into her chair. "Some kind of bird-banishing gizmo?"

"Works on the same principle as a dog whistle. It emits a

sound that humans can't hear and birds can't stand," replied Hitch, tucking the device into his shirt pocket.

Ruby was impressed — not a bad gadget to have up your sleeve when the wildlife went wild.

"I might have to get myself one of those," said Mrs. Digby. "Where'd ya buy it — SmartMart?"

"Well, they do say SmartMart's the smart place to shop!" said Hitch, quoting the store's tagline.

"Well, all I can say, child," said Mrs. Digby earnestly, "is that it's just as well your parents ain't here to see this. Your mother would have a three-cornered fit if she witnessed what those critters have done to her sheets."

Mr. and Mrs. Redfort were currently away — as they so often were — this time on a mini cruise that was taking them and the local historical society around Twinford's coast. Dora Shoering was giving a series of onboard lectures about the smugglers' caves, the famous Twinford shipwrecks, and various other seafarers' legends.

"Don't you give those sheets a second thought, Mrs. D.," said Hitch. "I'll get the laundry service to pick up the linen — no need for you to waste your valuable energy on that."

"Shucks and fiddlesticks," said Mrs. Digby. Which didn't really mean anything, but often translated as, *If you insist.*

It had been less than two months since Hitch had joined the Redforts as house manager (or butler, as Sabina Redfort preferred to think of him) but to look at Mrs. Digby you might have thought he had been there always. She had accepted him at once and woe betide anyone who said a bad word about him. As far as she was concerned, he was the best darned butler, house manager (or whatever else he wanted to call himself) this side of anywhere.

Of course, what Mrs. Digby didn't know was that Hitch was actually an undercover agent, sent by Spectrum to protect and work alongside Ruby. She had no idea that the butlering was just a cover — that really would have impressed her.

But it was a Spectrum imperative that Mrs. Digby should never know, never even suspect, that this alarmingly attractive man might not be all that he seemed. Although Ruby and Hitch had got off to a somewhat rocky start, they made a dynamic team. LB had seen this: she was a smart woman, and she knew that unflinching loyalty was what made a good agent, and agents who were loyal to each other made for a solid agency.

"So," said Hitch to Ruby. "How are you going to get yourself in and out of trouble today?"

"I'm not," said Ruby. "I'm gonna lie low, take it easy, probably hang out with Clancy."

She went over to where the kitchen phone sat, picked up the receiver, and dialed a number she had dialed approximately several thousand times.

"Hey, bozo, meet me, usual place, just as soon as." She replaced the receiver.

"And they say the art of conversation is dead," commented Hitch, shaking out the newspaper.

Mrs. Digby looked at Ruby and shook her head. "It's a crying shame," she said. "All life's good manners and fine etiquette gone to pot. I tried to raise this child a nice child, but I probably got to accept failure here."

"Ah, Clance don't mind," said Ruby. Which was true: Clancy Crew was Ruby Redfort's closest friend, and they understood each other without words — though that said, they spent most of their time "nonstop yacking" as Mrs. Digby would often comment.

For this reason there was very little Clancy Crew didn't know about Ruby Redfort, though another reason was that it was almost impossible to keep a secret from him. Ruby was good at keeping secrets, but Clancy always sniffed them out. So, despite all her efforts, Clancy had managed to find out about her recruitment to Spectrum. Ruby had been forced to assure LB that from now on she would keep her mouth shut, that she would not blab to him again, that she would keep it zipped at all times.

But Hitch was astute enough to know that this was a promise Ruby Redfort just couldn't keep. So they had made a little agreement: LB must never know that Clancy knew everything, and Clancy must never tell anyone anything, on pain of death. He never would; there was no question about that. Clancy Crew knew how to keep it zipped.

However, Ruby did still have one secret that not even Clancy Crew was aware of.

She kept it in her room under the floorboards, and not one living creature except perhaps a spider or a bug knew anything about it. Since Ruby was just a kid of four she had written things down in little yellow notebooks. Not a diary exactly, but a record of things seen or overheard, strange or mundane. She had just completed notebook number six hundred and twenty-three, which she had placed underneath the floorboards along with the other six hundred and twenty-two. The one she was working on now, six hundred and twenty-four, was kept inside a compartment concealed in the frame of her bedroom door.

Now, Ruby went upstairs and took the notebook out.

The way Ruby saw it, you just could never be sure when something inconsequential could become the missing link, the key to everything. **RULE 16: EVEN THE MUNDANE CAN TELL A STORY.** Though usually it was just inconsequential.

She opened the notebook and wrote:

```
Sixty or seventy seagulls invaded the yard.
```

She added other important details she had noticed and replaced the notebook in its hiding place. She was just about to exit via the window when she heard Mrs. Digby calling.

"Ruby, you troublesome child, you better not be about to climb out of that window! I want you down here on the double!"

Now, Mrs. Digby was one of the few people Ruby could not always twist around her little finger. Sometimes Ruby just had to do things Mrs. Digby's way, and today, unfortunately, was obviously going to be one of those days.

CHAPTER 5
The Shape of a Condor

AFTER APPROXIMATELY FORTY-FIVE MINUTES of running errands, dropping things off, and picking them up, Ruby finally pointed her bike toward Amster Green and rode the short distance to the small triangle of grass where a big old oak tree grew, its vast branches reaching off in every direction. She leaned her bike against the railings, quickly looked around just to make sure no one was watching, and then, in a blink, swung herself onto the branch above and up and out of sight before you had time to think you had seen her.

"What kept you?" came a voice from high in the tree.

"Mrs. Digby," said Ruby, climbing up the tree.

"Oh," said the voice. "I was about to give up on you. I'd just finished writing you a message."

"Yeah? What did it say?" she asked, still climbing.

"Here," said the voice, and a piece of paper fashioned into the shape of a condor came floating toward her. She unfolded it.

```
Ec spgkwv kxoss kzi ulabtwwyj'w klmj srv
hrvjv llw emiojkevsrpoc uej xo avv eedp*
```

"No kidding?" said Ruby, impressed. The paper, like most of the messages they left each other, was folded into an origami shape, the words encoded using their own Redfort-Crew code, which no one but no one knew how to decipher.

"So how did training camp go?" asked Clancy.

"Good," replied Ruby.

"Good? That's it?"

Silence, and then Ruby's head appeared through the leaves. She shuffled along the oak's limb to where a skinny boy sat, binoculars around his neck and a sun visor shielding his eyes.

"Good to see you, Clance. What's up?"

"Truth is, it's been kinda boring without you, but I've been making it work—getting by," said Clancy.

"Glad to hear it," said Ruby.

Clancy was eager to get back to the subject of Ruby's agent activity, but Ruby just wanted to hear about Twinford life and what was going on with Clancy and his efforts to train his dog, Dolly, and had his sister Minny managed to get out of trouble or was she going to be grounded for life?

*LIKE BOOK 1, THIS IS A VIGENÈRE CIPHER. BUT THE KEYWORD HAS CHANGED! IT'S NAMED AFTER A QUADRUPED. IT WAS ONCE ON THE SURFACE, BUT NOW IT'S ON THE BOTTOM.

CLUE: IT SWIMS IN THE SEA, BUT IT'S NAMED AFTER A QUADRUPED. IT WAS ONCE ON THE SURFACE, BUT NOW IT'S ON THE BOTTOM.

Clancy saw Ruby wasn't in the mood to talk about herself, and if she wasn't in the mood, then there was no point trying.

So instead they talked about Clancy's week, and after that they discussed Redfort home affairs: in particular how Consuela, the brilliant if temperamental chef loathed by Mrs. Digby, had resigned in the most dramatic of ways and left to go work for the Stanwicks.

And when they had exhausted these topics, they talked about the amazing events of just one month ago, the museum, the bank, the gold, and the Jade Buddha of Khotan. They talked about Nine Lives Capaldi and the diamond revolver she had held to Clancy's temple.

They talked about Baby Face Marshall, now safely incarcerated in a maximum-security prison somewhere far from Twinford. And they shuddered when they remembered the Count, still at large and free to practice his evildoing. Where in the world was he?

When the sun had gone down and it was beginning to get chilly, Clancy and Ruby climbed back down the oak, picked up their bikes, and set off in opposite directions.

"So see you tomorrow!" shouted Ruby.

"My place or yours?" Clancy shouted back.

"Mine!" called Ruby as she disappeared around the corner.

CHAPTER 6
An Ocean of Fear

THE NEXT DAY WAS A SCORCHER. It came out of nowhere, and the whole of Twinford seemed to have unfolded their lounge chairs and lit their barbecues.

Ruby Redfort and Clancy Crew were sitting on the roof, reading comics. It was late afternoon, but the sun was still warm and Clancy was sporting a pair of heart-shaped sunglasses; they were his sister Lulu's. Nothing wrong with a thirteen-year-old boy wearing heart-shaped sunglasses, nothing at all; plenty of hip boys his age might want to express their sense of style and individuality by wearing heart-shaped sunglasses. But Clancy wasn't wearing them as a style statement: he didn't know what a style statement was; they were simply the first thing in the form of eyewear that came to hand. No one could accuse Clancy Crew of vanity — he always wore exactly what he felt like wearing. Didn't matter how ridiculous he looked. It was one of the things that Ruby liked most about him.

"Hey, Rube," he said. Ruby was concentrating hard on the RM Swainston thriller she was reading and didn't respond.

"Rube! Can you hear me?" He prodded her with a stick.

"Huh?" She peered up at him. The large red floppy sunhat obscured most of her face, and she managed to appear at the same time comical and stylish — neither look, however, was intentional. Like Clancy, she wore what she liked; unlike Clancy, she had an innate sense of style. Style was just something she had. She even managed to lend a certain chic to her T-shirt, which bore the less-than-elegant words *shut your piehole.* Most of Ruby's T-shirts were emblazoned with upfront messages of this kind; her mother, in particular, loathed them.

"So?" said Clancy.

"Huh, what?" said Ruby.

"You were gonna tell me about your training in Hawaii, remember?"

"Oh, that," said Ruby. "It's kinda confidential. I'm sure you understand."

Clancy started flapping his arms. "What are you saying, confidential? You promised me you were gonna tell me — you promised, Ruby, you weasel."

"I'm just kidding with you. Don't get your underwear in a bunch," said Ruby.

She put the book, *The Strangled Stranger,* under her chair, took a breath, and paused; she did this not only for the sake of drama, but also because, well, everything she was about to tell Clancy was strictly confidential. Classified information. Spectrum had forbidden her to tell *anyone anything* about the code breaking and undercover work she was doing for them, but then Clancy Crew was not *anyone.* Clancy Crew knew how to keep his mouth shut. Clancy Crew would rather die a painful death than betray a secret.

Ruby sucked the last dregs of her banana milk up the clear curly straw sticking out of her glass, swallowed, and said, "OK, the training basically involved scuba diving."

"Really?" said Clancy. "That's kinda cool. So you actually went in the ocean?"

"Yeah, Clance, *I went in the ocean.* Where'd ya think I went, a kiddie pool?"

Clancy had a deep fear of the ocean: it wasn't just the sharks, it was everything.

Though it *was mainly* the sharks. He had once read a book when he was younger, a novel, that had given him cause for many sleepless nights. Admittedly, the book had been one his mother was reading and not recommended for fourth graders. He had spotted it on her nightstand and was lured in by the image of the huge shark's head shown on the front cover, its dead eyes staring up at a lone swimmer. It had made quite an impression. Clancy had found it to be unputdownable and read all six hundred and forty-nine pages in four sittings while locked in the bathroom. He had paid for this every night of his life for the next 1,366 days — his dreams invaded by this great white monster.

Ruby always did her best to reason with him.

"Clance," she said. "Sharks are not interested in human flesh — most attacks happen by accident. The shark spots a swimmer, mistakes it for a seal, and goes over to investigate. The problem comes because sharks explore with their teeth. More often than not they take a bite and think better of it."

"That's very reassuring, Rube — I feel a whole lot better. Just wait while I go dive into the ocean."

"What you gotta do," continued Ruby, ignoring her friend's sarcasm, "is try not to pee — they take this as a sign of vulnerability. Failing that, if he's got you in his jaws, bop him on the nose with your fist. The nose is very sensitive on a shark. He'll soon let go — on the whole sharks can't be bothered to fight. They're not used to it."

"Well," said Clancy, "that must be the only thing that sharks and I have in common."

"In any case, it's very rare. I mean, you probably have the same likelihood of being trampled to death by a rhinoceros."

"Yeah, well, the difference is I would see the rhinoceros coming. At least I could run for it."

"Well, you say that, Clance, but rhinoceroses are awful fast runners. Personally, I'd rather take my chances with the shark."

Perhaps *because* of his terror, Clancy also had a deep fascination for anything to do with the sea. He liked to read about all those things that kept him awake at night sweating with fear. Killer jellyfish, killer whales, poisonous coral, giant squid, killer squid, killer-giant-squid, tuna fish, anything aquatic. He was a bit of an expert.

So he listened eagerly as Ruby told him about the stuff she had learned, the dives she had been on, the depths she had swum to, and the things she had seen.

"So did you — you know — come face-to-face with any of our toothy friends?" said Clancy, his eyes all wide with anticipation.

"Yeah, but they were only small ones — just little reef sharks — nothing to write home about," said Ruby.

"You *wanted* to see them?" said Clancy, flapping his arms again.

"Sure I did. It's all part of the experience of the ocean."

"Prehistoric things with razor-sharp teeth swimming toward you—yeah, I can see how you wouldn't wanna miss *that* experience."

"Anyway," said Ruby, "I'm not a bad scuba diver now. I've done my advanced training, and I'm all set for nearly any underwater mission Spectrum chooses to send me on."

"So your next mission will be underwater?" Clancy shuddered.

"Well, I would hope so," said Ruby. "I'm gonna look pretty dumb in scuba gear anyplace else."

"So you aren't trained for anything other than diving?" said Clancy.

"Give me a break, Clance. I've only been in training a month—I guess I'll be covering other things soon. I mean, I'm not sure when they're gonna teach me skydiving, but I imagine jumping out of a plane is off limits until they have."

Clancy fanned his face with the comic he had been reading. "Boy! Am I burning up."

Ruby looked at him sitting under the giant parasol, his feet in a bucket of cold water, a glass of iced lemonade to one side of his lounge chair.

Just about her whole life Ruby had had to put up with her friend's complaints about being too hot, being too cold, not being just right; Clancy was a regular Goldilocks. He seemed to have been born without a thermostat.

"What's *wrong* with you?"

"Can we please go indoors?" he whined.

Ruby rolled her eyes heavenward and struggled up from her very comfortable deck chair.

"OK, OK, let's go watch some TV before you evaporate," she said. "At least it might take your mind off your ocean fears for five minutes."

But, as Ruby would be the first to point out: **RULE 1: YOU CAN NEVER BE COMPLETELY SURE WHAT MIGHT HAPPEN NEXT.** As it happened, Clancy's ocean fears were about to get a lot bigger.

CHAPTER 7
Dolphins, Sharks —
They're All the Same

RUBY LIFTED THE HATCH ON THE ROOF and, barefoot, the two of them made their way down the open-tread staircase to Ruby's room. It was perfectly cool in the house. Bug, the Redfort husky, was sleeping on the large beanbag that sat in the center of Ruby's bedroom. He pricked up his ears when he heard Ruby and Clancy's footsteps and decided to follow them to the kitchen. There was a good chance someone might drop a cookie on the floor, and Bug was quick. There was no chance of Mrs. Digby sweeping it up before he had gotten to it.

Ruby and Clancy padded into the kitchen, drunk from the sun and exhausted from doing nothing. The transistor radio on the counter was tuned to Twinford Talk Radio and was blaring out some news story about Twinford City Square. Mrs. Digby always had the set turned up too loud because she was a little hard of hearing — though she claimed it was " 'cause those radio folk always mumble."

"*SO, KELLY, HAVE YOU SEEN THOSE GULLS IN TWINFORD SQUARE? CREATING QUITE A RUMPUS I BELIEVE.*" "*YOU'RE NOT WRONG THERE, BOBBY. I CAN'T SAY I'VE SEEN THEM, BUT I'VE CERTAINLY HEARD THEM! NO ONE CAN FIGURE OUT JUST WHAT HAS BROUGHT SO MANY SEAGULLS INTO THE CITY CENTER. PERHAPS IT'S THE UNUSUALLY SCORCHING WEATHER. BACK TO YOU, BOBBY.*" "*THANKS FOR THAT INSIGHT, KELLY. MOVING ON TO ANOTHER ANIMAL-RELATED STORY, SEVEN DOLPHINS WERE DISCOVERED IN TWINFORD HARBOR THIS MORNING, AND DESPITE ALL BEST EFFORTS FROM THE AQUATIC RESCUE TEAM, THEY SEEM TO BE REFUSING TO MOVE ON.*"

Clancy grimaced.

"What's with the face?" said Ruby.

"Dolphins," said Clancy.

"What have you got against dolphins? Everyone likes dolphins. What makes you such an individual?"

"Just don't trust them," said Clancy.

"Oh, Clance, don't tell me you're scared of them — no one's scared of dolphins."

"I am," said Clancy firmly.

"Why?" said Ruby. "What possible reason could you have for being scared of a dolphin?"

"For the following reason: I could be out swimming one day and spot what I think is a dolphin, and get lulled into a false sense of security only to find out it's actually a shark." Just a month ago Clancy had been waiting at the dentist's office, killing time leafing through the old magazines, when he had stumbled across a story about a man who had unfortunately mistaken a shark for a dolphin. The consequences didn't bear thinking about, but Clancy couldn't stop thinking about them.

"And how is that the dolphin's fault?" asked Ruby.

"It's got a fin," said Clancy, folding his arms. "They make themselves look like sharks."

"The fin shape is totally different," said Ruby. "Look in any encyclopedia and you'll see."

"Oh, yeah, I'll remember to do that next time I'm swimming along."

"Well, you know what, Clance? It's never gonna be a mistake you get to make because you're never gonna be swimming along;

you never go anywhere near what might or might not be a shark. You never even dip your toes in!"

Mrs. Digby emerged from the pantry, where she had been lining up canned food in alphabetical order. The Redfort housekeeper liked to run a tight ship (as she put it) and keep an A–Z larder.

"Hi, Mrs. Digby," said Clancy.

Mrs. Digby put her hands on her hips. "Well, howdy. And what can I do for you? Since I don't imagine either of you have come in here to volunteer for potato peeling. Am I right or am I right?"

"Just wondering if you might have some kinda snacky type of a thing up your sleeve?" said Ruby, her eyes all big and innocent.

The old lady clucked her tongue, pretending to disapprove, but actually loving nothing better than preparing food for Ruby and her friends—they were always so appreciative.

Mrs. Digby had known Ruby since Ruby was a minute old, and there was nothing she wouldn't do for her. Not that she was any kind of pushover—she was most definitely not. One tough old bird, in fact. Only a month ago she had been accidentally kidnapped during a robbery, but it was like water off a duck's back to Mrs. Digby.

"Been through a whole lot worse during my long and mainly miserable life," was all she had said about the incident. Mrs. Digby always described her life as miserable, though in fact this was not the case, certainly not for the past fifty years anyway.

The housekeeper set about making what she called a "Digby Club," which was actually just a regular club sandwich, but with her own homemade mustard mayonnaise, and topped off with a gherkin. For some reason it tasted a whole lot better than any other club sandwich that you might ever have tasted, and anybody who ate one never forgot it.

"By the way," she said, pulling something from her apron pocket, "I found that watch of yours on the front stoop; you oughta be more careful with your possessions, child, or you'll have nothing left to call your own."

"Darn it!" said Ruby. "The clasp is all bent, so it keeps coming loose. I told them to fix it."

"Told who?" asked the housekeeper.

"Um . . . the fixers," said Ruby. She was being cagey because this watch was no ordinary watch; it was a Spectrum-issue Escape Watch (also known to agents as the "rescue watch") and had once belonged to the wonder kid Bradley Baker. It was a clever piece of equipment; it looked like nothing more than a child's watch, but this timepiece, though old and not the latest in terms of spy gear, was still a gadget to be reckoned with. It had saved more than a few lives in its time. It had a brightly striped strap and an interesting clasp. The second hand was a fly and the watch face was colored enamel with cartoon eyes. The eyes followed the hands as they ticked tirelessly around. Spectrum had repaired the malfunctioning rescue features, but had neglected to fix the faulty clasp, so it was always coming loose.

Ruby took the watch and fastened it around her wrist, making sure that the clasp clicked home.

"Well," said Mrs. Digby, "mind you fix it or you'll be sorry. A stitch in time saves nine, is what I always say."

The housekeeper popped the sandwiches on plates and slid them across the countertop like she was a short-order chef.

Ruby and Clancy were sitting at high stools still chatting about dolphins and sharks. They paused their conversation only to convey their appreciation, picked up their plates, and made their way to the living room. Mrs. Digby nodded and started chopping up vegetables for the evening meal.

Both kids flopped down on the floor and, propping themselves on their elbows, tackled their snacks. Ruby reached for the remote and flicked on the TV. Clancy gave directions through mouthfuls of Digby Club.

"Try channel three," he urged. "No, wait a minute, seven. Nah, maybe try nine."

Ruby looked at him. "You wanna stop barking orders and do it yourself?"

"Nah, you're doing great. What's on eleven?"

They finally settled on some lame show about a seal who solved crimes with his seal's sixth sense. The seal narrated at the beginning and the end of each episode, which made it all the more unbelievable. It was pretty bad, but Clancy and Ruby didn't mind that. They kind of liked bad shows, almost as much as they relished good ones — there was nothing as enjoyable as ripping a truly terrible show to shreds.

"Oh, like that would ever happen!" Clancy would say whenever anything super stupid occurred in the plot.

And Ruby was very fond of exclaiming, "Yeah, right, I totally would go out in the dark alone if there was a psychopath on the loose."

Watching this seal show was providing them with ample opportunity to make a whole lot of wise remarks. Splasher — the seal of the show's title — was busy listening to a conversation that some villainous-looking types were having on the harbor wall, and he was getting pretty distressed by what he heard.

Clancy was killing himself laughing. "Can you believe this show?" he squealed.

Bug, hearing the commotion, bounded into the room, stepping on the remote and changing the channel to the local news station.

The words **BREAKING NEWS** flashed up on the screen, and a windblown reporter was standing on Twinford Bay Beach talking into the camera.

"IT HAS JUST COME TO LIGHT THAT THE BODY OF A DIVER HAS WASHED UP ON TWINFORD BAY BEACH."

Ruby and Clancy sat up.

"IT IS NOT YET KNOWN HOW THE VICTIM DIED, BUT IT WOULD APPEAR THAT HE WAS JUST AN UNFORTUNATE CASUALTY OF THE SEA'S UNPREDICTABILITY. ALL WE CAN TELL YOU IS THAT THE DECEASED IS MALE AND OF AVERAGE BUILD."

"Like I was saying," said Clancy, letting out a long breath, "the ocean is a dan-ger-ous place."

**Meanwhile,
somewhere off the
coast of Twinford . . .**

it was a glittering day, and it seemed that most of Twinford's glitteringly wealthy were on board Freddie and Marjorie Humbert's sixty-foot yacht, the *Golden Albatross*.

"Isn't this just one hundred percent perfect?" said Sabina Redfort, smiling.

"More than that," said Brant Redfort. "It's at least two hundred percent perfect!"

"Perfect is perfect," said Ambassador Crew. "No more, no less."

"Exactly," agreed Sabina. "It's double perfect."

Ambassador Crew rolled his eyes. He found the Redforts very agreeable company, but frustratingly dim. Just how Brant Redfort had ever gotten into Stanton University he could not imagine.

It was the invitation of the season: a mini cruise along the Twinford coast, sailing the passengers as far as the Sibling Islands, taking in sights most Twinfordites rarely, if ever, got to see. It had been set up by the Twinford Historical Society, which for the first time in twenty years had had to turn away applicants — its membership having swelled threefold as soon as it was discovered that the trip involved ten days on board the Humberts' luxury vessel.

"Isn't it wonderful to see just how many people are actually interested in history?" said Sabina.

"Might have something to do with this million-dollar yacht we're on," replied Ambassador Crew. He was a very cynical person.

"Why, is it old?" asked Brant. "Gee, I didn't know it was of historical interest."

"Give me strength," muttered the ambassador.

Dora Shoering was giving a series of lectures on the facts, myths, and legends relating to smuggling, piracy, and long-lost treasure. The facts, it had to be admitted, were few and far between, but no one much minded as it was naturally a glamorous affair and everyone was having an elegant time.

Along with Brant and Sabina Redfort, the guest list included Barbara and Ed Bartholomew, as well as Mr. and Mrs. Gruemeister and their bothersome dog, Pookie. However, Mrs. Crew had declined the invitation due to a horrible problem with seasickness; the Sibling waters were notorious for their restless currents.

Dora Shoering, a self-proclaimed intellectual who had almost attended Berklard as a student, gave a fascinating, if not entirely accurate, series of talks, but it was that Sunday afternoon's lecture that sparked most chatter.

"Fascinating," said Sabina. "I just love the story of the lost treasure of Twinford. Of course, much of it I knew already, because you see it was my ancestor's treasure that was lost. Did you all know that?"

The others did know this, because Sabina had not stopped repeating it all through the lecture — how her great-great-great-grandmother Eliza Fairbank (she wasn't sure how many greats) had been lost at sea off Twinford on the way to South America along with all her gems; only her little daughter, Martha, survived.

"Utterly gripping," said Marjorie Humbert. "Wouldn't it be divine if it were true?"

"But there is every possibility that it is true," said Dora. "Though it has never been proved one way or the other."

"Why did no one look for it?" asked Brant.

"Well, of course they did," Dora replied. "But they never found a thing. Plus, they had a few other concerns."

"Such as?" asked Ambassador Crew.

"A giant sea monster," replied Dora. "It was said it guarded the treasure — sat on it, they say, and no one could ever retrieve the gems from its razor-sharp talons."

"Talons?" spat the ambassador. "You're saying that this sea creature was an aquatic eagle?"

Dora looked uneasy: she had made up the bit about the talons. "Or crab claws, no one knows," she said hurriedly.

Ambassador Crew couldn't help but display his utter pity for anyone who would believe such total garbage, but the rest of the party was electric with excitement.

"We should search for it!" said Brant. "Imagine — Sabina coming face-to-face with her own ancestor's jewels."

"Good luck to you," said Ambassador Crew. "It would be like trying to find a needle in a haystack. You'd have to search the whole ocean floor just to find the wreck, and in these dangerous waters I wouldn't fancy your chances."

"Gracious," said Sabina. "Sounds like quite a quest."

"Exactly!" said Dora Shoering. "It's no surprise no one's ever found it."

"A nice fairy tale is what it is," said Ambassador Crew.

"Hey, look at that boat on the horizon." Barbara Bartholomew was pointing to the southwest. "Doesn't it look romantic against the setting sun?"

"Yes," agreed Sabina, looking at the old-fashioned sailing ship. "One could almost imagine oneself back in pirate times."

CHAPTER 8
D for *Detention*

THE NEXT MORNING, WHEN RUBY REDFORT turned the corner of Amster Street, she walked on past the bus stop, crossed the road, and headed for the Double Donut Diner. She figured there was plenty of time to grab a shake and still make the school bus.

It wasn't that the Double Donut Diner particularly specialized in donuts — it was really because Marla, the owner, thought it was a catchy name, and apparently it was, because everyone in Twinford seemed to know the Double Donut.

The diner was popular with all sorts of locals, and Ruby liked to hang out observing the comings and goings of Twinford folk. It also did particularly good French toast — something Ruby's mother was very much against due to the quantity of maple syrup her daughter drowned it in.

Del and Mouse looked up as she came in. "Hey, Rube, how you doing?"

"Oh, you know, could complain, can't be bothered." She looked around. "Clancy not here?"

"He had to leave early," said Mouse. "Said he had to go and see Principal Levine, on account of flunking French, *again* — Madame Loup is *furieux*."

"How come he didn't tell me about that last night?" asked Ruby.

"He only just found out. Mrs. Bexenheath actually *called* the Crew household this morning," said Del. Del was the only person Ruby knew who could speak while at the very same time suck milk shake up a straw.

Ruby winced. "A little trip to the principal's office, huh? That's gonna get old Clancy's dad in a stew."

"Lucky for Clance his dad's off sailing the high seas with your folks," said Mouse.

Ruby nodded. Clancy's dad wasn't in the business of bringing up losers: at least that's what he was constantly telling his children. Ambassador Crew liked to think of himself as a winner, and that meant having children who were winners. Clancy, in this respect, often let him down.

"Poor old Clance," said Ruby, signaling to the waitress that she was ready to order.

Just then, in stumbled a girl with long copper hair, golden-brown skin, and gray eyes. It was the impossibly pretty but strikingly clumsy Red Monroe.

"Hi, Red. What happened to your leg?" asked Del.

"Oh, yeah," replied Red, looking down at her scuffed knee. "I tripped over a dog."

"That reminds me," said Del. "My uncle Charlie, you know, the one who's with the coast guard? He was saying how this shipment of dog food ended up in Argentina when it was meant to be delivered to Mexico, and how this shipment of bananas was meant to arrive in San Francisco, but ended up in Chile. I mean how about that!"

"So?" said Mouse. "What's the big deal? Mix-ups happen."

"Yeah, but my uncle Charlie was saying it's been happening a lot, I mean *a lot*."

Del tried to emphasize what "a lot" was by leaving her mouth hanging open when she had finished speaking.

"Oh, how interesting," said Ruby, yawning an exaggerated yawn.

"I'm telling you guys, this is a big deal," Del insisted.

"Give us some examples then," said Mouse, who was concentrating hard on her milk shake.

"Like a bunch of sneakers that ended up in Antigua instead of Seattle, and a whole load of corn that showed up in Miami."

She paused before adding, "Uncle Charlie told me a troupe of Indian elephants on their way to Baltimore still hasn't shown up at all."

Ruby looked at her with a tired expression. Del had quite a reputation for turning fiction into fact, and this just sounded like the usual garbage that she regularly spouted.

"For a start it isn't a troupe of elephants; it's a parade or herd," said Ruby. "And for seconds that has to be untrue."

"Ask anyone," said Del.

Ruby turned to Mouse. "So, Mouse, did you hear about the shipment of elephants that went missing between India and Baltimore?"

"Nope," said Mouse.

Del sighed. She knew when she was beaten. "Hey, how about some French toast? I mean there's time, right? We just need to eat quick; we can still make the bus."

Del Lasco could talk a cow into milking itself, and before they knew it they were all sitting eating a Sunday-style breakfast as if school was not even on the menu. When the hands of the clock got dangerously near pointing out eight o'clock, the friends slipped down off their stools and headed in the direction of Twinford Junior High.

The bus had long gone.

✤ ✤ ✤

"Late *again*! What a *surprise*," said Mrs. Drisco without one chime of surprise in her voice. "So what was it this time — the cat ate my homework?"

"Oh, we don't have a cat, Mrs. Drisco," said Ruby.

The teacher pinched her lips together sourly. "Well, that's a detention then," she said, writing a *D* in the register.

"I have a note," said Ruby.

"Well, unless it's from the mayor himself, then I really don't think I'm interested."

"Oh, it is," said Ruby.

She reached down to her satchel, opened it, and rifled through her notes and excuses section. There were notes inside for any occasion, arranged alphabetically. She selected the one she needed.

Pulling out a piece of paper from the bag, Ruby handed it to Mrs. Drisco. Mrs. Drisco looked at the piece of paper most carefully. She put her glasses on and took them off again, then sat down. The note was most definitely signed by the mayor himself. It wasn't a copy.

Just how Ruby Redfort had come by this note is another story, but suffice it to say, Ruby kept a lot of things up her sleeve or, more precisely, in her satchel. Who knew when they might come in handy? The Boy Scouts had it right: be prepared — it was front and center in the Boy Scout handbook, a little bland in its delivery but a good rule. Ruby had chosen it as her **RULE 11: EXPECT THE UNEXPECTED AND BE READY FOR ANYTHING.**

CHAPTER 9
All Out of Fish

SO HOW DID YOU PULL THAT OFF?" asked an impressed Del Lasco at lunch. "You know, the trick with the note."

"It's not a trick," said Ruby.

"So how'd ya get it?" said Del.

"Ah, I have my sources," replied Ruby.

"Yeah, well, a truly 'good' friend would share those sources with her closest and mostest," said Del.

"If you need me to get you out of a jam sometime Del, all you gotta do is make it worth my while," Ruby said with a smile.

Clancy arrived at the lunch table, his tray teetering with high-calorie food. He was looking to put on a little weight, but the effort would no doubt prove fruitless, for it seemed no matter how much he ate, Clancy never got wider than a string bean.

"So, Clance, you gonna watch the swimathon on Saturday?" asked Del.

Clancy shivered. "No siree. I've got no interest in watching kids from Twinford Junior High get devoured by oversize fish."

Del looked at him like he had lost a few marbles. She turned to Ruby.

"What's with him?" she said, pointing her thumb in his direction.

"You know Clance, a boy with a fearful persecution complex — thinks the whole of marine life's out to get him," said Ruby.

Del punched him on the arm. "Get a grip, Crew. Nothin's gonna bother taking a bite out of your shrimpy body." She took a big chomp out of her sandwich and continued to talk. "I wish it was *our* grade taking part in the swimathon; too bad only the kids in ninth grade get to swim." Del was captain of the eighth-grade swim team, and she relished any chance she got to compete.

The ninth grade had been training for this for the past few months and, as a team-building exercise, Coach Newhart was taking them for a seafood cookout — not that he touched mollusks or crustaceans himself. Coach Newhart only ate "real food" and to him that meant food that walked on all fours on dry land — no fins, no feelers.

Elliot came and joined them. "Hey, where're Mouse and Red?" he asked, looking around as if they might be under the table.

"Chess club," said Del.

"Red plays chess?" he said.

"She's good actually," said Del. "Well, when she's not knocking the pieces all over the board, she tends to win."

Elliot nodded, surprised but impressed. "So, Rube, how was your vacation?"

"You know, good," she replied.

"So what did you do?" he asked.

"Swim," said Ruby.

"Anything else?" he inquired.

"Cleaned the bathroom a few times," she said.

"Well, thank you for that detailed account of your spring break," said Elliot. "That all sounds *really* interesting." He turned to Clancy. "So what did *you* do?"

"Hung out mainly — with my sisters," replied Clancy through mouthfuls of fries. "My dad's taking this Historical Society cruise; left on Friday, so he didn't have time for us all to go away on a family vacation before — too busy."

"What's the deal with that?" asked Del. "He gets a vacation and you don't?"

"My dad says it's not really a vacation; they're learning about the legends and history of the Twinford coast. He says it's good for the ambassador to be seen on a trip like this," said Clancy. "Ruby's mom and dad are on it too."

"Sounds like a riot," yawned Del.

"Actually, the Sibling treasure legend is pretty interesting," said Ruby. "You should read up about it; as legends go, it's a good one. Besides, it involves one of my ancestors."

"You're kidding," said Clancy.

"No way!" said Elliot.

"I don't think you ever mentioned that before," said Del. "Well, maybe once or twice or perhaps three million times!"

"Oh, ha-ha," said Ruby flatly. "You guys just wish you had some kinda historical intrigue in your families; ain't my fault that you got nothing to talk about."

The details of the legend were roughly this: Ruby's great-great-great-great-grandmother, Eliza, was sailing to South America on the family ship, the *Seahorse*, with all her worldly goods (very valuable ones by all accounts), when the boat was attacked by pirates who slaughtered all on board. However, Eliza's four-year-old daughter, Martha, who was a smart child, the smartest anyone could remember, escaped death by hiding in a barrel of apples.

When the pirates had finished raiding and murdering, they began collecting the spoils from the *Seahorse*. But unfortunately for them, they hadn't quite murdered everyone on board. A few of the *Seahorse* crew who were still belowdecks took the remaining pirates by surprise, and a violent battle broke out. Most of the pirates had already returned to their galleon, but those who were left fought to the death until the *Seahorse,* engulfed in flames, sank below the waves.

Miraculously, the child, Martha, managed to escape by floating in the apple barrel before eventually washing up in Twinford.

The whole story sounded very far-fetched to Ruby, but she couldn't deny its appeal. One intriguing part centered around something little Martha claimed to have seen. She was quite convinced of the fact that she had watched her mother being carried from the boat by the pirates, kicking and screaming. Martha would not be dissuaded on this point. She was sure that her mother was still alive, although no one else believed it.

The postscript to the story was also intriguing since it became a tale told to children all over the region. It was said that not so long after the *Seahorse* was wrecked and plundered, a beautiful woman was seen aboard a pirate vessel, raiding any ships that dared to sail in pirate waters. Some said they had seen her brandishing a cutlass and slitting men's throats, others that she was held captive, destined never to tread dry land again.

Clancy's day was marred by his extra French tutoring and, just to add insult to the occasion, a nasty run-in with his two least favorite Twinford Junior High pupils.

"Oh, look who it is! Nancy Drew, Redridingfort's little helper! Look, he's just been to his 'French for duh brains' tutorial."

The girl jeering at him was Vapona Begwell (or Bugwart, as she was known by most of the school), one of the few kids who did not like Ruby. But then Vapona didn't particularly like anyone. Vapona Begwell was an unfortunate-looking girl, sour-faced and mean with it. Tall but strangely lumpy with a sort of leery stoop that made her look very much like a cartoon bully — which was sort of what she was. She hung out with Gemma Melamare, a total viper with cute blue eyes and a snub nose, who lurked at Vapona's side and leaked poison into the schoolyard, spreading rumors and setting friends against friends. It never worked on Clancy and Ruby; they were wise to the Melamare menace.

"So, Clancy, I notice you and Ruby haven't been hanging out so much lately. Was it because she said that thing about you being too dumb to be seen with?"

Clancy looked at Gemma blankly.

"Oh, you didn't know?" said Gemma, her sugary voice feigning apology.

He smiled as he pulled his bike from the bike stand; saying nothing was his secret weapon; he knew it made Gemma Melamare crazy. Still smiling, he headed off toward the torture that was an hour's violin lesson, his face not for one second belying the hell he was about to endure or how much he wanted to sock Gemma with the aforementioned instrument.

When Ruby arrived home from school, she found Mrs. Digby singing along to the radio, which was tuned to Chime Melody. Chime Melody was her favorite station for tunes, Twinford Talk Radio for talking. Talk radio she loved, but Chime Melody was her guilty pleasure. It played the old tunes, and Mrs. Digby adored the old tunes. And what's more, she seemed to know every one of them.

She always said, *"If I hadn'ta been so busy cooking you Redforts your every morsel, I would have sung for my supper and made a bundle on Broadway."*

"Anything happen while I was busy learning stuff?" asked Ruby, opening the refrigerator.

"Only that the fish store was all out of fish. I ask you, we live practically in an ocean, but I swear there's not one single sprat for sale. In my day, fishermen *knew* how to fish. They could catch a catfish in a rain puddle."

"Don't sweat it," said Ruby. "I'm not in a fishy frame of mind tonight."

"I don't care what frame of mind you're in, child. It's what you need that counts, and you need fish or that little brain of yours is going to shrivel up like a raisin." Mrs. Digby was a great believer in fish oil.

"So what are we having instead?" asked Ruby.

"*You* will be having a spoonful of cod-liver oil and some cabbage soup," said the housekeeper firmly.

"You have to be kidding!" said Ruby.

"Your mother's orders," said Mrs. Digby, her hands on her hips, prepared for the inevitable argument. "Your ma said fish or cabbage and I gotta abide by her rules."

"But what you are actually saying is fish *and* cabbage — that's not the deal," said Ruby.

"I'll grant you that." Mrs. Digby nodded. "Cabbage it is. Cod-liver oil will have to wait."

Mrs. Digby was a stickler for abiding by Sabina Redfort's dietary rules, so there was no getting away from it: cabbage was on the menu and that was that.

"Oh, I almost forgot," said Mrs. Digby. "That Elaine Lemon stopped by wondering if you'd like to babysit Archie."

Ruby made a face. "No way, no day," she said firmly. "Uh-uh."

Mrs. Digby chuckled and started chopping cabbage.

It was at supper that night that Ruby got the message. She looked down into her unfortunate cabbage soup to see a fly struggling to make it to the rim. It was making good progress, but just as it was about to reach the bowl's edge, it would change direction and stupidly end right back where it started.

"There appears to be a fly in my soup," said Ruby, looking directly at Hitch, who had joined them for supper and was taunting Ruby by devouring a steak cooked medium rare, fries on the side.

He winked back. "I had a premonition that that might happen. Let me substitute it for something less cabbage," he said, removing the offending liquid and replacing it with food that told her all she needed to know.

It was a slice of toast, and into it was grilled a message:

Be ready: 2:30 a.m. Bring your waders.

The note had been toasted into the bread by the Spectrum-issue toaster fax machine. A discreet way of conveying information — and what's more, you could eat the evidence, which Ruby promptly did.

Finally, the toast she had been waiting for: Spectrum had a mission for her.

CHAPTER 10
Sea Division

AT 2:30 A.M. RUBY GOT OUT OF BED, pulled on her jeans, sneakers, a T-shirt printed with the words *excuse me while I yawn,* picked up her jacket, pushed open the window, and climbed down the eucalyptus tree. Its limbs stretched toward the west side of the house, providing a perfect ladder for the able tree-climber.

Hitch was already sitting in the silver convertible, its engine turning over so quietly you hardly knew it was running.

"Nice of you to show up," he said.

Ruby looked at her watch. It was 2:32 a.m. "Give me a break," she said.

"Lives have been lost in two minutes," said Hitch.

"Oh, come on, man. What's the big deal?"

"The 'big deal'?" pondered Hitch. "Let me think . . . well, I hear you can only breath-hold for one minute and one second, so imagine if you were waiting for me to rescue you, and you were stuck underwater, and I took a whole two minutes to get there. You'd be all out of air, kid."

"You were waiting in the car. You weren't exactly in total mortal danger."

"You didn't know that."

"OK, OK," said Ruby. "I'm sorry. I won't do it again."

"I wouldn't bet on it," said Hitch. "Listening to advice isn't what you do best."

"Well, since we are busy 'sharing' here, then might I suggest that giving people the benefit of the doubt isn't one of your strengths?"

Hitch pointed at Ruby's T-shirt and said, "Your T-shirt is on the money, kid. So zip it."

He backed out of the driveway and they drove in silence to Desolate Cove. As the name suggested, no one really visited this place—it had no sand and was nearly always windswept and rarely warm. Hitch parked behind a steep bank of pines, the vehicle hidden from view, and he and Ruby set about zipping their jackets and pulling on the rubber waders that had been stashed in the car's trunk. In silence, they walked across the pebble beach until they reached the place where the cliffs met the water.

"Stay close to the rock, kid," warned Hitch. "There's a sudden drop to the left—very deep water, and I'm not sure I can be bothered to fish you out." The sound of his words was almost drowned out by the sound of the sea as it dragged through the stones of the beach, relentlessly pulling and pushing, almost like a chorus of whispering voices.

Here you could almost believe in fishermen's legends of sea devils and sea witches.

The water reached almost to the top of Ruby's waders, and she just barely managed to keep from getting soaked. She had no idea where they were headed or why, but she guessed there must be a pretty good reason for this little jaunt.

They made it around the next sharp corner, and there it was: a hidden low opening in the cliff, not so much a cave, more like a large niche, just big enough to conceal . . .

a scuba-sub.

"Kinda cool," said Ruby.

"You have no idea," said Hitch.

A metallic pod-like thing, the sub had a reflective glass dome on top.

"The glass is four inches thick," said Hitch. "Allows the sub to dive to depths of five miles. When submerged, the light bounces off it in such a way that it is just about invisible."

"Even cooler," said Ruby casually, like she'd seen a whole bunch of scuba-subs in her time.

Hitch raised his eyes heavenward and depressed a button on his watch, and the glass lid slid back. There looked to be enough space to seat three passengers comfortably and four at a squeeze. It looked worryingly unstable, and Ruby was concerned that it would tip as she climbed in.

"Plenty of agents bigger than you have found themselves jumping into this thing, trying to make a fast getaway," said Hitch. "And I can assure you, kid, it never rolls over . . . so long as you don't slip, you won't drown. If you do, it's anyone's guess."

Ruby gave him a sideways look, then climbed in very carefully and buckled up. Hitch took a key from a well-concealed compartment, slotted it into the ignition, turned it this way, that way, and then another way before the engine began to purr.

After fiddling with some switches, and once the roof was locked into place, Hitch pushed a lever and they moved forward, dipping smoothly under the waves. The cliff ledge suddenly disappeared, and the sub moved into deep water.

"Keep your safety belt fastened!" said Hitch as he pulled on another of the controls and the scuba-sub suddenly jetted forward at great speed, silently cutting through the ocean. Things on either side of them vanished into a blur as they passed by.

"How do you avoid colliding with a whale?" asked Ruby,

who was sort of pinned to her seat, enjoying the ride, but not yet entirely relaxed.

"Automatic Avoidance Sonar," said Hitch. "I've never hit anything yet, kiddo!"

It was a thrill to travel so fast—better than any amusement park—but Ruby wouldn't have minded slowing it down a little, taking some time to look at the scenery. In the blink of an eye they reached another rock face; this one seemed to be covered in petrified insects—sort of prehistoric-looking flies and insect fossils.

"We're stopping here?" asked Ruby.

"Not exactly," said Hitch, pressing one of the buttons on the control panel. What looked like solid rock suddenly corkscrewed open, and they entered a water-filled tunnel.

They navigated their way up the passage until they reached a dead end, a round pool. Hitch switched off the engine and a platform under the sub lifted them and their vehicle out of the water.

They had arrived.

Ruby assumed this entrance must be the latest way in to Spectrum HQ, since it was not unusual for the location to be moved several times a month.

"So this is Spectrum?" said Ruby.

"Not exactly," said Hitch again.

"What does that mean?"

"This, kid, is Spectrum's Sea Division, Spectrum 5. Sea Division, as the name would suggest, is always located somewhere at sea."

"So, given that we work for Spectrum 8, what are we doing here?" asked Ruby.

"Spectrum 5 has been working on a case that might cross over with a case that Spectrum 8 has been looking into. LB thought it might be a good idea to join forces."

As they walked, some of the slick white corridors became clear glass-tube passageways, and fish swam by on the other side — sunfish, rockfish, cardinalfish, garibaldi, stingrays, and a thousand others. It was sort of like being in a giant aquarium, though the fish might well conclude it was the *people* who were the exhibits here.

It was strange for Ruby to enter Spectrum as a fully paid agent in training. She stifled a smile, remembering that at the tender age of thirteen she had already achieved her lifetime ambition of becoming an undercover secret agent for one of the most undercover and secret of secret agencies in the world.

She looked around her at the huge domed space with its glass floor and sea life moving underfoot.

"Hey, kid!" shouted Hitch. "Want to look lively? LB's waiting."

Ruby had taken off her jacket and slung it over her shoulder so it was again possible to read the slogan written in bold letters across her T-shirt: *excuse me while I yawn.*

Hitch paused a minute. "Kid, my advice? Put your jacket back on and zip it right up. LB sees that and she might not find it so funny."

"She not in a good mood?" Ruby called across the hall.

"I doubt that sincerely, kid. That diver who just washed up dead on the beach—he was one of ours, and losing an agent always puts a crimp in her day."

CHAPTER 11
Seriously Strange

HITCH LED THE WAY DOWN A STEEPLY SLOPING PASSAGE
that wound around and around and seemed like it must spiral
right through the seabed. When they reached a black circular
door, Hitch punched in some numbers and they were admitted
to a screening room.

The room was full of agents and Spectrum staff, sitting in
cinema-style seats that all faced a large white screen. There was
a buzz in the air, everyone knew something big had happened
but few knew exactly what had gone down. Ruby tried to get her
bearings, looked around — unfortunately straight into the eyes of
Agent Froghorn (he of the silent *G*). He made much of pointing
to his watch, indicating that it was way past her bedtime, and
Ruby mouthed a word not to be repeated. Agent Redfort and
Agent Froghorn were not likely to ever exchange birthday cards.

Sea Division headquarters had much in common with
Spectrum 8 HQ, but there were some very obvious differences,

the main one being when you looked out of the window you saw water. Agent Trent-Kobie, head of Sea Division, had been called away on urgent business, and so the briefing was to be given by the boss of Spectrum 8.

LB.

Dressed all in white, LB walked into the room — and instantly the chatting stopped. LB had this effect on people. She was immaculately dressed but for her feet, which were bare with red nail polish perfectly applied to her toes. The head of Spectrum 8 did not much care for shoes of any kind and was rarely seen in footwear.

When she reached the front, where the microphone stood, she dropped a file onto the small table at her side and launched right in.

"So, as you will know by now, Agent Trilby's body was found on Sunday evening — he had been diving off the coast not far from Twinford Bay Beach. During the past month he has been investigating unusual ocean activity — strange behavior of marine life. There has been a lot of unusual ocean activity recently, and it can all be found in Agent Trilby's report." She continued to go through example after example of things that had been occurring just off the coast of Twinford.

Dolphins refusing to leave the bay, seagulls flocking inland, fishing stock low.

"As we all know," continued LB, "Trilby was a very proficient diver, and it is highly unlikely that he would have drowned in normal circumstances. We are still waiting for the autopsy results, but it would seem that he was unfortunate enough to come into contact with something like a stingray or an electric eel. There is evidence of bruising to his leg that still needs to be explained, but we feel it's likely that he encountered this sort of creature and this either led to a cardiac arrest or a severe shock that in turn led to drowning."

It couldn't have been a stinging creature that killed him, thought Ruby, *Trilby would definitely have utilized his Spectrum-issue anti-sting Miracle serum.* It was a comfort to know that every diving agent had this lifesaver with them even if it couldn't guard against shocks and bites.

LB pushed her glasses back up to the bridge of her nose. "Yes?" she said, spotting a raised hand.

"Do you think the strange ocean activity is linked to something else — some dark plot, I mean — or do you think it's all just a consequence of some natural event throwing things off course?"

The question came from Agent Blacker, a disheveled-looking

man in a crumpled jacket — an agent Ruby admired. They had worked together on the Jade Buddha case, and he was not only a smart person, he was a nice guy. He had a laid-back manner, but was as sharp as a tack.

"There is nothing to suggest that Trilby was the victim of foul play, if that's what you're getting at," replied LB. "However, I am interested in his findings in the context of other unusual activity. Some of you will have been party to the ongoing investigation into the missing or scrambled coast-guard signals and reports of disruption with shipping vessels; cargo going awry, turning up in the wrong place."

She listed the coast-guard reports — and the list was long. Shoes, coffee, corn, bananas, you name it, it seemed to have ended up in the wrong port.

"Even a six-ton elephant on its way to Baltimore has gone astray," concluded LB.

Ruby made a mental note to apologize to Del Lasco: give or take a few elephants, she had actually been telling the truth.

LB wound up her talk and removed her glasses, hooking them onto her shirt. "To be honest with you," she said, "we really have no idea what might be going on. To date we are not investigating any criminal activity. All we know is that Agent Trilby was monitoring unusual events at sea and regrettably died. If it wasn't for the coast-guard reports, we would continue monitoring marine life and not look any further."

Blacker raised his hand again.

"Yes?" she said.

"So you *are* looking to make a link?" said Blacker.

"Either that or to establish that there isn't one—it could all be a coincidence," she replied.

"But link or no link, you'll be wanting me to plot through Trilby's findings and see where they take us?" said Blacker.

"Correct. Meanwhile, I understand that Agent Kekoa from Sea Division will take over Trilby's ocean research. She intends to make sound recordings—this way we hope to learn just what is causing the marine disturbance. If the strange sea life occurrences are just a series of natural blips and shifts, then so much the better; the information will be passed on to those who deal with such things, and we will concentrate on the shipping alone."

LB stepped to one side and Agent Kekoa walked to the front. Ruby's dive instructor looked shorter out of the water and less assertive. You could tell she wasn't particularly comfortable standing there talking. She clearly wasn't really comfortable out of her wet suit. In fact, clothes made her look strangely out of her depth.

"There have been reports of a sound, a whispering sound," said Kekoa. She clicked the remote and up popped a slide showing a freckly kid of about seventeen, his photo alongside a map of the Twinford coast, and an arrow pointing to the sea beyond Little Bay.

"Tommy Elson was swimming out past Little Bay and reported a whispering sound coming from under the water."

Click: Slide of a young couple in beach gear. The map showed that they were on a sailboat far out at Rock Point.

"Same story with Hallie Grier and Lyle Greene."

Click: A surfer girl with a couple of missing teeth. She was smiling and shielding her eyes from the sun.

"Billie-May Vaughn was surfing with her dog and heard a noise that she described as someone calling, but calling in a whisper; she dove under the water but could see nothing to explain it. She claimed her dog reacted to the sound too."

There was some snickering in the audience that could have come from Agent Froghorn, but Kekoa took no notice.

"The girl alerted the lifeguard, who swam out but found nothing to substantiate what Billie-May had told him."

Kekoa clicked through some more pictures that showed various fresh-faced-looking people and the location references.

"The sounds have generally been heard when people are

swimming a mile or so from shore, or on boats farther out to sea. One person, Danny Fink Junior, heard the sound when fishing on a rock which juts out into the ocean, almost an island, but that's the only example of anyone hearing the sound on dry land."

"Have *you* heard it?" asked one of the agents.

"No," said Kekoa.

"And how many years have you been diving in those waters?" asked another.

"Seven," said Kekoa. "But I've been in Hawaii the last couple of months."

"Yet you yourself have heard nothing?" said the first agent. "Even since you got back?"

"No," said Kekoa.

A rippled whisper went through the audience.

"So have you considered that these accounts could all be bogus? I mean, some of the people who reported it are just little kids," continued the first agent.

"Yes," said Kekoa. "But I consider it unwise to disregard them just because *I*, just because *you*, have no personal experience of them."

Ruby couldn't agree more strongly with this statement. There were people who made wild claims about spotting aliens and spacecraft, and there were other people who claimed that this was nonsense and that aliens and spacecraft didn't exist, but either way what you had to accept was that these people had seen *something*. **RULE 5: REMEMBER, THERE IS MORE TO LEARN THAN YOU CAN EVER KNOW.**

"In conclusion," said LB, stepping back in front of the screen so the smiling face of Danny Fink Junior was projected across her white suit, "I want this case wrapped up all neat and tidy AS"—she rapped the file with her fountain pen—"AP." She couldn't have looked more serious.

"One of our agents is dead. Spectrum needs to know if it was foul play or just plain bad luck. The coast guard needs to know if all this disruption to the cargo shipping is incompetence or something a lot more serious. The fishing industry needs to know where all the fish have gone. I want to know if I have a team smart enough to give me some answers. If I don't get the right ones, then I'm not happy; if I'm not happy, some of you are going to have to take a walk."

"Yikes," whispered Ruby. "What's LB like when she's unhappy, I mean, *really* unhappy?"

"You don't want to see it," said Hitch.

Ruby was glad she had taken Hitch's advice and zipped her jacket up. LB was in one very bad mood.

CHAPTER 12
Consequences

THE SUN WAS ALREADY COMING UP by the time Hitch and Ruby turned the corner into Cedarwood Drive.

The discussion had gone on well into the early hours, and it was almost time for Ruby to be up and ready for school. The two of them sat at the table and, over eggs and toast and maple syrup, discussed the Spectrum briefing.

"So what thoughts are jangling in that teenage mind of yours, kid?" asked Hitch, pouring coffee, his fifth cup this morning.

Ruby sucked hard on the curly straw that stuck out of her peach-and-cranberry juice blend. When the glass was emptied and the straw had begun to make an ill-mannered gurgling sound, she looked up.

"Huh? You say something?"

"You clean your ears out lately, kid? I was saying, do you believe Trilby's death was accidental?"

"Maybe it was, maybe it wasn't," said Ruby. "The question

is, do I think the marine activity and the confused shipping are connected to his death?"

"That's the question?" said Hitch.

"Yes. I think it could be a mistake to assume that they are, but on the other hand, one thing could be triggering the other. What if there is one thing going on, which is man-made, and another that is a consequence of the man-made?"

"So . . . connected but not intentionally?" said Hitch.

"Yeah, let's say someone is interfering with the shipping radar and signals somehow, perhaps with a low-frequency signal, a sound to block sound. The idea being to disrupt the shipping, I guess, but I don't know why. Anyway, this in turn is making the sea life crazy, which results in Trilby getting killed. The seagulls coming inland en masse, dolphins swimming into the harbor — all because of sound."

Hitch nodded. "It's certainly a theory. I have no idea if it's a good one, but it's a theory."

"It could mean that Trilby's death, though accidental, was actually the consequence of something bigger," said Ruby. "Something sinister. So I guess what I am suggesting is, yes, in a way his death could be an accident, nothing sinister. But in a way it perhaps wasn't and is."

Hitch raised an eyebrow. "I'm barely following."

Ruby looked at him like he was a few blocks short of a load. "Maybe you need another cup of coffee or three," she said.

"Maybe." He took another slurp. "And the whispering?"

"I don't know." She was thinking, trying to tunnel down to some lost thought, but whatever it was, was lurking deep in the furthest depths of her mind, and she could not reach it. So she just said, "Could be entirely imagined, of course."

"Yes," said Hitch. "One person says they've heard something — then a whole lot more people imagine that they've heard the same thing."

"Yeah, happens all the time," said Ruby, nodding. "People are very suggestible."

"It's true," said Hitch. "I mean, if I start mentioning the words *jelly* and *donut,* do you find yourself kind of yearning for one?"

Ruby gave him a look. "You got one?"

He shook his head. "So what do you think — did those people hear the whispering or not?" asked Hitch. "That little Redfort brain must be thinking something. You have any kind of gut feeling on this?"

Ruby looked at him straight in the eye. "My brain is telling me I should be asleep, but my stomach is telling me that I sure could do with a jelly donut and a glass of banana milk."

"Well, let's make it happen, kid."

**Mrs. Gruemeister's dog,
Pookie, was barking. . . .**

In fact, he had been barking for quite some time, but everyone aboard had chosen to ignore him, it being 5:46 a.m.

"Probably seagulls," murmured Mr. Gruemeister, pulling the blankets over his head. "That dog will bark at any little thing."

"I've tried my darnedest to train him," sighed Mrs. Gruemeister. "Only bark at intruders. That's what I taught him, but he doesn't listen."

In cabin 4A, Brant Redfort sat up in bed, yawned, and rubbed his eyes. He switched on the radio, but to his great disappointment the only station he could get any reception for was one playing the most awful music. In fact, he wondered if it was music at all.

"What is that dreadful noise?" moaned Sabina. "Sounds like violins having the most vivid of disagreements."

Brant switched it off in disgust. He had been looking for a pleasant sound to block out the barking dog, but it wasn't going to happen.

"I can't take much more of this yapping," he said. "How about an early breakfast up on deck, honey?"

"Good idea, Brant. That bow-wow is beginning to give me the most dreadful headache. Honestly, you'd think they would have raised him better. Can you imagine if Ruby yelped like that?"

"Well, no, honey. But then, she isn't a dog."

"But you know what I mean, Brant."

"Sure I do, honey; Ruby is a far better daughter than Pookie would ever be."

At that moment there was a large thud on deck, followed by more thuds, a yelp, and a heavy splash. The barking stopped. Sabina and Brant looked at each other for a split second before struggling into clothes and hurrying toward the noise.

That's when the screaming began.

CHAPTER 13

-... . .- - / .. - --..-- /
-. --- ... . -.-- / .-.- .- .-. -.- . .-.

POOR CLANCY. If only he had known what was in store
for him that day, he doubtless wouldn't have made it out of bed.
Morning class was interrupted by an in-person announcement
from Coach Newhart.

It seemed that the whole of the ninth-grade swim team
had come down with mollusk poisoning at last night's
clambake — except for Denning Minkle, who was allergic to
seafood. The doctor had advised that no one take part in the
swimathon for fear of weak limbs and consequent drowning.

Coach Newhart wasn't to be defeated by this alarming news.
Coach Newhart was rarely defeated by anything. To Coach
Newhart, this was a challenge, and a coach's job was about
nothing if not challenges. So what if grade nine was all getting
up close and personal with their latrines — he still had grade
eight, and they looked to be fighting fit; a bit weedy perhaps, but
no one was throwing up.

"So can I count on all o' yous for the Twinford swimathon?" bellowed Coach Newhart. "I am determined that this year we will beat Branwell Junior High."

Clancy tried to make himself very small and very invisible, but it didn't work.

"Crew! I'm including you in this. I want you out in that bay, front and center, swimming as if your life depended on it."

Clancy had a premonition that it probably would. The idea of getting in that ocean scared the living daylights out of him—but then at this precise moment, so did Coach Newhart. Coach Newhart was not a man one said no to. No siree.

"So, Crew, you gonna be there?"

Clancy nodded. But that wasn't good enough for Coach Newhart.

"I can't hear you, sonny."

"Sir, yes sir," shouted Clancy, like he was on a parade ground.

"That's more like it," said the coach, nodding. Then he turned to Ruby. "And you, Redfort. I won't be accepting a note from the governor this time. Everyone swims. And that includes you."

"OK," said Ruby, shrugging. She really didn't mind—she was a good swimmer. In fact, so was Clancy; it was a curse for him that despite appearances he was actually very athletic and surprisingly fast in water. For someone who hated water as much as he did, this was a real problem.

Once Coach Newhart had finally stopped barking, Twinford's very own chief lifeguard, the implausibly named Slicker Dawn, gave a little briefing about bay safety. Slicker delivered all information at top volume, probably because he had spent much of his time shouting instructions at swimmers; he liked to repeat things too, so what should have been a five-minute briefing took a good half hour.

"Anyway," concluded the lifeguard, "Twinford Bay is one of the safest in the county. I repeat, one of the safest in the county. So long as you stay between the flags, you will not get sucked out to sea by the riptides and you will not get dragged down by the undertow."

"Oh, boy," muttered Clancy. "I don't stand a chance."

"Just to reassure you," shouted Slicker Dawn, "we haven't had one Mayday call or rescue in three weeks, not one! That's a record right there."

To Clancy this just made it all the more likely that there would be one soon. According to probability, a rescue was surely due.

The announcement over, Clancy tried to go back to concentrating on class, but however much he tried to engage with the subject at hand, he found that right now the life cycle of the Peruvian tree frog didn't really have too much to do with the life prospects of a shrimpy boy from Twinford City.

When the bell rang, he slowly pushed his chair away from the desk, picked up his bag, and walked out into the corridor. He was so lost in thought that he didn't see his longtime enemy lumbering toward him.

"Crew, you look like you're about to pee your pants," sneered Bugwart, blocking his path.

"No, I'm about to throw up, actually. So if you don't want to get puked on, I'd get outta the way." As soon as he had uttered these words, he realized that he *was indeed* about to throw up. Looking at him, Vapona could *also* see that this was in fact *more* than likely and immediately stepped to one side as Clancy made a dash for the restroom.

When Clancy finally made it to music class, everyone else was already in their places. Ruby, who was on xylophone, was sitting on the other side of the room from Clancy, who was to be on kettledrum. She could see his face, all scrunched up with anxiety, and it was pretty obvious what he was thinking about.

Ruby tapped out a message in Morse code*:

-.-. .-.. .- -. -.-. .-.- --.-- / -.-. ....-.. .-.. / --- ..- - /

-- .- -. .-.-.- / -.-- --- ..- / .-.. --- --- -.- / .-.. .. -.- . / -.-- --- ..- .---. .-. . /

.- -... --- ..- - / .- -- / -.. ... .

Clancy looked up. He knew right away what she was saying, and his reply was this:

- .... .- - .---. .... / -.-. .- -... / .. / .- - / .- -... --- ..- - / - --- /

-.. .. . -.-- / - .... / .... .- - .-. -. .-. -. .-. -.-- / -- --- -. -. .. -. -.

So Ruby tapped out another that went:

- .... . -.- . / .- -.- . / -. - --- / ... .- -.-. -.-- ... / .. -. /

- .- .. -. .-. -- -. .-.-.- / -.... .- -.-

And in return got this back from Clancy:

.-. -. --- ..-. . / .. -

Boy, was he the most stubborn kid she had ever met.

Mrs. Courtenay-Clack rapped her conductor's baton crossly on the side of her music stand.

"When you are quite ready, Ruby, Clancy — we are all waiting."

Ruby looked around the room. It was true: everyone was waiting for her to lead into this rather modern piece by Fenton Schreiber.

She picked up her stick and banged out what were meant

*GO TO PAGE 408 IF YOU WANT TO KNOW WHAT RUBY AND CLANCY SAID!

to be the first few notes of *Elastic Movement in G,* but was in fact another message for Clancy.

--. . . --.. --..-- / - .... . -.- / -.-. .- .-.. .-.. / - .... / -- ..- ... .. -.-. ..-..

He smiled.

The teacher rapped her baton again.

"Ms. Redfort, will you please get with the program!"

"Sorry, Mrs. Courtenay-Clack," said Ruby, pretending to leaf through her music score. "I think I skipped a page."

CHAPTER 14
Another Twinford Bay Casualty

THAT TUESDAY AFTERNOON WAS MARKED by another Twinford Junior High swimming-related event. It seemed someone (probably Dillon Flannagon) had thought it would be amusing to dress a mannequin in the school mascot costume (a squirrel suit) and place it in the pool. The janitor got quite a shock when he saw a giant squirrel in the Twinford Junior High pool floating facedown in the water.

On a board drifting next to this unusual scene, the culprit (surely Dillon Flannagon, it really looked like his handwriting) had written in huge letters, ANOTHER TWINFORD BAY CASUALTY. To make matters worse, the blue paint (believed to be toxic) that the giant sign was written in was dissolving into the pool water. This made it a health and safety concern, and therefore the pool would have to be drained.

Principal Levine had not seen the funny side. Whoever it

was, was really in for it. When Ruby passed Dillon in the corridor, she whispered, "Run, Flannagon. Run."

After class, Ruby and Clancy fetched their bikes and wheeled them out of the gates and along the sidewalk. Clancy didn't have the energy to pedal; he was too depressed.

"Oh, brother! What am I going to do about the swim meet? There's no way I'm getting in that bay. No way."

"I'll look out for you, Clance," said Ruby.

"Oh, yeah?" said Clancy. "There are gonna be like a hundred kids all swimming out there in the bay. No way you can keep an eye on me the whole time."

Ruby looked at him hard. "You can do this, Clance. It's just mind over matter is all."

"That's easy for you to say," grumbled Clancy. "The water doesn't bother you—nothing bothers you."

This wasn't true of course. It was just that Ruby had spent a whole lot more time thinking about this stuff. She had a notebook full of rules, and one of them was **RULE 12: ADJUST YOUR THINKING AND YOUR CHANCES IMPROVE.** She had learned this from Mrs. Digby, a wise old buzzard if ever there was one.

"All I'm saying, Clance, is your chances are better if you go into it in the right frame of mind."

"Don't you get it, Rube? My chances are a whole lot better if I never get in that ocean in the first place. My chances of having a heart attack are greatly reduced if I don't even get my feet wet."

Ruby gave him a reassuring pat on the back. "Your chances of suffering a lifetime of grief from Coach Newhart increase by about a thousand percent if you don't."

"I know," sighed Clancy mournfully.

"Come on, let's go get a fruit shake," said Ruby, pulling him toward the Cherry Cup. "On me."

When they got to the Cherry Cup, they took the high stools at the counter and Ruby reached for the drink menu. Clancy was swiveling his seat distractedly and muttering to himself.

"Hey there, you guys, what can I get you?" called Cherry.

"I'll take a Strawberry–Pineapple–Fiesta, and I reckon Clance could do with a tranquilizer."

Cherry looked hard at Clancy. "You all right, pal?" he inquired kindly. "You look kinda strung out."

Cherry was a man in his late fifties—graying hair and the sort of face that made people want to confide in him.

Clancy spilled the beans about the swimathon while Cherry blended fruit.

Meanwhile, Ruby thought about Spectrum. She was thinking about the briefing. *Is there a connection? Is there something in the deep blue ocean causing disruption to sea life? Possibly. Could it be caused by the moon, the tides, an earthquake on the other side of the world even? Possibly.*

But the shipping confusion? That has to be man-made. The question is, is it man-made by accident or man-made by design? If it isn't an accident, then one can only conclude it has to be sinister.

She was jolted from her musings by Clancy.

"So have you been into Spectrum yet?"

"Could you keep your voice down, buster? I'm not supposed to talk about this stuff," hissed Ruby.

Clancy looked around. "No one's listening," he said, pointing at Cherry's busy establishment. Everyone was chatting or engrossed in their magazines or menus.

"That's what you think," said Ruby. "How do you know that woman over there, the one with the little curly kid, isn't keeping track of everything we say?"

"I can tell," said Clancy. "I mean, look at her — all she's interested in is her baby."

"That's how much you know," said Ruby. "I happen to be aware that she is a sector seven agent and that old curly top is just a cover."

Clancy's eyes grew to saucer size. "No way?" he said. "Really?"

"No, not really, Clance, but don't just assume that someone's not listening just because they look like they're not listening."

It was one of her rules, and an important one.

RULE 9: THERE IS ALWAYS A CHANCE THAT SOMEONE, SOMEWHERE IS WATCHING YOU.

Or, in this case, listening to you.

Ruby had ignored the rule a few weeks ago and had ended up tied to a chair by an evil count and almost buried in a ton of sand, all because someone had been listening in while she yacked away on the telephone to Clancy. She had every right to be cautious, even though the woman in question was actually Mrs. Frast from her mother's bridge club. However, the worry of being overheard only made up part of her reason for keeping it zipped; the truth was that what Ruby really wanted to do was sit in her room and give the briefing some clear thought, puzzle it out.

"Look, Clance, don't take this the wrong way, but I just need to sit and churn a few things over. You understand, don't ya?"

"I guess," said Clancy.

They finished their drinks, and Ruby rode on home.

She walked into the house and up the stairs to the kitchen. She was pretty hungry, and something smelled good. Mrs. Digby was nowhere to be seen. But on the bright side, there were some homemade pizza slices, just cooked, on the table, and a note that said, *Dig in, why don't you?*

There was a PS. It said, *Mrs. Lemon called again. She wants you to sit for that fat baby of hers. I told her you had an infectious skin condition and it didn't look like it would clear up for a week or two.*

Ruby smiled. "Nice going, Mrs. Digby." She loaded her plate with pizza and poured some banana milk into a glass, then, holding an apple in her teeth, she maneuvered her way up to her room. She closed the door firmly behind her, retrieved her yellow notebook, and set about making lists, and then used the elements from the list to make a spider map. She always found it useful to see problems visually.

First she drew a picture of a diver; he was at the top of the page. Then she wrote three headings:

CONFUSED SHIPPING

Spidering out from that heading she wrote every single incidence of confused shipping she had heard of.

The next heading said:

UNUSUAL MARINE ACTIVITY

There were a lot of these too.

The last heading read:

SEA SOUNDS

Branching out from this were all the names of the people who had heard the strange whispering in the ocean.

And then a question:

ARE ALL THESE HAPPENINGS CONNECTED?

AGENT TRILBY: drowned

Bruising to leg

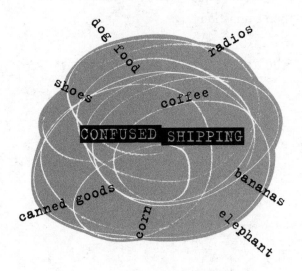

dog food

radios

shoes

coffee

CONFUSED SHIPPING

canned goods

corn

bananas

elephant

ARE ALL THESE

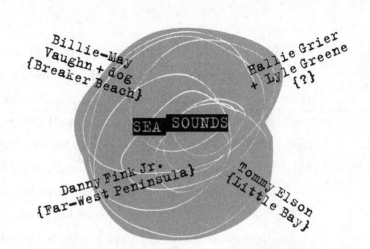

Billie-May
Vaughn + dog
{Breaker Beach}

Hallie Grier
+ Lyle Greene
{?}

SEA SOUNDS

Danny Fink Jr.
{Far-West Peninsula}

Tommy Elson
{Little Bay}

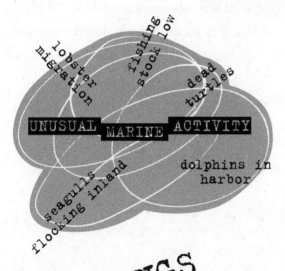

lobster
migration

fishing
stock low

dead
turtles

UNUSUAL MARINE ACTIVITY

seagulls
flocking inland

dolphins in
harbor

HAPPENINGS

CONNECTED?

Ruby sat staring at her own question for some minutes before catching sight of the time. She quickly reached across and switched on the portable TV that sat on her bedroom floor. The title music to *Crazy Cops* blared out, and the face of Detective Despo filled the screen. She sank down in her beanbag and let her mind concentrate on the life-and-death matters of a fictional cop.

The great advantage for Detective Despo was that he had a team of TV writers who made sure his cases were all tied up neatly by the end of each sixty-minute episode. Right at that moment Ruby envied him; she couldn't help wishing that she had a writer on board to make sure her latest case came out right in the end, but regrettably for her, she didn't live in a fictional world.

Mrs. Sylvester was up on deck,
as indeed were all the other passengers,
though she was a good deal more
hysterical than most and was
screaming. . . .

"Pirates! Pirates! They'll rob us blind, cut our throats, and leave us for dead! They've already thrown that poor dog overboard."

On hearing this, Mr. Sylvester fainted.

This all provided an excellent distraction, one that Sabina Redfort made good use of. She very quickly and very quietly made her way to the wheelhouse, snatched up the ship-to-shore radio, and sent out a Mayday call to the coast guard.

"Mayday, Mayday. This is the *Golden Albatross*. Do you read me? Over."

She got no reply, but she wasn't going to give up. Someone was bound to pick up the distress signal sooner or later.

"Mayday, Mayday. This is the *Golden Albatross*. Do you read me? We are in deep over-our-heads trouble. Over."

Still no reply. This was very odd. The coast guard was supposed to answer immediately. Sabina's voice rose louder.

"Mayday, Mayday, I repeat, do you read me? Over."

"Yes," said a voice — unfortunately not a voice from the radio, but rather a deep voice from just behind her. "It's certainly over for you, lady!"

Sabina spun around, and there, standing a few feet away, was a smartly dressed young man who looked like he would be more comfortable in an office than on the deck of a pirate boat; he did not look one bit like the murderous type. However, the man at his side did. He was smiling, revealing a mouth full of gold teeth, some chipped, some missing. He was a small man, but he seemed to easily occupy the cabin with a monstrous malevolence.

In his hand was a very shiny and very sharp-looking knife.

"I was just . . . trying to cancel a . . . dental appointment," stammered Sabina, not at all sure what she was saying, but she was staring at the man, and dental hygiene was the first thing that had come to mind.

The man snickered cruelly. "No need for teeth where you're going."

Sabina didn't like the glint in his eye. He was obviously a man who enjoyed throwing dogs into the ocean; no doubt women, too. He grabbed her arm and pushed and dragged her back to the deck.

"Watch it, would you, Captain Hook; you're wrenching my arm out of its socket."

"No need for arms where you're going," laughed the pirate. Then he spied the gem on her finger. "Now give me your ring!"

Sabina shook her head. "But this is a family heirloom. It belonged to several of my great-grandmothers, and if you think—"

"You hand it over," growled the pirate, "or I'll kill everyone on board."

"But . . . it won't come off my finger," protested Sabina.

"No need for fingers where you're going!" he said, flashing the knife.

Goodness, thought Sabina, *there's not going to be much of me left.*

"Let me cut it off. Save you the struggle." He laughed again.

"You'll do no such thing," said Sabina, clenching her fists. The pirate lunged toward her, and Sabina lashed out, clocking him on the jaw. Sabina Redfort packed quite a punch, and the ring, which was diamond, gashed a scarlet ribbon across the pirate's cheek.

"Oh my, that was an accident," said Sabina a little nervously. "I was about to say, if you want this ring, you had better get me a little soap and water."

The pirate didn't look like he was about to oblige, but then he grinned.

"OK," he said. "Here's the water; good luck finding the soap."

And with that he picked her up and threw her overboard.

Brant Redfort, horrified, bellowed, "Honey, don't think of drowning! I'm coming to save you!"

And he did a swan dive from the bow of the boat and disappeared beneath the waves. The pirates, sensing they had in some way failed to create an atmosphere of blind terror, began shooting into the water. They continued to shoot for some minutes, wanting to be sure that these two have-a-go heroes would never resurface.

"We won't be worth much to you if we're all dead!" screamed Mrs. Sylvester. "Hostages have to be alive, remember."

"Who said anything about hostages?" snarled the pirate.

This had the desired effect, and all the remaining passengers trembled and awaited their fate.

CHAPTER 15
Clutching at Straws

RUBY WOKE ON WEDNESDAY MORNING to hear her radio making an unpleasant noise, like an orchestra tuning up. She lifted her head wearily from the pillow and through the blur of her poor eyesight saw a gray furry shape.

"Bug," she groaned. "You wanna switch that off?" It was a trick of his to step on the radio, turning it on. It usually got Ruby out of bed.

The dog ambled over to where she lay and licked her nose.

"Cut it out, would you, Bug?"

She dragged herself up, then tripped over the happy husky and landed on her behind. *Darn it!* She crawled over to the radio and blindly fiddled with the dial.

"If you're gonna switch the radio on, at least tune it to something that sounds like a tune." To her surprise she found it *was* tuned. Mrs. Digby had obviously been in with the vacuum, since the dial was set to easy-listening Chime Melody. However, the track that was playing was anything but easy listening: it sounded like a whole bunch of grasshoppers were playing badly tuned violins.

Jeepers, is that enough to give anyone a sore head.

Ruby looked at herself in the mirror.

"I guess I'm up," she muttered. She showered and dressed and fixed her barrette in her hair, then looked at herself in the mirror.

Better, she told herself. She pulled on a T-shirt that said ***wake me if things get interesting.***

School that day basically involved trying to coax Clancy out of packing his bags and heading for the hills.

"I think I should just get outta here, make a run for it," he said. He seemed to mean it. "I won't survive two minutes in the ocean, not two minutes."

"Clance, you're overdramatizing. The worst that could happen is you get stung by a jellyfish."

"A jellyfish!" squealed Clancy, by now flapping his arms furiously. "I don't like the sound of that. No, I'm gonna head for Colorado—it's landlocked. I could camp out for a few months until this whole thing blows over."

Ruby rolled her eyes. "Clance my friend, you're beginning

to lose it. It's just a *school swimathon*." But Clancy Crew could not be calmed.

"You know how I am about jellyfish; if I get stung, I'll most likely have an allergic reaction and sink."

"You can borrow my Spectrum anti-sting canister, how about that? That's gotta reassure you," said Ruby.

By Thursday, Clancy was worse: he was hardly able to speak, and in physics when Mr. Endell asked him what he would do if an asteroid struck Earth, Clancy replied, "Thank my lucky stars."

Elliot tried to jolt him out of it by making him laugh, but most of his jokes seemed to revolve around some poor bozo meeting a gory end, and so his efforts resulted in Clancy Crew sinking lower into his sweater. He actually looked like he was shrinking.

By Friday, Clancy had adopted the demeanor of a condemned man. He had stopped wrestling with his fate and seemed to accept that there was no way out; he was going to have to swim that swimathon even if it meant swimming heroically — or perhaps weeping like a coward — toward certain death.

After school, just as Clancy was leaving for home, Ruby caught up with him.

"Hey, Clance, do you want me to come over?"

Clancy shook his head. "Nah, that's all right, Rube. I gotta get my sleep; it's my only chance."

"You know you're not gonna die, Clance; you're being awful pessimistic."

"Can you guarantee that?" asked Clancy, searching her face for assurance. He wanted to believe her, he really did.

"I gave you my anti-sting; there's no way you can die of a jellyfish attack," said Ruby.

"I know," said Clancy. "But there's worse than jellyfish out there."

As she looked into his desperate eyes, she thought of that old saying: a drowning man will clutch at straws. Clancy needed a straw right now, one that he could put all his faith in: **RULE 20: NINETY PERCENT OF SURVIVAL IS ABOUT BELIEVING YOU WILL SURVIVE.**

Ruby reached into her inside jacket pocket and unclipped something from the lining.

"Here," she said. "Why don't you take this? It's the luckiest thing I got." She handed him a tiny tin button. It seemed to be totally plain, just an ordinary white button, until you held it in your hand and felt something embossed on its surface. Ruby had found it when she was just a little kid, next to the sidewalk on Cedarwood Drive. She had kept it all these years; she wasn't exactly sure why. She usually had it pinned to the inside of her jacket, a habit started when she was a toddler and aware that her mother would consider the pin a hazard and take it away. Now that she was grown there was of course no need to hide it, but it had become a "thing"—something she did—and so the button remained out of sight. "Just don't lose it, and give it right back, OK?"

Clancy looked at this small object lying in his hand. He believed her about the luck. Ruby could see that in his eyes. *This tiny object might just save my life.* That's what he was thinking. "Really?" he said, and his face looked brighter. "I can borrow it?"

"Yeah, take my good luck, why don't you."

He smiled. "Thanks, Rube."

She walked off, then stopped and called out, "So remember, if anyone's gonna get chomped tomorrow, it's me!"

Ruby was slowly riding her bike home when she noticed the stranger standing on the corner of Bamboo and Rose. She had seen him a few times now without really taking notice, but this time she *was* taking notice: Twinford was a big place, but this guy seemed to be frequenting a lot of the same places Ruby did.

Is he tailing me?

She had first seen a weathered-looking guy soon after the dolphins took up residence in Twinford Harbor. Earlier this week she had spotted the same man on the corner of Amster, drinking a small cup of coffee. He wore a hat and sunglasses (even though the sun had already sunk low in the sky). He was tanned and lithe, but the hair that stuck out from under his cap was gray and he looked like he had seen many a scorching summer's day, his skin leathery and worn. She had spotted him in the middle of town too, outside the library and then again down near the harbor.

Nothing to be suspicious about, you could say, but Ruby had picked him up on her internal radar, and once she had seen him a couple of times, she realized she was seeing him over and over. She had never observed him with anyone, nor had she heard him speak, not even to the waiter at the coffee shop. When he ordered, he pointed; when he thanked, he nodded; when he paid the check, he paid silently and left with a wave of the hand.

OK, so there was no law against drinking small cups of coffee in the Full-O-Beans coffee shop, but though Ruby had never caught him looking in her direction, she had this weird feeling that this man was watching her, like he knew who she was. If she was right about that, then what was he doing? And was she in danger?

Why would he be tailing me? she thought.

For now, she couldn't do anything more than add him to her list.

Once back on Cedarwood Drive, she scooted up the stairs to her room. She retrieved her yellow notebook and marked the "stranger" sightings on her city map. Having stared at the map for some time, Ruby put down her pen, folded the map, and returned it to the hiding place. She went down to the kitchen to find Mrs. Digby and food.

She found Mrs. Digby boiling pasta and scolding the radio.

The radio presenter was saying:

"We at Chime Melody apologize for the interference to our broadcasts during this past week. We are trying to correct the problem. Meanwhile, don't go twisting that dial, we'll miss you."

"They shoulda sorted this issue before now," said Mrs. Digby. "It's more than an old person can stand, this squawking coming at you every time you step into your kitchen. No wonder my noodles are overcooked." She twisted the tuner to Twinford Talk Radio.

"SO BETTY, I HEAR YKK 672 IS ABOUT TO PASS PRETTY CLOSE TO EARTH?" "THAT'S RIGHT, KEN." "BETTY, IS IT POSSIBLE THAT THE ASTEROID COULD BE INTERFERING WITH CHIME MELODY 204 FM?" "INTERESTING THEORY, KEN, BUT I DON'T THINK THE SCIENTISTS WOULD AGREE THAT THE TWO THINGS ARE RELATED."

"Asteroid, my foot." Mrs. Digby clunked the off switch with her ladle and went back to salvaging her noodles.

But Ruby's mind was no longer on food; it was far too busy trying to decide if Ken might just be right. Maybe the asteroid did have a part to play in this whole mystery.

Or maybe it was just a cold bit of rock floating through space, and Ruby was no closer to working out what in tarnation was going on.

**Ambassador Crew did not
consider himself the type of man
to be commandeered by pirates.
It just wasn't in his game plan. . . .**

The captain of the *Golden Albatross* — a cowardly little man — might have surrendered immediately, but Ambassador Crew was no coward, and he would *not* give in so readily.

He had had enough of dancing to their tune. He stood up from where the Twinfordites were huddled and strode out to confront the head pirate. He drew himself up as tall as he could. He towered above these scoundrels, and it made him feel confident. He would get what he wanted — he always did.

"This will not stand — do you hear me? I insist that you release me and drop me back on terra firma. I have a job, and it's an important one. Oh, and these people need to get home too." He waved his hand, indicating the cowering cruise passengers. "Some of them have jobs, and most of them have commitments of sorts."

The pirates merely laughed.

"Who is this bozo with the snapped arm?" jeered the pirate with the poor dental work. He was pointing at Ambassador Crew's plaster cast — an injury sustained in a squash match.

"Now, just look here —" began Ambassador Crew.

The pirate snarled a menacing snarl that came from deep inside. "You are not the boss of this boat — I am. And if I say you need to keep your big mouth shut, you shut it — understood?"

Ambassador Crew glanced at the silver knife glimmering in the pirate's hand, and he kept his mouth firmly shut.

"And if I say you jump up and down, then you jump up and down, got it?" said the pirate.

Ambassador Crew nodded.

"So jump up and down," snarled the pirate.

Ambassador Crew jumped.

CHAPTER 16
Don't Look Back

IT WAS 8 A.M. ON SATURDAY MORNING, and Clancy Crew was doing as Coach Newhart had suggested: swimming as if his life depended on it. At this rate he was going to win the trophy for Twinford Junior High single-handedly. He was way out in front and almost at the buoy. He even thought he could hear Ruby's shouts, urging him on, but of course he couldn't, not with the earplugs in. What he *could* hear was the thumping of his heart and the voice in his head that said, *Why am I in the water? Am I out of my mind? I'm going to die!*

A couple of times he thought he saw something; a couple of times he thought he felt something brush past him. He tried to focus on a rule Ruby had taught him many, many years ago when he was just a tiny kid at a Halloween party. It had been his turn to stick his hand in the Halloween barrel; the barrel always contained everyday items — like a hard-boiled egg with shell removed — but your imagination could easily lead you to believe that it was a misshapen eyeball you were holding. Sometimes, it is important to shut down the creative part of the brain, just tell yourself it's OK and you will find that it is OK. **RULE 21: DON'T THINK BACK; DON'T THINK AHEAD; JUST THINK NOW.**

So Clancy tried to do just that. Things went fine until he got to the marker, turned, and began to swim back to shore. This was the worst part, the part he dreaded. Now he couldn't see what was in the open water behind him; now he would never know if some large fish with big sharp teeth was following him, waiting for exactly the right moment to open its jaws and bite down on a leg, or worse, his whole body. He imagined the blood gushing up out of his mouth, the feeding frenzy that would ensue.

Clancy closed his eyes and swam.

He swam so hard and so blindly that he only realized that he had reached the beach when he felt the rough sand graze his stomach and the strong hand of Coach Newhart pulling him to his feet.

"Nice swim, Crew. I knew you had technique, but I had no idea you were fast." The coach draped a towel around his shoulders and slapped him on the back. "Grab a hot drink, son, and get warmed up."

Clancy staggered toward the support team, all of them smiling and cheering congratulations, but Clancy was only aware of the sensation of sand underfoot; feet, all two of them, back on terra firma. He was alive.

When the swimathon was over and all the participants were out of the water and back on the beach, pulling on their tracksuits, Clancy went to find Ruby. She was sitting on the beach, her head resting on her knees, her eyes focused on the horizon. She looked up, smiling. "See Clance, I told you you could do it!"

"Can we just get out of here?" he pleaded.

Once they were safely installed in their favorite booth at the Double Donut, Ruby picked up the conversation. "Mind over matter is all it took you — of course, guts too," she added. "I don't deny that."

"Well, never again," said Clancy, clutching a mug of hot chocolate. He was still shivering even though it was eighty degrees outside.

"Don't let Coach Newhart hear you saying that," said Ruby. "He thinks he just discovered the swim talent of the century. My guess is he's got big plans for you, my friend."

"Can we please talk about something else?" pleaded Clancy. He was beginning to turn green. It was fair to say that Clancy Crew looked all washed out, which wasn't surprising since he had just faced his biggest fear and lived to tell the tale. Ruby thought about *her* darkest terror, the total fear of being buried alive. Would she have fared so well if forced to confront her own nightmare? She decided to cut Clancy a little slack and changed the subject.

"So I'm guessing Spectrum might issue me with some new spy gadgets—you know, dive-related ones."

"Speaking of which . . ." Clancy pulled something out of his pocket. "I found this on the beach. You musta dropped it." It was the rescue watch.

"Thanks, Clance! I didn't even realize I'd lost it. It's the clasp—the darned thing keeps coming loose. Hey, but that little problem with the retractable grab cable should be all hunky-dory, now so I can rappel out of anywhere."

"Wish you'd grabbed me out of the ocean an hour ago," muttered Clancy.

"Nah, you didn't need me—you swam your way out of that just fine."

"It was the button," said Clancy.

"Well, you're the one who did the swimming," said Ruby.

"It was the button," repeated Clancy.

They were both silent for about twenty seconds, and then Clancy said, "So that was pretty nice of LB to let you keep it. The watch I mean."

"Yeah," said Ruby. "The 'great' Bradley Baker's rescue watch, who would have thunk it." She said this with more than the smallest hint of sarcasm.

"You said it's pretty special to her?"

"Seems so," said Ruby. "BB and LB were kinda close."

"So is it true that they were sweethearts?" asked Clancy.

"Sweethearts!" Ruby spluttered. "No one says sweethearts, Clance—not unless they're at least ancient, like two hundred."

Clancy looked indignant. "Mouse used the word *sweetheart* just yesterday."

"Yeah, well, I'll bet she used it in a cool way, you know, being ironic or something."

"You saying I'm not cool?" said Clancy.

"Clance, I'm not saying that—I just meant you were using the word *sweetheart* in an old lady type of way."

"I'm using it in its technical form," argued Clancy. "It's technically correct."

"Yeah, if you're listening to Chime Radio or something. . . . Speaking of which, did you happen to tune in lately?" said Ruby.

Clancy looked at her like she had lost at least one or two brain cells. "What? Are you crazy? Do I look like I'm a senior citizen?"

"It happens to play some great numbers," said Ruby. "For anyone with an eclectic taste in music—I rate it."

"Yeah, I agree actually, but not in the afternoon. The afternoon show is super lame — cheesy beyond cheese puffs."

"OK, I'll give you that, but I wasn't asking if you had *listened*, I asked you if you had happened to tune in; they're two different things."

"How'd ya mean?" asked Clancy.

"OK, so a few days running this weird thing has been happening where Chime broadcasts tunes that aren't tunes."

"What? I don't get it," said Clancy, scrunching his face up like he had just eaten a bad snail or something.

This always got on Ruby's nerves: trying to explain something when someone was looking at you like this was off-putting. "Quit making the face, would ya?" said Ruby.

"Sorry," said Clancy. "I don't do it on purpose; it's just how my face goes."

Ruby continued. "I mean the music is untuneful, as in very un-Chime-like, sorta avant-garde — *like* music, but super modern," she said.

"Has anybody been complaining about it?" said Clancy.

"They apologized on the show, and Talk Radio said it might be due to asteroid interference."

"So maybe that's it," said Clancy. "Maybe it's just some old asteroid."

Ruby didn't say anything, but Clancy recognized the look in her eye. "What are *you* thinking it is?" he asked.

Ruby sighed. "I'm thinking there are a lot of strange things all going on at once, and it's hard to imagine they aren't all connected in some way."

They were deep into this animated discussion when Red and Del showed up. They slid into the seats next to Clancy and Ruby.

"So Coach is pretty over the moon," said Del. "Says he hasn't had so many great swimmers all in one grade for at least a decade. He can see big opportunities for the Twinford swim team — wants to make sure old Crew here joins up. Says he's a great ocean swimmer, which means he wants you coming to swim practice. You ready for that, Crew?"

Clancy put his head in his hands.

"What's the matter with him?" asked Del.

"He's just feeling lucky to be alive," said Ruby.

"And this is how he expresses it?" said Del.

"You mean something happened out there?" asked Red.

But Clancy didn't want to talk about it.

"He thinks there's *something* out in Twinford Bay that might nibble him," said Del.

"You know what?" said Red. "I think he might be right. I heard something when I was swimming. Something not normal."

"How could you?" said Ruby. "You were wearing earplugs."

"Well, that's the thing," said Red. "I lost them."

Ruby wasn't surprised to hear that; Red lost things a lot. She was a dropper, a breaker, and a loser of stuff.

"When I was almost out to the buoy," said Red, "I heard this kind of singing."

Ruby sat up. "Really? What do you think it was?"

"Could have been a mermaid or something. It was kind of sad-sounding," said Red.

"Oh, geez!" said Del. "Trust you to believe in mermaids."

"I'm not saying it was one," said Red. "I'm saying it coulda been one, if there were mermaids, I mean. I'm not saying there are, but if there were."

"There aren't," said Del. "Not even slightly, you can take my word for it." Ruby agreed with Del on this point. Red's mermaid theory was unlikely, but it *was* kind of strange that she claimed to have heard a voice in the ocean. Ruby was thinking back to Agent Kekoa's briefing — the strange sounds people had been hearing in the bay. *Could Red have heard the same thing?*

Clancy was feeling a little cheered by this conversation; he didn't mind talking about mermaids because, as far as he understood it, all they did was sit around brushing their hair. They weren't particularly threatening as sea creatures went, and what's more they didn't exist, so it wasn't really something he had to worry about.

"Hey you guys, I've been looking all over for you!" said Elliot, spotting them at their table. "Do ya wanna come to my place later this afternoon? We're having a barbecue. Mouse'll be there."

Clancy looked at him warily. "Seafood?" he asked.

"Burgers," said Elliot.

"Sure." Clancy smiled. "That would be great."

However, it turned out not to be so great because Elliot's mother's friend Tilly Matthews dropped by to update the world and his wife on the latest rumor going around Twinford. Tilly Matthews had a lot of time on her hands, and most of it was spent telling folks other folks' business; this time, though, she had some real news.

"Apparently, fourteen-foot sharks have been spotted moving along Twinford Bay. And not one or two either, a whole batch of them."

Ruby was considering correcting Tilly on the collective for sharks, but was interrupted by the clattering of Clancy's salad fork as it fell from his hand onto his plate.

"Are you OK, sweetie pie?" asked Elliot's mom. "You look like you might actually faint."

"To tell you the truth, Mrs. Finch, I don't feel so good," replied Clancy earnestly.

His imagination had instantly supplied him with an image of him being swiftly devoured by a fourteen-foot-long shark, and he couldn't think of anything a whole lot worse than being eaten by a fourteen-foot shark. Perhaps being eaten by *a whole batch* of fourteen-foot sharks would be worse, but it was marginal.

"Would you mind if I called a cab and went on home?" he asked.

"Well, now I'm really worried Clancy. Do you want to lie down?" asked Mrs. Finch.

"No, I'll be fine," said Clancy, who then promptly fainted.

CHAPTER 17
Something Fearsome This Way Comes

WHEN RUBY WOKE UP THE NEXT MORNING, she called Clancy right away, but he wasn't answering his phone. In the end she had to call the main line and ask Drusilla, the housekeeper, to get him to pick up.

"Hello," came a weak voice from the end of the line.

"Clance? What are you doing?" demanded Ruby.

"I feel lousy," said Clancy. "Real sick."

"You're not sick, you're just freaked out. Yikes, Clance," she said. "I mean, I knew you were shark phobic, but I didn't think that just talking about them could actually be terminal."

"That's not it," said Clancy. "It's just that I knew I shouldn't swim in the ocean. Now, it turns out I was right. I came *this* close to actual death."

Ruby, of course, didn't see it this way. To her it just went to prove what she had always known: that sharks were not man's predators. She had read countless books on the subject, and no one worth their marine biologist salt thought sharks were out to eat *people*.

"You're OK, Clancy," she said. "Stop freaking out."

"I'm sick," insisted Clancy. "Super sick."

Ruby sighed. "I'm coming over."

She went downstairs and found Mrs. Digby sitting talking to Hitch—unusual only because Mrs. Digby rarely sat down. She usually drank her morning beverage while vacuuming, but this was a Sunday—a day on which she allowed herself a little luxury. She was poring over the papers as she swigged a cup of strong-looking tea that had been stewing in a large silver teapot, the sort of teapot a dormouse might live in. Mrs. Digby was discussing with Hitch the gossip that made up every local news headline that day.

```
SHARKS SPOTTED IN TWINFORD BAY
SWIMATHON KIDS SWIM FOR THEIR LIVES
MARINE LIFE OUT OF CONTROL
MONSTERS ON THE LOOSE
PANIC!
```

The *Twinford Mirror* went on to say: Local fisherman very fortunate not to drown when a pod of dolphins rocked him out of his boat yesterday evening.

"I thought dolphins were meant to be man's best friend," said Mrs. Digby.

"No, that's dogs," said Ruby.

"Well, I never heard of dolphins trying to drown folks. What in high heaven is going on, for Jiminy's sake?" Mrs. Digby asked the papers.

"Well may you ask," said Hitch. "It says here that three fishermen sent out distress signals, but no one registered their alert."

Ruby made a mental note to add these latest events to her sheet of paper — she was going to have to extend it. But not right now — right now, she had to go buck up Clancy.

She fetched her bike and rode over to the Crew home. The front door was opened by Drusilla, who informed Ruby that Clancy was feeling "under the weather."

"If you can get him out of that bed, I'll give you a medal," Drusilla added.

"I'll give it my best shot!" called Ruby, running up the three flights of stairs that led to Clancy's room.

She opened the door.

Clancy raised his head from the pillow. "Rube, that you?"

"Give me a break, Clance, and quit the feeble routine, would you. You didn't get attacked by fish yesterday, and there's no chance of it happening while you're lying in bed."

"I don't feel so good, you know," said Clancy. "I think I'm going to stay here. I need to recuperate."

They argued for nineteen minutes before Ruby threw in the towel.

She wasn't about to waste her entire Sunday sitting at Clancy's bedside listening to total horse manure; instead she would check out what Del was up to.

It was late Sunday afternoon, and Ruby had been playing Del Lasco at table tennis for more than a few hours. They had come out even, winning seventeen games each. By the time she climbed on her bike, Ruby was flat-out tired and finding it a struggle to turn the pedals, but as she reached the corner of Amster, she saw the stranger again; he was getting into a car. Maybe it was time to turn the tables, tail *him* for a change and see how he liked it.

The car's engine started, and the car pulled out from the curb and drove north up Bleaker. Her heart was beating pretty fast and adrenalin pumped through her.

What do I do when I catch him?

But this wasn't going to be a question she needed an answer for.

Ruby kept up OK until he turned onto Flower, which was a pretty steep hill, one of the steepest in Twinford. Her legs, after thirty-four games of Ping-Pong, were never going to chase a car up a hill, and as the gap between them grew, she accepted defeat and freewheeled back down, gliding on home to Cedarwood Drive.

On Monday, while Ruby was brushing her teeth, she switched on the radio, turning the dial until she reached Twinford Talk Radio. There was a jingle playing, some commercial about the benefits of eating cereal with raisins in it if you wanted to have a productive day at school. Ruby couldn't see it herself; she had always felt that raisins had no business being in breakfast cereal. *Who wants to eat a shriveled grape floating in milk?*

The commercials over, the voice of Greg Witney, the TTR anchorman, came back on the air.

"SO, SHELLY, WHAT DO YOU THINK HAPPENED TO THESE GREAT OCEAN PREDATORS?" *"IT'S HARD TO DRAW ANY FIRM CONCLUSIONS, GREG, BUT THEY DO SEEM TO HAVE BEEN SAVAGELY ATTACKED BY SOME OTHER PREDATOR. JUDGING BY THE STATE OF THEM, CERTAINLY SOMETHING FEARSOME."* **"BUT JUST WHAT CREATURE COULD TAKE ON A TIGER SHARK? IT DOESN'T BEAR THINKING ABOUT, HUH, SHELLY?"**

"IT CERTAINLY DOESN'T, GREG. TWINFORD FOLK MIGHT WANT TO KEEP OUT OF THE WATER UNTIL THIS VERY STRANGE MYSTERY IS SOLVED. NOW BACK TO YOU."

Jeepers. Clancy is never going to get out of bed again.

Ruby got dressed: today's T-shirt kept its insult short and simply said **bozo.** She stamped her feet into her well-worn Yellow Stripe sneakers and skittered downstairs.

Hitch was sitting at the kitchen table, polishing some silverware and looking for all the world like an actual butler.

"I think you may be getting too into your cover story," said Ruby, her nose in the refrigerator, searching for the juice.

Hitch shrugged. "Mrs. Digby runs a tight ship."

"Yeah, but she already *believes* you're a butler; you don't need to make out you're the best entire one to ever polish forks on this earthly universe of Twinford."

"And I don't want her thinking I'm a lousy one either. My life wouldn't be worth living, kid."

Ruby shrugged and sucked on her drinking straw. When she came back up for air, she said, "So did you hear the story about the attacked sharks?"

Hitch looked up from his polishing. "Yes, that is strange. Sounds almost supernatural."

"Yeah," mused Ruby. "Almost like there's some kinda giant sea monster swimming about offa the Twinford coast."

"You telling me you believe in sea monsters, kid?"

"Not really, but stranger things have happened," said Ruby.

"This city's going to the dogs," said Mrs. Digby, walking into the room, bucket in hand. "The dogs, I say."

Bug registered the word *dog* and looked at her hopefully.

A tiny glow came from Hitch's sleeve, and he furtively looked at his watch.

"Well, this is all very intriguing," he said, swiftly putting the silverware back where it belonged. "But I really better get going — that laundry won't drive to Crisp 'n Clean by itself."

"I wouldn't be so sure of that," said Mrs. Digby. "Some of it looks like it's crawling with life. Bacteria gone wild."

"I better step on it then," Hitch called, and he was almost running. Despite the wisecracking, it was pretty obvious that Hitch actually was in a hurry, and Ruby was certain that it had nothing to do with laundry.

"You need me to assist?" hissed Ruby, following him to the front door.

"I appreciate the offer, kid," said Hitch. "But I reckon Mrs. Drisco might be kind of disappointed if she doesn't see your bright and smiling face in class this morning."

Drat. She had forgotten that today was Monday, and therefore she was expected at school.

"I could cut class," Ruby suggested. "I mean, it would be no big deal, not if Spectrum needs me to work on something?"

"Spectrum can handle this, kid," assured Hitch. "I'll radio you if things get tricky. Just concentrate on your cover story; act like a schoolkid for a while." He patted her on the head and disappeared out the door.

"Could you be slightly more patronizing?" muttered Ruby as she straightened her barrette.

She walked back into the kitchen, swallowed the last mouthful of her cereal, and slung her satchel over her shoulder. "OK, Bug, I'll take you for a sprint."

"I hope you're not thinking of being late for class, you little insect," said Mrs. Digby, fixing Ruby with the old Mrs. Digby X-ray stare. When the housekeeper looked at her like that, Ruby could almost believe that she could read her thoughts.

"Course not, Mrs. Digby. I won't go far, and I'll send Bug back on his own. I'll make it on time, I swear." She gave Mrs. Digby her "trust me" look, but Mrs. D. wasn't born yesterday.

"Don't give me those big eyes of yours," she said.

"OK," said Ruby, spitting into her hands and pressing them together. "I promise in spit. Satisfied?" This was how the Digby family sealed their oaths; a promise sealed with spit was a promise to be kept.

Mrs. Digby sniffed. "All right, but I better not be getting calls from that Mrs. Drisco. I haven't got time to listen to her blathering; she's a very disagreeable woman."

"You hear me arguing?" said Ruby.

Mrs. Digby sniffed and switched on the radio, and out came that same strange sound.

"Not again! Why are you spouting out this plainly diabolical earache? If I wanted to listen to this kinda terrible assault to my ears, I would have bought myself a cockatoo." She banged it with her rolling pin. "That's me and Chime Melody through. I warned you," she said, snapping the radio off and marching out of the room.

"Weirder and weirder," said Ruby to herself.

CHAPTER 18
White Noise

RUBY HEADED OFF IN THE DIRECTION OF LITTLE BAY. She needed to take a look at the ocean before she went to school; not that it was likely to tell her a whole lot, but she just felt it might help to go and sort of drink it in.

She climbed on her bike and whistled to Bug—he liked to run alongside, and a sprint out to the ocean was nothing for him. When they got within a quarter mile, they both sensed something pretty strange.

It was a sound, a sort of clacking sound.

As they got nearer, Ruby figured out what it was. Hundreds upon hundreds of crabs, all making their way along the sands. "That's kinda weird, huh Bug?"

The dog went to investigate, sniffing at the creatures and backing off as they snapped their tiny claws at his nose.

Ruby let go of her bike and slowly picked her way through the crabs, expecting to come to the place where they ended—but they didn't end, they just kept on coming.

Then, far, far on the other side of the beach, she saw a diver walking toward the ocean. She called out to him, but he didn't hear her, and before she could reach him he had ducked under the sea's surface. A few yards up the beach sat a large yellow carryall—the diver would be coming back for it, she imagined, but Ruby couldn't wait. She had promised Mrs. Digby that she would not be late for school, and a promise in spit was a promise to be kept.

Ruby made it into school just seconds before the bell sounded, dashed into her classroom, and slid into her seat, smiling at Mrs. Drisco, who scowled back. She looked for Clancy, but he wasn't there. He was never late for class, so she guessed he must be off sick, or (more likely) was still faking it.

Still freaked out? she wondered. *Or avoiding something?*

It didn't take her long to figure it out.

The bell rang, and Ruby spilled out of her homeroom with all the other kids. She made her way to physics, and as she turned the corner, heard a familiar voice shouting.

"Hey, Redfort, are you planning on showing for swim practice this evening?"

Ruby turned to see Del Lasco, tall, sporty, and kind of in your face, coming down the main stairway.

"I said I would, didn't I?" replied Ruby.

"Yeah, well, you say a lotta things, and I haven't seen you show for practice once this season."

Ruby had been kind of busy with Spectrum, and it was true she had simply not had time for Junior High commitments.

"I did the swimathon, didn't I?"

"Sure. And got beaten by Clancy Crew. He isn't even on the swim team! You need to train. Sharpen up."

"I'll be there tonight, *OK*?" assured Ruby as she made for the door.

"I notice Crew's skipping off today too, which is just swell."

"And how is that my fault, buster?" called Ruby, disappearing into class.

If you didn't know it, you might imagine that Ruby Redfort and Del Lasco weren't even friends at all — but they were. Good friends in fact. Del Lasco had a mouth on her, that was for sure, but she was also very loyal. No one could deny that if the chips were down, you could count on Del to wade in and punch someone on your behalf, even if you didn't want them punched.

Mr. Endell was talking about white noise today. Which was pretty interesting, as it turned out, and sort of helpful given what Ruby was investigating for Spectrum. White noise, according to Mr. Endell, was a kind of noise produced by combining every frequency together, from high to low — like someone playing every key on a piano at the same time.

What was interesting to Ruby was that white noise could be used to *mask* other sounds, including voices. This was because the ear was so busy dealing with so many different notes and tones, all sounding at once, that it couldn't manage to tune in to just one voice.

Mr. Endell demonstrated this by turning on his desk fan, which he pointed out produced a kind of white noise, and then speaking at a normal volume.

He said, "   ."

"What?" chorused the class.

"I was saying," said Mr. Endell, turning off the fan, "that spies and secret agents have actually manufactured white-noise machines to stop other spies and secret agents from listening in to their conversations. Think of white noise as thousands of voices all talking at the same moment. It's possible to tune in to one voice in a group of chatting people. But there's no way you can tune into one voice in a crowd of a thousand."

Kinda fascinating, thought Ruby. Could someone be using something like this to block Mayday calls and cargo signals and reroute shipping? There was a good chance.

❅ ❅ ❅

It was three o'clock, and Ruby grabbed her swim bag out of her locker and hurried out to the waiting bus. Swim practice was going to be at the municipal pool due to the Dillon Flannagon Twinford Junior High pool incident. Ruby went to get changed, stuffed her bag in the locker, and walked toward the Olympic-size pool. She could hear Coach Newhart shouting instructions and generally bossing the team into shape.

Ruby got into the water and did a couple of lengths to warm up. She had her swimming goggles on and couldn't see too well, but she was aware that the lifeguard was blowing his whistle. Someone had committed some pool misdemeanor, and she looked up to see who the culprit was. Through the blur of the water she saw the lifeguard frantically signaling to her to get out of the pool. "Man! What have I done!" she muttered to herself. These municipal pool lifeguards were a royal pain in the behind. Ruby swam to the side and immediately began to remonstrate with the whistle-blowing bozo.

"What? I didn't use the verruca footbath with enough due care and attention, or was I splash . . .?" Her voice tailed off as she lifted her goggles and found herself staring at a familiar face.

"Oh, brother! It's you."

"Hey, kid," said Hitch. He was wearing the blue shorts and logo-printed T-shirt just like all the other lifeguards, and with his suntanned skin he blended in perfectly and no one gave him a second look.

"What are you doing here?"

"I'm here to suggest that you go tell your coach that you need to get the nurse to take a look at that bump on your head."

"What bump on my head?" said Ruby.

"The bump you need to convince Coach Newhart is giving you so much grief that you have to see the nurse about it."

"Oh, man! You know Del Lasco is going to actually kill me. You want that on your conscience?"

He threw her a towel.

"I'd be more worried about Coach Newhart if I were you."

"Thanks. I appreciate your concern," said Ruby.

"You signed up for this, kid. I warned you, but you wouldn't listen; this job can play fast and loose with your social life."

"It's not my *social* life that I'm concerned about; Del can punch, man. I mean really punch."

Hitch pulled Ruby out of the water, and she staggered off to try and act her way out of swim practice. Ruby Redfort was a first-rate actress, and she did a good job of persuading Coach Newhart that she would be dead in the water if she so much as doggy-paddled. Then she made for the changing rooms; she could feel Del Lasco's eyes boring into her back as she limped away.

Hitch and Ruby met in the corridor, both now changed, Hitch in a suit and tie and Ruby in jeans, jacket, and *bozo* T-shirt. Hitch raised an eyebrow when he saw it, but didn't comment.

He led her through a door marked MAINTENANCE, which housed various pieces of equipment and pipes and tanks and all kinds of things that presumably kept the swimming pool clean and warm and full of water. Almost invisible behind one of the largest pipes was another door. It looked like it hadn't been opened in quite a while, and several dead flies were clustered on the floor in front of it.

He took out a key chain holding several identical-looking keys.

"This is a door to Spectrum? You're kidding me," said Ruby. She was well aware of Spectrum's ability to create tunnels and entrances to the agency HQ — and all seemingly at a moment's notice — but this was the Twinford City swimming pool.

"You know Spectrum, always likes to keep you on your toes," said Hitch as he unlocked the door. It was made of thick steel, and it closed behind them with a satisfying *clunk*. They were at the top of a pure white spiral staircase, not an open-tread iron one. This staircase was completely enclosed and made of a material like molded stone. Without a word, Hitch descended.

CHAPTER 19
Strange and Old-fashioned

THEIR FEET SOUNDED LIKE TAP SHOES on the hard steps. The staircase seemed to be endless, almost dizzying, and Ruby had to concentrate so as not to lose her footing. Hitch was already out of sight.

"I hope you're not gonna ask me to return the same way!" shouted Ruby, her voice spilling after him.

"Don't worry. There's an elevator," he called.

"What? So why are we using the stairs?" Ruby whined.

"All part of the training," said Hitch. "You never do know when running down stairs really fast is going to save your life."

"Or kill you," said Ruby flatly.

They finally walked through a small white curved door so discreet that you might never discover it if you didn't already know it was there. It opened into the vast Spectrum atrium, the white floor covered in black concentric circles.

While Ruby waited for Hitch to sort out her authorization

band, she tiptoed along the lines, pretending that her life depended on keeping her balance. And then she noticed something she had never noticed before: a tiny mosaic right in the center of the final circle. She bent down to take a closer look; it was a perfect little housefly.

In the far corner sat a woman who seemed to be growing up through the middle of a round desk, rather like a mushroom. The desk was dotted with telephones of every color. Ruby called out to her.

"Hey there, Buzz."

The mushroom paused mid-dial and peered over the top of her ugly glasses. For such a young woman she really did dress very dowdily. She raised her hand, a lazy attempt at a wave, as if she could hardly be bothered with the effort of it, and continued to make her call. Buzz was sitting doing what Buzz was supposed to do, answering brightly colored telephones and speaking down the receivers in every possible language. Hitch strode over and announced Ruby's arrival.

"He's not here yet," said Buzz, her voice nasal, her tone unapologetic.

"You're saying he's late?" said Hitch.

"I am," said Buzz. The orange phone rang and she picked it up and began speaking Portuguese.

"Who's he?" asked Ruby.

"You'll see," said Hitch.

"Great, now you're being covert about a meeting I'm about to have in two minutes," muttered Ruby.

"Let's go see Blacker while we wait," said Hitch. "He'll be glad to see you. I told him I was bringing you in." He beckoned Ruby to follow him. "Looks like you might be here a while; seems like you're in demand today, kid."

They headed off in the direction of the blue corridor, passing doors in varying shades of cyan until they got to the one he was looking for. Hitch knocked, but didn't wait for an answer.

Blacker was sitting in a large round room, its ceiling curved, its floor flat glass, and under the glass the room continued its curve. Blacker flicked a switch, and the sphere they stood in was suddenly covered in coastal maps. They were inside a giant sea globe.

"Hey there, Ruby. Nice to see you again. I thought you were going to Department Seven first?" said Blacker, looking at Hitch.

"He's late," said Hitch.

Ruby looked at Hitch. "You mean I could be at swim practice after all?"

"I was told to get you here by three thirty. I can't help it if people don't show when they say they're going to show," said Hitch.

"Well, no matter, early or late," said Blacker. "I'm glad you're here. We got a lot to do, and I sure could use your brain."

Hitch walked to the door. "See you in a while, kid. Be smart." He left the room.

Blacker pushed a chair in her direction, and Ruby sat down. "Here, have a jelly donut—it'll help you think," he said, handing her a fat sugar-dusted donut. "So, they fill you in on what's going on?"

"Nuh-uh," said Ruby.

"OK, so let me," he said. "I have been looking into the Mayday call those fishermen sent out last night. They claim to have made several attempts to contact the coast guard, and when their distress signal was not answered, they tried to get the attention of another boat. This vessel, however, did not come to their aid, although they insist it must have seen their predicament."

"What did this boat look like?" asked Ruby.

"*Strange and old-fashioned* is what they said, though they didn't get to see it up close."

"So where exactly was the fishing boat when they called in to the coast guard?"

"Exactly here." Blacker pointed to the wall at an expanse of sea not so far from the Sibling Islands on the north side. There was a little red light illuminated, indicating the tiny fishing vessel.

Another light, this one green, represented the boat the fishermen had tried to make contact with; not so far away, but to the east side of the islands.

For the next two hours Blacker and Ruby worked together, reading out coordinates and marking them with lights. By the end they had almost thirty markers glowing on the glass walls around them, showing the locations of cargo boats that had drifted off course, other boats that had sent out unanswered Mayday calls, and rough locations for sightings of strange marine-life activity. They covered quite an area, and it wasn't clear what it really meant, though there was a clustering in the deep waters half a mile from the Sibling Islands.

"What's out there?" asked Ruby.

"Not a whole lot," said Blacker. "Cargo ships sail close, but not directly into those waters; they always travel to the west side of the islands. The ocean is deep on the east side, but there are too many rocks just under the surface to be safe for very large shipping. The currents can be dangerous for recreational sailing — you need to know what you're doing."

Ruby did know; she had heard people talking about it all her life. *Beware the Sibling tides* — it was one of those old sayings people handed down to their children. The point was that it was not a good idea to go out there unless you really knew what you were up to. The waters were dangerous, and there were outlandish tales spanning the centuries of people mysteriously going missing—all greatly exaggerated no doubt, but nonetheless true, at least in essence.

"What about the actual Sibling Islands? Aren't they kinda worth a visit?" suggested Ruby. "I mean, don't people head out there to see them? I'm sure my parents are passing nearby on this yacht tour they're on, learning about history and stuff."

Blacker licked the donut sugar off his fingers; it was getting all over the keyboard. "I guess if you have the inclination to go and stare at two giant rocks sticking straight up out of the ocean—very few tourists bother to go that far, your parents excepted, I guess. It takes a long time to get there and you can't land or anything and you certainly can't swim. Sure, they're sort of impressive to look at, but they don't usually attract a lot of sightseers. It's geologists who are interested, and marine life experts; as I said, the water goes very deep, and there are a lot of unusual species of fish. Apart from that it's pretty dangerous out there; plenty of ships used to get wrecked in olden times."

They both sat and stared at the maps now dotted with red, green, pink, yellow, and violet lights, all representing a different type of disturbance or unusual occurrence.

The telephone rang, and Blacker picked up. "OK, I'll send her over." He put the receiver down.

"Do you think you can make it to Department Seven? It's in the violet zone — room 324, if you're going by numbers."

"I reckon I'll find it," said Ruby.

"You sure?" said Blacker, getting to his feet. "You want me to walk you?"

"That's OK," said Ruby. "I'm good at finding my way."

She was pretty sure she knew where she was going, but even if she hadn't had a clue, she would have said she did. The truth was, Ruby wanted to stop by somewhere.

She could have just turned left down the corridor the way she had come, but what would be the fun in that? She was a slave to her curiosity — as Mrs. Digby so often observed, *"Curiosity will be the death of you, young lady."*

This prophecy had almost been borne out just a matter of weeks ago. Ruby was lucky to be alive, and she knew it, but it hadn't changed a thing. She was as big a snoop as ever. So instead of turning left out of the door, she turned right.

It took some time, but after what seemed like miles of passageway and a zillion closed doors, she finally reached one she recognized. It was bright orange, and it was the Spectrum gadget room.

She looked at the Bradley Baker rescue watch, tapped the exact time into the keypad, and the door clicked open. The code had not been changed.

Ruby had been told not to take anything without proper permission. That meant filling out a form — in triplicate — and getting it signed by the correct authority. But the person in charge, what's-his-name (she had never actually met him), wasn't in Spectrum today, and when was she going to get the opportunity again?

As she walked past them, the display cases and glass drawers all lit up. Ruby moved past the rows of low glass counters, slowly eyeing their contents. She was looking for something in particular, something she had seen on her first visit to Spectrum. It was in the section devoted to gadgets for use in the ocean.

THE BREATHING BUCKLE.
To be used underwater. Slip buckle off belt, place between teeth, and breathe comfortably for twenty-seven minutes, two seconds.
WARNING! NO RESERVE AIR CANISTER.

Ruby could see that this device might well come in handy, and she was sure that the person in charge would sign it out if she requested it — so what was the harm in taking it? She was a bona fide agent, after all, and she had done her dive training. So what was the big deal? She cast her eyes over the other glass drawers and cases. There was an intriguing label next to a small bag that looked to contain marbles.

LIMPET LIGHTS, ALSO KNOWN AS HANSEL AND GRETEL FIND-YOUR-WAY-HOME TRAIL GLOWS. Underwater phosphorescent lights to be used to make a trail. Guaranteed not to move. Duration five hours.

She might as well grab them too while she was at it, since she was going to get in a whole lot of trouble anyway. In for a dime, in for a dollar. She slipped the "borrowed" treasures into her pockets and checked her watch.

Oops, didn't mean to be gone so long. The time had slipped through her fingers. Peeping through the spyhole, she checked to make sure the coast was clear before opening the door. Then she walked swiftly down the corridor and up to Department Seven, violet zone. She knocked before entering room 324.

"Late!" said a voice.

"Oh, geez," said Ruby. "Does it have to be *you*?"

CHAPTER 20
A Real Potato Head

RUBY COULDN'T BELIEVE HER DUMB LUCK. Was she really going to have to suffer the company of the Silent G?

His name was Froghorn, but the *G* was silent — something Ruby chose to ignore, which was just one reason their relationship was so bad. The other being that Froghorn was a petty-minded bully. At twenty-three he had been the youngest agent currently in Spectrum employment, but then Ruby had come along and spoiled all that, and he was *not* happy about it.

"You should be grateful, little girl — I'm actually handing you some real work on a real case. This is your lucky day."

"Oh, I'm really stoked," said Ruby. "Being shut in a tiny room with you is my *definition* of a lucky day."

"Oh, dear. Now you're getting your hopes too high. I won't be babysitting. I have *important* things to work on, and I think even you can manage to listen to tape recordings by yourself."

Ruby looked at the desk, covered in batches of tapes.

"What are they?" she asked.

"You have to listen to them."

"What are they?" said Ruby again.

"Tapes — of radio shows, the kind of shows that people with very little musical taste might tune in to."

Ruby considered this for a moment. *Was he talking about what she thought he was talking about?*

"I guess you're referring to Chime Melody?"

Froghorn wrinkled his nose, evidently surprised that she was aware of the Chime situation. "Oh, I'm sorry — no insult intended," he said, not the merest hint of apology in his voice. "Apparently you're a listener?"

"Sure, I listen," said Ruby. "It's important to have an open mind, otherwise one walks around like one knows it all when one is actually a total potato head, no insult intended."

Froghorn's mouth went very small, but he chose to ignore Ruby's jibe.

"There seems to have been some interference of some kind — highbrow music playing on a lowbrow show. It could be accidental, just two radio frequencies clashing. However, due to all the other unusual activity, LB assigned me the job of listening to each and every tape just to make sure there isn't some underlying voice message or communication."

"She assigned you? So what am I doing here?" said Ruby.

"You're here because I've delegated this task to a junior agent."

"Are you palming this work off on me, Froghorn?" she said. It was clear he thought it was a dead-end job.

"Not at all. It's just the kind of chore a less able person should be doing, and your name came to mind. All you have to do is listen, though I realize this is not something you're skilled at."

"Jeepers, Froghorn, did your mommy not love you enough? You got some serious ego issues, man."

Froghorn pursed his lips so his mouth went even smaller. He didn't like this Ruby Redfort girl undermining him. Who did she think she was marching in with her big mouth, mocking him, making him feel stupid?

"Next time, don't be late." The door slammed as he left.

"That's the best you got? Don't be late? You need to brush up on your insults, potato head," said Ruby to no one but herself.

She stared at the piles of tapes.

She felt not unlike one of those fairy-tale characters who ends up left with some impossible task — to weave straw into gold or peel 1,500 carrots before dinnertime.

Might as well buckle down. She inserted the first tape in the machine, put on the headphones, and sat back in the chair.

It was going to be a long, long night.

CHAPTER 21
Get Zuko

THE DOOR TO RUBY'S BEDROOM FLEW OPEN.

"Child, get yourself up and at it; your parent-folks will be arriving home today, and I want to get your room looking like a room before your mother has me fired and run out of town."

Ruby lifted her head from the pillow and rubbed her eyes. She was exhausted from her long night of listening to Chime Melody's peculiar sounds.

Mrs. Digby, who of course knew nothing about that, was standing in the doorway, pink rubber gloves up to her elbows, bucket in hand. Through the blur that was Ruby's eyesight she looked like some kind of gunslinger.

Ruby groped for the clock. "Mrs. Digby, it's only five fifty-nine in the a.m., what are you doing?"

"That's right, plenty of time to do a little spring-cleaning, now up and at it!" said the housekeeper, marching straight into Ruby's closet. "I'll start here; you can pick the debris from off of the floor."

Ruby muttered under her breath, but she got up all the same. "You know you're turning out to be a lot like Consuela."

Mrs. Digby snorted. She did not like to be compared to the Redforts' ex-chef. Consuela was a woman she did not care for, and she had been glad to see the back of her and didn't make any bones about saying it.

However, not everyone felt the same. Consuela was an incredible chef, and Brant and Sabina would pay double what the Stanwicks were paying if only she would come back.

Ruby did as she was told — it really wasn't worth the argument. By the time she left for school, her room was looking like it belonged to one of those perfect kids you saw in the commercials, those ones who smiled all the time. Ruby, dressed in a T-shirt emblazoned with the words *dying of boredom here*, looked about as far from being a "commercial kid" as any kid could.

At the same time that Ruby was cleaning her room, Hitch got out of his car and looked out to sea. He could make out the Humberts' yacht, the *Golden Albatross,* coming in from the west. As it got nearer, he couldn't help noticing that the vessel was looking less than shipshape — a little battered, a little worse for wear, a little war-torn.

Hitch had been casually leaning against the car, arms folded, drinking in the sun, but now he was suddenly alert. As the boat moved into the harbor, he could make out the faces of those aboard, and no one was looking very happy. He cast his eyes over all the passengers, but could not see the faces of Brant and Sabina. He began to walk toward the yacht, picking up the pace with each step. By the time he got to the quayside, he was flat-out running.

He watched as Freddie and Marjorie Humbert wearily disembarked.

"What happened?" he asked.

Marjorie Humbert looked at him. "Pirates," she uttered.

Hitch scanned her face. "Is everyone OK?"

The Humberts looked at each other.

"The Redforts?" asked Hitch.

Freddie turned to him, his eyes welling up. "They didn't . . ." His voice caught in his throat. "They didn't make it," he stammered.

"What do you mean, 'didn't make it'?" said Hitch, a sudden fear shooting through him. "You're saying they're not with you?"

"Sabina was pitched overboard. Brant dove in to save her, but then . . ." Poor Freddie, he couldn't find the words.

"The pirates shot them," said Marjorie, her voice barely audible. "Right there in the water. They didn't stand a chance."

"You *saw* them get shot?" asked Hitch.

Marjorie looked at him with her kind eyes. "No, we did not see that, and I'm grateful we didn't." She was ashen-faced and looked close to collapse.

But Hitch needed more; he needed to know for sure. "But you didn't see them, see their bodies I mean; you never saw them dead?"

Marjorie winced, but bravely held his gaze. Freddie looked away. "No," she said in a whisper. "We never saw them dead, but we never saw them again. I want to tell you something good, Hitch, something hopeful. But I can't."

Freddie nodded, took her by the arm, guided her down the gangplank, and together they staggered safely to shore.

Hitch didn't miss a beat: before he had gotten five feet from the quayside he had radioed in to Spectrum and was put through to LB. He explained the situation and then put in his request.

"We need to conduct a search," he said.

"I'll get someone to contact the coast guard at once," said LB.

"No, that's not what I mean," said Hitch firmly. "This is the kid's parents we're talking about. *We* need to conduct a search. Alert Sea Division; we need backup. If they're alive at all, then they won't be for long."

"Hitch, this isn't what we do; this isn't part of Spectrum's remit. I'm sorry for the Redforts, I'm sorry for the kid, but these people are not part of our work here. The Twinford air-sea rescue squad will deal with the situation; they're professionals when it comes to general civilian safety."

"You know these folks don't stand a chance if we don't step in; they're more than likely dead already."

"Yes, my point exactly, they're most likely dead already. So why would we rally our agents, and in so doing possibly blow our cover by making such an obvious and overblown search of the area? I respect your desire to make things right for the kid, but sometimes it just isn't possible. Sometimes we have to take it on the chin and move on."

Hitch knew she was right. No one in Spectrum could afford to get sentimental; you start getting mushy and it was time to hang up your agent-issue watch.

"I hear you," said Hitch. "But listen — how do we know this doesn't have something to do with Agent Trilby? How do we know the pirates who threw the Redforts overboard aren't somehow also causing all this marine disturbance?"

Silence from LB. Then: "Go on," she said slowly.

"How about if I get Zuko to go in?" said Hitch. "Undercover, I mean, as relief air-sea rescue. He knows what he's doing and can fly one of our helicopters dressed up like it's air rescue, and he can search with the best equipment. No one need know, and it's just one agent."

LB was quiet for a moment and then said, "OK. That could work. The fine details are your business. Keep it covert and keep it untraceable, no link to Spectrum. Anything goes wrong, it's your head, not mine."

"I appreciate it, LB." He hung up, got back in his vehicle, locked the doors and mirror-glassed the windows, then he pressed a button on the dashboard. The dash front slid up to reveal high-tech Spectrum equipment. He fed in Agent Zuko's code name and badge number and was instantly given his coordinates.

Zuko was not on mission; instead he was relaxing upstate, on standby and awaiting orders. Hitch buzzed him, and not ten seconds later Agent Zuko's image appeared on the miniature screen. He was wearing a blue checked shirt and looked like he might be fishing. Zuko was an old buddy of Hitch's. They had been through some tough times, gotten each other out of plenty of scrapes, rescued each other from certain death on numerous occasions, and there wasn't a favor too big to ask of each other.

Hitch told him the deal, and in just a few minutes it was all arranged and agreed. Zuko would conduct the most thorough search of the Sibling waters; he had twenty-four hours, that was all.

With a heavy heart, the Redfort "house manager" drove back to Cedarwood Drive and to Mrs. Digby.

Now for the hard part, he thought.

Mrs. Digby took the news stoically. She didn't interrupt, she didn't let out a cry, nor did she move a muscle. She just stood there in the middle of the kitchen, her feet planted firmly on the floor. She didn't breathe a word until Hitch had said everything he was going to say.

"They'll be right as rain," she said. "Mr. R. doesn't give up so easily, and Mrs. R. doesn't give up at all. Most tenacious woman I ever met. Besides, they met while diving in Italy. They know how to swim. I'm not a water person myself, can't abide swimming about in the ocean. If God wanted us in the ocean, he wouldn't have made the land." She was burbling on while she busied herself like nothing was amiss. "Those two, they could swim in molasses."

Hitch didn't contradict her, but he wasn't feeling so confident. There had been shots into the water, a whole lot of bullets. It wasn't the swimming he was worrying about. If they were swimming, then that meant they had survived the pirates, and that seemed unlikely. Pirates were not nice people, never had been. All those books you read about them, all those films that made them out to be funny and romantic, they weren't true. Pirates were cold-blooded killers only interested in what they could steal.

He got up from the kitchen bar stool and reached for his keys.

"I better get down to the school — pick up Ruby. I don't want her hearing about this from anyone else."

Mrs. Digby nodded. "I'll be here," was all she said.

CHAPTER 22
No News Is Good News

WHEN RUBY TRAILED OUT OF TWINFORD JUNIOR HIGH, Hitch was waiting there to meet her. She spotted him across the schoolyard, standing by the car, and quickly called good-bye to Red as she hurried toward him.

"So something happening at Spectrum? We gotta get somewhere? 'Cause you know I was hoping to see Del later. I said I'd play her at table tennis to make up for swim practice; promised I'd destroy her, but I guess that ain't gonna be on the cards. Boy, was she ever mad at *me*, didn't believe the whole thing about the bump on my head, said I was gonna have to . . ."

Ruby slowly stopped talking.

"You OK, Hitch? You look like someone just ran over your goldfish."

Hitch didn't know what to say. How do you tell a kid her parents are missing and presumed dead? He struggled to find the right words, but there *were* no right words, so he just said it.

She looked at him. Her face belied her thoughts. *How could this have happened?* One minute the girl who had it all, the next the girl who had lost the two most precious things in her life.

Hitch put his arm around her and said, "They're just missing, kid. No one's saying more than that."

But what Ruby heard was the little voice in her head. She knew that things were not looking good for her parents' safe return, didn't matter what "no one" was saying.

Ruby didn't need to ask where their boat had been at the time; she was pretty sure it would be somewhere not so far from the Sibling Islands in those dangerous waters with the tricky currents, with the undertow every sailor feared.

"Look, I spoke to LB," Hitch said. "She has authorized a Spectrum agent, using Spectrum equipment, to scan the Sibling waters for your parents. If they *can* be found, we'll find them. You can be certain of that, kid."

Ruby just nodded. They got in the car and drove back in silence.

Mrs. Digby opened the door before Ruby was halfway up the steps.

"Don't you torture yourself up with worry, Ruby; they'll be

back before you know it. I can feel it in my bones, and my bones ain't never wrong."

Hitch made his excuses to Mrs. Digby and headed back out. He couldn't sit around — he had to do something, even if it was just taking the Spectrum dinghy out and scouting the waters. The chances of finding anything were remote, but at least it was something to keep his mind from believing the worst.

The old housekeeper and Ruby ate supper accompanied only by the noise of the ticking clock and the intermittent ringing of the phone. Ruby barely touched her food. When she was done trying, she climbed the stairs to her room and flicked on the TV.

The story of the pirates and the survivors of the Humberts' yacht was headline news. There was an interview with Ambassador Crew, his arm in a fresh black sling and a patch over one eye, ironically making him look distinctly pirate-like.

The conch shell in Ruby's bathroom rang, and she picked it up at once.

"Ruby, my dad told me everything."

"Hello, Clancy." She sounded like every drop of energy had drained out of her.

"This is awful, Rube, just awful."

"Yeah," said Ruby.

"I can be at the tree in ten," said Clancy.

Silence.

"Wanna meet me there?"

Silence.

"Rube . . . ?"

"Yeah," said Ruby, replacing the handset.

Clancy arrived at the oak tree on Amster Green just nine minutes later. Ruby was already there, sitting up on the highest climbable branch. He clambered up and slid along next to her.

"But no one's saying they're dead," said Clancy. "They're just missing is all."

"How many people can swim for seven days without life jackets, without rescue?"

It wasn't a question that Clancy wanted to answer.

Instead he said, "But maybe they've been rescued. You yourself always go on about how lucky your folks are — maybe they got lucky one more time."

"Then why don't we know about it? Why haven't they radioed in?" challenged Ruby. "They would radio, they would. If my mom's an expert at *anything,* it's picking up a phone."

They talked for a while before Ruby felt an overwhelming need to be alone.

"Gotta go, Clance. You know, just gotta go."

"I know," he said.

As she made her way down to the ground, Clancy called out.

"Rube, you know I got a hunch they made it out of there alive."

She looked up at him, her face suddenly full of hope, wanting to believe.

"And you know what I'm like with my hunches, don't you?"

"Yeah," she replied. "You're usually right."

"Correction!" he called. "Always right. I have an unblemished record. Remember that."

She smiled at him sadly, got on her bike, and rode back toward home.

Hitch's car was not in the driveway, and the lights were off in his apartment. It looked like he would be gone all night.

At 2:43 a.m., Ruby woke up cold and sweating. Her dreams had been turbulent. First she'd had the recurring nightmare, the one where something pulled her down into deepest indigo, something whispering, something with eyes that never blinked.

Then her parents had appeared, they were wading through the surf, calling to her, but she couldn't hear what they were saying. She walked toward them, but no matter how many steps she took, she could not get any nearer. Then suddenly a huge wave engulfed them, and when it retreated, they were gone.

Ruby snapped the light on and reached for her glasses. She looked around for Bug, but he must have gone downstairs to his basket. She couldn't shake the image from her head, so she climbed out of bed, and went down to the kitchen.

Bug lifted his nose and got to his feet, yawning.

"Hey there, Bug." She stroked him behind the ears, trying to bring to mind exactly what Clancy had said. *Did he really have a hunch, or was he just being kind?*

She switched on the radio. There was a late-night quiz show aimed at security guards and insomniacs; the questions were pretty dumb, but they were some distraction.

"WHAT WOULD YOU CALL A BABY WHALE?"

"A calf," said Ruby automatically.

"WHAT WOULD YOU SAY IF YOU STEPPED ON A GERMAN'S TOE?"

"*Entschuldigung*," said Ruby. "No, wait, *verzeihung*."

"WHAT WOULD YOU DO IF YOU WERE A COOPER?"

"Make barrels."

"WHAT WOULD YOU BE IF YOU WERE ON CHARON'S FERRY?"

"I know this one . . . what is it?"

Suddenly a news announcer's voice broke in.

"WE ARE SORRY TO INTERRUPT THIS PROGRAM FOR SOME BREAKING NEWS. TWO BODIES HAVE BEEN FOUND BY A FISHING CREW TWENTY MILES OUT TO SEA. THEY HAVE NOT YET BEEN IDENTIFIED AND AT THIS TIME WE CAN ONLY SAY THAT THEY ARE A MAN AND WOMAN OF APPROXIMATELY MIDDLE AGE."

Ruby didn't hear anything more of the broadcast; all she heard was the answer to the quiz show question pinging into her head.

"Dead," she said.

She leaned back against the wall and let herself slide down to the floor.

CHAPTER 23
Love Without Words

RUBY DIDN'T SLEEP ANY MORE THAT NIGHT. She sat in her bedroom in the dark just staring out of her window, waiting for dawn to come.

At 6:30 a.m. on Wednesday morning, the phone in her room rang. *Clancy*, she thought, but she didn't pick up. She couldn't talk to anyone, not even Clancy Crew. Talking to people meant listening to them telling her it was going to be all right, and she knew it wasn't. It wasn't all right at all.

At 6:39, Hitch knocked on her door. He could tell just by looking at her face that she must be aware of the latest reports.

"I heard the news, kid."

She blinked back at him.

"I agree it doesn't look good," he said. "But we don't know, not for sure. No one's been identified."

She didn't speak.

"I spent all night in the boat, and I found nothing. Doesn't mean it's over; 'nothing' can also be good. Zuko's out in the chopper now; he's a good agent with good eyes, good instinct. If there's anything to find, he'll find it."

They went down to the kitchen, and Mrs. Digby came right over and kissed Ruby on the top of her head and squeezed her cheek, like she always did, always had done from the first day she was born.

"I'm not going to school," Ruby said.

"Course you're not, Ruby. You're staying here with me," said Mrs. Digby, nodding her head. "I'm making you French toast and proper English tea."

The housekeeper didn't want to let Ruby out of sight, but at about a quarter to noon Ruby managed to give her the slip. She wanted to be out in the fresh air where she could think, where she wasn't surrounded by everything that was her mom and dad.

She took a walk down to Amster Green. She nimbly climbed the old oak, and when she reached the topmost climbing branch, she sat down. She felt around with her left hand, reaching for the deep knot in the bark. She pulled out a neatly folded origami turtle. The coded note said,

```
ec hbbtzik erl ocoeqw rpuyl
```

She took out her pencil, crossed out the code and wrote,

```
Commiserations, you now have
     a blemished record.
```

She climbed back down, got on her bike, and rode out to Twinford Harbor.

For some reason it was the only place she wanted to be. Maybe because her parents had always loved boats, had always loved the ocean, or maybe it was because this was one of the last places Ruby had seen them alive.

The Redforts had met in the ocean, and now they had died in the ocean. What had been the most romantic of beginnings was now the most tragic of endings.

Her parents had told the story so many times Ruby could almost hear their voices explaining how they had met off the Tuscan coast of Italy.

SABINA: *It must be seventeen years ago now. Boy, was your dad ever handsome.*
BRANT: *And your mom, she was a knockout.*

SABINA: *Brant was working as a diver, for that marine biologist.*

BRANT: *Yes, and you, honey, were sailing single-handed around the Mediterranean coast. What a gal!*

SABINA: *I was trying to become fluent in Italian, but I never really got further than the word* ciao.

But as it turned out, she hadn't needed to. They had met underwater, and it was love without words.

Somewhere far off, Ruby thought she could hear a dog barking. A *real yapper,* she thought.

"Could you give it a rest already!" A loud voice belonging to a woman scolded the dog, and the dog stopped yapping.

Then . . .

"Ruby Redfort! Ruby! Ruby Redfort!"

Ruby looked up, but the sun was shining directly into her eyes, blinding her. All she could see was a tall silhouetted figure, a woman in a long, voluminous robe who appeared to be waving.

"Ahoy there!" came another voice, deep and sort of fat sounding.

Ruby squinted into the bright light, trying to make out the callers.

"Nice of you to come meet us." It was Bernie and Eadie Runklehorn, friends of Ruby's parents.

"Look who we fished out of the drink!" bellowed Mr. Runklehorn.

And then two other figures came into view, followed by a little dog.

"Hey, honey. How did you know we would be sailing in today?"

"*Mom? Dad?* Are you really alive?"

Her father glanced down as if checking. "Last time I looked," he called back.

CHAPTER 24
Just Plain Lucky

IT WAS AGENT ZUKO WHO HAD SPOTTED THEM. The
Runklehorns' yacht's engine had failed, and due to the lack of
wind, they were making slow progress back to shore. Zuko had
landed the sea chopper on the water and fixed the engine. Not
long after this, the yacht cruised into the harbor. Everyone safe,
everyone sound. Brant had swung Ruby up over his shoulder
and mussed up her hair in the way he always did, always had
done since she was just a little kid — but for once she really didn't
mind one bit.

"I owe you one, pal," said Hitch, shaking Zuko's hand.

"Hey — easy job. You owe me nothing," said Zuko.

When things had calmed down and Ruby and Hitch were
alone, she said, "Hey, you know — thanks."

"All part of the job," he replied.

"No," said Ruby. "I know it's not, so thank you."

He winked at her. "Consider it my pleasure, kid. I happen to like your folks a whole lot. Your mother can be a little persnickety, and I can't stand your father's whistling, but on the whole I'd rather not do without them."

Of course, it was important that Brant and Sabina should be debriefed as soon as possible, before they forgot anything that might prove vital to catching those responsible for their near-death encounter. Both the police and the coast guard were keen to get some kind of description of the assailants, but the interview was not going well.

Ruby sat in on the debrief. Partly because it was so nice to see her not-dead parents, but also because she was intrigued to hear what they had to say.

"He had terrible dental work," said Sabina, wrinkling her nose. "I mean, he went to the trouble of having five or six gold teeth fitted, but the front one was very discolored, and a couple of the lower ones were missing altogether, and talk about halitosis. I don't think he had so much as sniffed a bottle of Mint-Mouth his whole criminal life."

The police detective felt Sabina was getting sidetracked by teeth and tried to bring things back to more useful territory.

"Try, Mrs. Redfort, if you will, to focus on the overall

appearance of the man — how tall he was, for instance. Was he stocky? Was he lean? How was he dressed?"

"Oh, he was dressed appallingly. Nothing went together. Lots of things that didn't make sense, very tasteless; not that the clothes themselves were all bad, but they didn't work as an ensemble."

Brant thought it might be time for him to chime in.

"I think what Sabina is getting at is that the man had a somewhat haphazard appearance. He was small yet tough; no one doubted his strength. His clothing suggested that much of it was stolen — or acquired. Maybe he saw things, took them, and wore them."

"Yes, well put, honey," agreed Sabina. "That's exactly it! He's not a shopper." She stopped as if remembering something important. "But his colleague was."

"Colleague?" queried the detective.

"His cohort, accomplice, whatever you call these pirate types." Sabina waved her arms. "What I'm trying to say is that there was a fellow on board who did not look one bit like a pirate, yet he was in with them."

"So what did he look like, Mrs. Redfort?" asked the detective.

"Sort of collegey, educated, respectable, nicely dressed, kinda like Brant," said Sabina.

Now, this was interesting. *What was a guy like that doing with a bunch of pirates?* thought Ruby.

"And how many of these pirates would you say there were?" asked the detective.

"Forty, I'd say, at least. Would you agree, Brant?"

Brant nodded. "Give or take—perhaps more like twenty."

"And would you say that these pirates were even slightly interested in kidnap and ransoms? I mean, did you think it crossed their minds?" the detective asked.

"No, that wasn't my impression," said Brant confidently. "They had no idea who Ambassador Crew was, and they seemed to have not one jot of interest in us, just our wallets."

"And jewelry," added Sabina, looking down at the ring still firmly jammed on her finger, her finger still firmly attached to her hand.

"And their boat?" asked the detective. "Could you describe that?"

"Pirate-like," said Sabina.

"What do you mean, *pirate-like*?" said the detective.

"The sort of vessel," said Brant, "that you might expect a pirate to sail in. It was dramatic, sort of corny almost."

"Like in a film," said Sabina. "Old-fashioned. Lots of rigging and sails — you know, crow's nests and the like — all it was lacking was the Jolly Roger."

The detective wrote that down. It was something, and they didn't have a whole lot to go on.

Old-fashioned, thought Ruby. Wasn't that exactly the way the fishermen had described the boat they spotted in the distance, the one that failed to pick them up? Ruby found herself mulling this final fact over and over in her mind. There was something intriguing about it.

Like in a film, she said to herself.

CHAPTER 25
Once in a Blue Moon

AT ABOUT SIX O'CLOCK THAT EVENING, Ruby was lying on her parents' bed: her mother was sitting at the dressing table brushing her hair. Brant Redfort was choosing a necktie from his very large collection of neckties. They were all looking forward to a fun evening with the Runklehorns, who were expected within the next half hour or so.

"So," asked Ruby, "what exactly did you learn out there— the whole history deal I mean?"

"Some pretty fascinating stuff," said Brant.

"Oh, my! Did we ever," agreed Sabina. Ruby waited for her mother to launch into the story of the treasure of the *Seahorse,* a legend she was prone to talking about whenever she got the opportunity. Sabina was very fond of this tale because the legendary treasure—in particular, a priceless ruby necklace—supposedly belonged to her great-great-great-grandmother, Eliza Fairbank.

Tonight Sabina was particularly excited because during the cruise Dora Shoering had confirmed that the story was a lot more than legend. It was all, most probably, true. The fact that Dora Shoering knew no more about history than the next man or woman didn't seem to bother Sabina.

"Of course, they were my great-great-great-grandmother's rubies." Sabina paused. "Or were they my great-great-great-great-grandmother's? Either way, people say they were the most stunning jewels this side of India."

"What was the whole big deal about them?" asked Ruby, who of course knew the whole big deal, but her mother liked to explain, and Ruby was feeling kind enough to ask.

"They were flawless — crystal clear and *flawless* — big, too," replied her mother. "They would have been yours, of course, eventually." She sighed. "They would have gone so well with this Marco Perella dress." Sabina was scrutinizing herself in her dressing-table mirror.

"Oh, you don't need jewels, Mom," said Ruby. "You always knock 'em dead — rubies or no rubies."

Her mother smiled. "As long as I have my little Ruby Redfort," she said, hugging Ruby. "Who cares about stones?"

Ruby didn't usually go in for this sort of schmaltzy convo, but tonight, well, tonight her parents had come back from the dead, so Ruby *was* easing up on the teen attitude. She did actually *mean* every nice word she said, but she also wanted to get out of having to wear the flouncy yellow blouse her mother had picked out for her. It was touch and go as to whether this strategy would work, but it was worth a try.

"So," said Ruby, "tell me again, what exactly happened out there?"

"Oh, come on, Rube!" said her mother, laughing. "We've told you at least four times!"

But Ruby couldn't get enough of the story — she was kind of proud that her parents had survived such a dicey situation. There was of course another reason for wanting to hear it over and over; it was **RULE 14: VERY OFTEN PEOPLE NEGLECT TO TELL THE MOST IMPORTANT DETAIL.** She'd learned this from Detective Despo; *Crazy Cops* might just be a TV show, but if you wanted to learn about detective work, then this show was packed with an awful lot of good tips.

"Well," said her father, "I woke up to hear that little dog yapping . . ."

They went through the whole terrifying ordeal again. How, as the pirates started shooting into the water, both of them had escaped the clutches of almost certain death by diving deep down under the boat and holding their breath.

"The pirates left us for dead, no life preservers, no nothing," said Brant. "But we managed to grab onto Ambassador Crew's luggage. The pirates had thrown it overboard. I think he might have been getting on their nerves; Lester can do that to people."

"Yes, we were very lucky with the suitcase," said Sabina. "It floated beautifully — it's top-quality luggage, you know. Good luggage is always a good investment. The three of us, that's Pookie, your father, and I, clung on for dear life."

"Pookie?" said Mrs. Digby, who had just come in to collect the laundry.

"The yappy dog," said Ruby.

"What kind of creature suits a name like Pookie?" sniffed the housekeeper.

"Pookie," said Ruby.

"Well, I pray I don't meet him," said Mrs. Digby, picking up a basket and making her way back to the kitchen.

"Yes, the three of us managed to paddle toward the Sibling Islands, though why they call them islands I don't know; they're nothing like islands, just big old rocks — there's absolutely no sign of life there. You can't even climb onto them, unless of course you happen to be Spider-Man." Her mother was dusting her nose with powder.

"But I thought the waters near the Sibling Islands were

supposed to be super dangerous, what with the currents and tides and all?" said Ruby.

"Well, that's true enough," said her father. "But the darnedest thing must have happened — the currents were still, totally still. Something to do with the moon, or is it the stars? I forget what causes it, but something up there." He pointed vaguely above him.

Of course, thought Ruby. He wasn't exactly on the money with his explanation, but it was close enough. *The asteroid!* **YKK 672.** She had read somewhere that large asteroids, passing close enough to Earth, could modify the local attraction of the moon and stop water currents for as long as the asteroid stayed near the atmosphere.

"It can last several days, or just a matter of hours, you never can tell," continued her father. "For just a short window of time the currents calm, and you can actually swim without getting sucked under, and hey, presto! Your parents don't drown!"

"Yes, were we ever lucky with that!" said her mother. "Your dad and I are excellent swimmers, but no one can swim in the Sibling waters when the currents are strong. What are the chances?" Her mother grinned and powdered her nose some more. "This happens once in a blue moon, and we get lucky. Who could believe it?"

Ruby could: her parents were born lucky.

"So how come you know all this info on the tides and currents an' all?" asked Ruby.

"It all comes from his days aboard the *Sea Wolf.* You remember, your dad worked for that diver guy in Tuscany, Italy?" said Sabina. "Of course, he already had a free-dive scholarship at Stanton too."

Ruby did remember this, but she had no idea Brant had actually taken any of it on board—her dad wasn't exactly the smartest fish in the barrel.

"I studied under a genuine marine genius. Well, actually, I worked for his marine genius co-divers. Francesco Fornetti rarely spoke to me, I was too junior." Brant sighed.

"He was a terrific breath-hold diver," said Sabina. "Too bad about what happened to him."

"Yes, too bad—he knew more about ocean life than just about anyone around," added Brant.

"Why, what happened to him?" said Ruby. "Did he die?"

"Professionally, I guess," said her dad.

"Meaning what?" asked Ruby.

"It happened in Twinford, actually. We'd seen him a couple of times. We went on . . . um . . . a sailing trip with him. Then he started jabbering on about something he'd seen, some weird creature, couldn't stop going on about it. He got laughed out of the ocean by a bunch of marine-life experts. They all said he had gone crazy, swallowed too much saltwater or something," said Brant. "It was too bad; he just sort of disappeared after that."

"Anyway," said Sabina excitedly, "I just wish he'd been there when we saw the worrying thing in the water. He might have been able to identify it."

"What worrying thing in the water?" asked Ruby. This was a new detail—they hadn't mentioned the worrying thing in the water before.

"Well," said her mother, "there we were, just swimming around the Sibling Islands, trying to find fresh water—which you might think impossible."

"Fortunately for us, it wasn't," said her father. "There was a natural stream that ran down the north side of the north rock into the ocean; we found an old plastic bottle that we filled to the very brim, and that's what saved our lives."

"Terrible how people litter," said her mother. "Although we were very grateful for it at the time. Without it we might have perished of thirst."

"But what about the thing?" asked Ruby, impatient for them to get to the point.

"Oh, yes, there was definitely a thing in the water," said her father. "Pookie heard it—you know what a dog's hearing is like."

"Very sensitive," agreed Sabina.

"But what was it?" asked Ruby.

"We didn't exactly see it," said her mother.

"I felt its vibrations," said her father. "Like it was moving toward us. Our chances were looking really quite deathly, and then something really strange happened. This sort of indigo cloud—like dye—kind of appeared in the water."

"Like squid ink?" asked Ruby.

"Well, sort of, but not," said Brant. "It was like no squid ink I ever saw before. And blue, not black."

"It got all over Pookie, and he didn't like it one bit," said her mother. "Kept trying to lick it off, and the more he licked, the more he yapped."

"Boy, did that dog yap," agreed Brant.

"Though thank goodness he did," said Sabina. "Because the Runklehorns heard it—they were sailing past the far side of the islands, and the next thing we heard was Eadie Runklehorn's voice calling, '*Ahoy there, Redforts! Just the people we were looking for. We need a couple to make up a bridge four! We're getting very bored playing Snap on our own.*'"

Brant was laughing at the very memory of it. "You know

Eadie," he said. "Such an original sense of humor—there we are, clinging to a suitcase, practically drowning, and she makes a joke!"

Ruby was looking at them wondering if too much sun and saltwater had made them insane. Not many drowning people would see the funny side, but she guessed this was the old Redfort survival instinct kicking in; keep laughing and nothing can ever be as bad as it seems. She had read about this in the *SAS/Marine Survival Handbook*. It said there that the trick to surviving a life-and-death situation was ninety percent attitude—same as her Rule 20.

"So then what?" asked Ruby.

"And then, ta-da, they rescued us!" Sabina said this last part with a flourish of her powder brush, as if it was the most natural thing in the world to be rescued from a sea monster.

"Yes, and back in time for cocktail hour," said Brant.

"So if you got rescued at four p.m. on Friday, how come you didn't make it back here until lunchtime the following Wednesday?" asked Ruby.

"Oh honey, you know what the Runklehorns are like," said her father. "Wouldn't put us ashore until we'd played a dozen rounds of deck quoits and several hands of bridge. Then, of course, we remembered the pirates."

"You *forgot* them?" said Ruby.

"Well, it was all so exciting bumping into the Runklehorns like that," said Sabina. "The pirates clear went out of my mind. Anyway, we all decided we had better sail the long way around since we didn't want to get captured again, and that's when that nice fellow with the helicopter showed up."

"Supper was the only disappointment," said her father. "The chef had been having trouble trying to catch a single fish. We ended up eating canned tuna."

"I guess *something* was scaring the fishes," said her mother.

Water, water everywhere and not a fish to eat, thought Ruby. She remembered the other week when Mrs. Digby had threatened her with cod-liver oil because the fish store was out of fish. *Weirder and weirder still.*

The doorbell chimed.

"Oh, that will be the Runklehorns," said Sabina. "Go put on that nice yellow number, would you, honey?"

Ruby opened her mouth to protest, but before she could say anything, caught sight of herself in the mirror. The T-shirt she was wearing was printed with the word **duh.** She would make her mother's day perfect and go change.

CHAPTER 26
Cerebral Sounds

THE DINNER CONVERSATION WAS OF COURSE LIMITED to the subject of pirates, rescue, and lost treasure.

"What gets me is why the coast guard didn't pick up my Mayday call," said Sabina.

"Yes, that is a mystery," agreed Brant.

"And Bernie sent message after message when our engine went kaput, but no one responded," said Eadie.

"It was pure chance that we got rescued. The guy in the chopper just happened to be flying by," said Bernie.

"Shame, it was a lovely spot," said Brant. "We were really having a high old time, weren't we, darling?"

"Oh, yes," replied Sabina. "A swell time."

While her parents and the Runklehorns laughed, Ruby was beginning to put things together in her head. She was sure that the pirates had to be responsible for the lost Mayday calls: it made sense; this way they could rob and hijack vessels without being disturbed. But how were they doing it? From her mother's description, they didn't sound like the most sophisticated villains at sea, and surely, if they were going to all the trouble of blocking Mayday calls, they must have a bigger target in mind than cruise boats and cash.

Like Blacker said, it wasn't like many pleasure boats sailed in those waters.

"Sabina was so heroic." Brant gripped her hand and smiled. "You should have seen her out there, quite an inspiration."

Her mother's family had *always* had confidence, but what they were famous for was their guts, the kind of courage that inspired awe — after all, there were legends about it. No one could be sure that these weren't just tales told by drunken sailors, but Ruby chose to sort of believe them; they sounded just far-fetched enough to be true. And it wasn't impossible that her mother's relative had also survived a pirate attack, though when she looked across at Eliza's great-great-great-granddaughter, sitting there in her cerise Marco Perella evening dress, it did seem unlikely. However, though Sabina Redfort might not have inherited her great-great-grandmother Martha's brains, she had certainly inherited her courage. Sabina Redfort was no wuss, no siree.

Later, when dinner was over and Ruby's parents were sitting chatting with the Runklehorns, she went upstairs to her room and pulled out the list and the spider map. It seemed likely that the dead couple, the couple who turned out not to be Ruby's parents, were also the victims of the pirates, judging by the state of their yacht, the *Swift*, which had been ransacked. They too had been thrown to the waves, but they were not such able swimmers, and with no ambassadorial luggage to cling to, drowning was their fate.

Ruby added them under the heading *pirate attacks*.

The facts on the piece of paper were growing, and things were beginning to add up. Though she still wasn't sure to what.

THE DROWNED AGENT DIVER

CONFUSED SHIPPING

UNUSUAL MARINE ACTIVITY

SEA SOUNDS

MISSED MAYDAYS

THE STRANGER

PIRATE ATTACKS

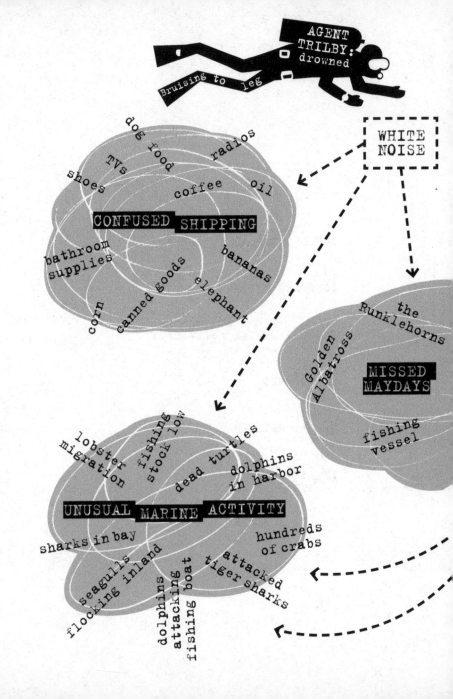

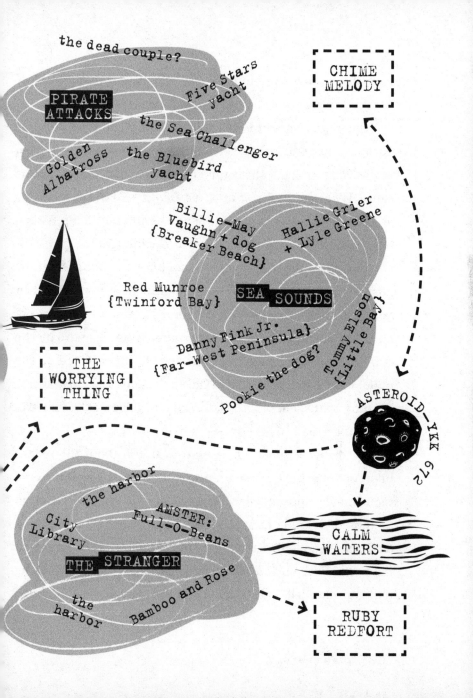

Ruby fell asleep without difficulty and slept soundly until an hour before dawn, when her dream took a puzzling turn.

She found herself in her music class. Clancy was tapping out a message with a drumstick. Ruby was frustrated: she knew Morse code well, but she couldn't decipher this, it just made no sense. *What are you trying to tell me, Clance?* He was just looking at her like she was super dumb and continued to tap. Was it nonsense, or was she not as smart as she thought?

She woke up, but the dream continued . . . or at least the tapping did. It was coming from the bathroom. Ruby fumbled for her glasses, got up, and switched on the light. It was the faucet, not quite turned off, and a steady drip was drumming onto a plastic cup that was upside down in the sink. Ruby switched on the radio, which was still tuned to Chime Melody, and a reassuring old tune wafted out of the set, the kind of golden oldie that Mrs. Digby adored.

As Ruby listened, she began to think about the recent interruptions, the strange un-music-like music playing on the radio, music more suited to the classical radio channel Cerebral Sounds. The kind of music that had no business being played on Chime. Suddenly Ruby froze, and she felt those tiny hairs on the back of her neck prick up. She could see it now, this thing that had sounded like a jumble of notes, a mess of sounds; she had heard it with her own ears, but failed to understand.

She ran to the wall of books that covered one side of her room and pulled at the quarterly code magazines that dated back several years. She remembered reading an article about something, something that might help her chase down the thought she couldn't catch. She spread them out across the floor until she caught sight of the one she wanted. In this old edition was an article on musicians who had encrypted music and so passed secrets across the airwaves without anyone ever suspecting that these tunes were not just tunes. One of the most famous was a composer called Arvo Pärt, but there were many others: the highly successful composer and double agent Sarå H. Stein, and Roberto Bowerbeck and Tristan Delaware to name a handful. At the back of the magazine was a seven-inch plastic record: low quality, but it should still play.

Ruby put the record on the turntable and the needle automatically lowered itself onto the disc. The piece was by I. Zac-Gardner: *Preamble in Three Equally Divided Halves*.

It sounded very much like the kind of thing Chime had been playing—music without melody.

Ruby pulled on her sweatshirt and ran down the stairs right to the bottom of the house. She moved lightly and almost soundlessly, and only Bug heard a footstep.

She tapped lightly on Hitch's door. She heard him put something down on the table, a cup or a glass.

"Ruby?" he said quietly. "That you?"

She opened the door; he was still dressed from the night before, or maybe he was *freshly* dressed for the coming day. He looked only mildly surprised to see her.

"Hey, kid," he said. "What got you up before dawn?"

Ruby sat down in one of the two easy chairs that furnished the compact yet stylish apartment.

"I figured something out," she said. "At least, I think I figured something out. I just got to prove it is all."

"I'm all ears, kid." He sat down in the opposite chair.

"This Chime Melody thing I've been working on for Froghorn — I suddenly get it. It's not interference, it's not someone disrupting the airwaves — it's more than that."

"More how?" asked Hitch.

"Well, old Froghorn dumped me with the job of studying each tape, each piece of music, trying to listen for a voice masked by the music, but that's not what's going on here."

"It isn't?" said Hitch.

"No," said Ruby. "The music isn't covering up the communication, the music *is* the communication. It's a code."

"You know this?" said Hitch.

Ruby shook her head.

"But you're pretty sure?"

"Eighty percent. I figure each note is a letter. Could be more complicated though. You know, like when a note lasts for two beats, you skip a letter, or it changes into a number, or something."

"I don't know," said Hitch. "But if you say so, I believe you."

"So I gotta listen to the tapes so I can figure out how it works."

"That all? You can go in and listen to them any day you like."

"I mean I want to bring them home; it would give me more time."

He paused, considering the request; it wasn't strictly protocol, but it was practical. He took a deep breath. "I can get them."

"What about Froghorn? Is he gonna make trouble?"

"No, leave Froghorn to me. I can handle anything he cares to throw."

"And maybe . . ." said Ruby, "don't let's say anything until I've got proof. I'd hate to give him the pleasure of knowing I'd got it wrong."

"I'll keep it zipped, kid. You can count on it."

They went up to the kitchen and sat there for a while drinking tea and talking things over until they were interrupted.

"Well, knock me down with a feather!" Mrs. Digby said. "This child is up before the sun — I must be dreaming."

CHAPTER 27
An Unblemished Record

RED DROPPED BY JUST AS RUBY was about to leave the house on Thursday morning. "I thought I'd come by and see how you were doing. I tried calling, but you didn't pick up."

"Yeah, sorry about that," said Ruby. "It all got kinda busy, you know."

Red nodded. "You must be so relieved. I mean, how dreadful thinking you'd never see your mom *and* your dad again, neither one of them."

Red's own dad had gone missing one day, just up and left, and she had never laid eyes on him since, so she knew what she was talking about.

"It was pretty bad," said Ruby. "Kinda the worst day of my life, you know?"

Red nodded again. "So you wanna grab some breakfast at the Donut?"

"Sure, why not," said Ruby. "Might as well celebrate."

It was nice to join her friends for breakfast, just like always.

"So," said Clancy, "my record is unblemished. I told you I had a hunch your folks were alive, and I was right."

"Yeah Clance, I'll give you that — you were right," said Ruby.

"As always," said Clancy.

"As always," agreed Ruby.

Yes, life was good. The specter of death having receded for now, far into the future. Laughing and yacking like worries were a thing of yesterday, which they sort of were. . . . Well, except for the ruthless pirates and the weird shark action, dead divers, and ransacked pleasure cruisers — apart from those things, everything was rosy.

The trees looked greener, the sun felt warmer, school seemed a tad more fascinating, and Vapona Begwell . . . well, she was as objectionable as ever.

"So, Redridingfort, I hear your parents almost got chomped by sharks," she hollered across the cafeteria.

Ruby decided not to tell Bugwart where to stick it, it was too nice a day, but as it happened, Del stepped in, and then things got kind of ugly anyway.

Del's food fight with Bugwart sort of escalated. At one point Ruby saw several chicken wings fly across the dining hall. These were followed by a considerable number of pizza slices — and resulted in several detentions for a number of students; the ringleaders spent the afternoon cleaning the school cafeteria.

Apart from that, nothing much truly happened school-wise.

Ruby had to drop her plan of hanging out with Clancy at Del's house, but as it turned out, that was just as well. The Bradley Baker rescue watch flashed green in music class, and that meant no hanging out with anyone. Ruby made a promise to Clancy that she would catch up with him on Friday, and as soon as the school bell rang, made her way back to the pool, back to Spectrum.

She rode swiftly, shortcutting through quiet residential streets, zigzagging through back roads. When she got to the main square, she saw the stranger again.

This guy is starting to bug me, Ruby thought.

He was sitting reading what looked like a map, a large yellow carryall at his feet. Where had she seen a yellow bag like that before? By the time she made it to the Twinford City pool, she had it: Little Bay Beach; this guy was a diver. Was it relevant to anything? Why should it be? It was just that she had this feeling. She slipped through the door of the maintenance room, making sure it clunked shut behind her, and took the elevator down to HQ.

On arrival, Buzz informed Ruby that LB wanted a word, and she was to wait outside her office. Ruby stared at the huge optical painting that hung on the wall in the waiting area. She didn't hear the soft padding of her boss's bare feet, not even when they were just two steps away.

"Pleased to hear your parents aren't dead, Redfort." And that was about as touchy-feely as the head of Spectrum 8 was ever going to get. LB moved right along as if personal talk was in some way distasteful.

"It's my thinking that this case is about a whole lot more than confused shipping and pirates and pleasure boats. Would you agree?"

Ruby nodded. LB was looking at her in that LB way as if she expected Ruby to produce the name and address of the person responsible. The Spectrum 8 boss paused for a second and then said, "We have a list as long as a clown's arm of strange ocean occurrences, but what does it all add up to?"

Ruby didn't have an answer; she felt like she was thinking through molasses.

"You're going to need to step it up, Redfort. Stop paddling around, and start using that brain of yours. Get involved."

Ruby nodded dumbly. "Sure," she said. "I mean, I will. I am. I'm working on something actually."

"One would hope so," said LB. "Spectrum doesn't employ you to sit on your behind twiddling your thumbs." She walked to the elevator and pressed the button, then turned and said, "Oh, and by the way, a fisherman was found drowned in his own rowboat, how's that for a puzzle? The report's on my desk, you might want to read it." The elevator door slid closed, and she was gone.

Ruby *did* find that curious. It was like one of those riddles, similar to that one about the diver found drowned in the middle of a fire-ravaged forest. There was always a logical explanation if you thought about it long enough. To have drowned in your own boat, alone, meant there must have been water on board. A person could drown in just a few inches, but anyone but a baby would have to be unconscious to do so. She walked into LB's office, picked up the file from off the desk, and began reading immediately.

The report said nothing about signs of a bump to the head or the man having been drunk; this was no accident, far from it. However, there were clear signs that someone had tried to strangle him, but not with their hands, the injuries didn't fit with that. Perhaps the assailant had given up with the strangling and decided to drown him instead.

The conundrum was that the boat was found way out at sea and there were no signs to suggest another occupant. So therefore, the fisherman must have been attacked either by a diver, who then swam away, or by someone who sailed by, boarded the boat, drowned him, and left the scene. But then this didn't make sense. Why would you drown a man and then pop him back in his boat? Why not make it look like an accident?

It was the sort of thing that happened in a Sherlock Holmes mystery, not just off the coast of Twinford.

"Rats!" said a voice, a man's voice, sounding flustered.

She looked up to see Blacker hurrying across the Spectrum hall. He was balancing drinks and donuts, and some hot coffee had just spilled down his sleeve.

"Sorry, Ruby, I've been with Sea Division and I couldn't get the darned scuba-sub to start and everything sorta slid from there. Boats and submarines just aren't my thing."

Once they were comfortable in the globe room, they started trying to figure out what they knew and what they didn't know.

"No one responded to the Mayday call sent out by your mother, or the ones sent from the Runklehorns' yacht, because it transpires that we were right: all Maydays were blocked — deliberately blocked."

Ruby nodded. "That figures."

"Given that your parents are not the only ones to have tussled with pirates — there have been several incidents — I think we can begin to imagine that pirates might be to blame for the blocked Maydays."

Ruby nodded again. "I thought so too. I guess they don't want anyone to come to the victims' rescue while they're busy with their plundering. But why aren't they going after the shipping?"

"Yeah, I agree," said Blacker. "That doesn't make sense. These men live to rob. It's what they do — like sharks swim and eat, these men sail and steal, but why don't they bother with the more valuable spoils?"

Ruby sighed. "It would mean there has to be something else they're after, something that's worth more to them than random cargo."

Ruby and Blacker worked together for the next couple of hours, and as they worked, they began to see a clear pattern evolving. The only boats that were attacked by pirates were *small* boats that came directly into the waters within a mile or so of the Sibling Islands. The larger tankers and shipping vessels couldn't come as close because of the rocks, but anything that sailed within sight of the Sibling Islands was steered off course, taking them as far away from the area as was possible.

It looked random, but it really wasn't.

"They're trying to keep people *away* from the waters around the Sibling Islands," said Ruby. "They aren't particularly interested in robbing them, they just want them gone."

"And that isn't too hard generally," said Blacker. "Most ships avoid the place anyway, apart from fishing boats, and even the fishing hasn't been good lately. Most of the big shoals have gone."

"Yeah, Mrs. Digby's all upset about it," said Ruby.

"Keen on fish, is she?"

"Swears by it," said Ruby.

"Well, Mrs. Digby would be reassured to know Kekoa is investigating that," said Blacker. "But so far she still isn't sure if the problem's man-made or caused by some natural phenomenon." He tapped his pencil on the desk as he thought. "But what we *do* know is these guys must really want to keep folks away from the islands; they don't want a soul observing what they're up to."

"But what exactly could that be?" pondered Ruby. "The islands are just rock."

"Yeah, and the waters around the islands can be very dangerous if you don't know what you're doing; the swells and currents are pretty strong," added Blacker.

"Well, except for right now," said Ruby.

"That's right, your folks got lucky. Kekoa told me about that asteroid."

"Yeah," said Ruby. "Galactic activity certainly seems to be fitting in with someone's plans."

"But plans for what?" said Blacker.

That question Ruby didn't have an answer for, but she knew a good place to start looking.

RULE 53: IF SOMETHING IS WORTH KNOWING, CHANCES ARE IT'S WRITTEN DOWN SOMEWHERE.

CHAPTER 28
I Speak the Truth

TWINFORD WAS AN OLD TOWN, now considered a city: one that continued to grow and sprawl desert-ward. Tall, sleek buildings appeared to the north side, but the center of town was carefully preserved and protected by the Twinford Historical Society. The buildings — old, beautiful, and full of history — attracted tourists from far-flung places as well as neighboring towns.

In the very middle of Twinford, just near the city museum and city bank, stood the city library. A magnificent and imposing piece of architecture that announced its importance in Latin, via the motto carved across the front: *Ipsa scientia potestas est.*

Ruby loved this place, and always had: so many books, so much knowledge to stuff your brain with — and the comforting sounds of the creaking floorboards and discreet whispers provided a certain intimacy. It was also open late into the evening, sometimes all night, and that suited Ruby very well indeed.

Ruby dumped her coat and satchel on one of the many

chairs flanking the long wooden table that stretched almost the length of the library floor. Green-shaded reading lights illuminated the surface, giving the place a cozy glow: it was a nice place to study.

Ruby walked between the rows of hardback spines, all sitting in perfect order on the ancient-looking shelves of beautiful dark wood, handsomely crafted a hundred years ago. Some volumes had been waiting many, many months to be chosen; some would stand untouched from this year to the next. She chose with great care, methodically scanning the books, studying each one before adding it to her pile. Forty-five minutes later she had a stack of twenty-two, one on top of the other, sitting in front of her on the table.

Then she began reading. Book after book. She read about the time when sailors risked life and limb to sail the high seas, when the only way for people to move from country to country was by ship. The journeys that could take months, the passengers who died on the way.

As she read her way through the more *ancient* books, Ruby stumbled across various writings describing the wrecking of the *Seahorse* and the looting of the Twinford treasure. They tended to differ in detail, but most seemed to agree on two things.

One: That the *Seahorse* must in truth have been wrecked many miles to the north of the Sibling Islands; it was just not possible for the ship to have sailed into those waters at the spot the child, Martha Fairbank, described — it was far too dangerous, and the captain was experienced enough to know that.

Two: That pirates brought about the ship's destruction by attacking the crew and setting the ship alight, and that most of the treasure must have sunk without a trace.

Yet no one believed the little girl's tale about rubies and a sea monster — just a child's wild imaginings. As for her mother being taken alive? This was the wishful thinking of a four-year-old girl who had lost everything.

Ruby didn't feel she had discovered anything she didn't already know until she opened a book written by a certain John Elridge Featherstone, a physician who claimed to have treated Martha for ravings and fever after she washed up on Twinford's shore. He had spoken at length with Martha's governess as well as the child herself and had gleaned some interesting facts — information Ruby had not read anywhere else.

In *this* account it was Martha Lily Fairbank who took center stage, and while Featherstone clearly didn't believe all she had to say, he had at least listened: *Martha insisted that once the pirates believed that they had murdered all on board, they began carrying supplies from the ship, and along with these supplies they carried her mother, kicking and screaming, "My daughter, my daughter, she cannot be dead." But little Martha did not call out to her; she stayed perfectly silent, stock-still in her barrel.*

Those pirates who remained aboard went belowdecks to search for gems and gold and treasures, and that's when they were taken by surprise. A violent battle broke out, for it seemed they had not slaughtered all of the Seahorse crew. The men — pirates and sailors — fought to the death as the burning ship sank beneath the waves. Though it was true that most of the treasure was lost with the ship and most of those on board went down with it — some of the pirates did survive. They escaped clutching the priceless Fairbank ruby necklace and a casket of rare gems. Martha saw it all from where she hid, safe in her apple barrel.

This much of Martha's story Ruby knew already. But then it got more interesting.

According to Martha, this small band of pirates clambered aboard a makeshift raft, clutching the treasure that was the Fairbank rubies and Eliza's casket of gems. The barrel Martha had hidden in was also brought, along with the other supplies, and the pirates floated on their raft to a secret cave in the rocky Sibling Islands. Which of the two sister islands they rowed to Martha did not know since she could see very little from where she crouched, peering through cracks inside the barrel. All she said was, "We sailed to the rock guarded by the golden bird." She also described the cave the pirates paddled toward. "It had a big rock ledge that overhung the entrance like a porch or a lintel — a giant's door."

Martha could hear from the echoes that she was now inside a deep, enclosed, cavernous space. The pirates' voices were clear, and she listened as they talked of the treasure they had salvaged and how they would make good their escape. "No landlubber will find this place, so secret is it. A cave like this cannot be found by town-dwellers. We will stow the treasure here," they said, "high above the tidal pool. The captain will come for us soon enough."

Several times Martha feared that she would be discovered, knowing that before long the barrel would be opened. That night she bravely crept out of her hiding place while the pirates slept, hoping she would be able to escape the cave.

She walked down many of the tunnels, scratching her initial as she went. Being an unusually intelligent child, she knew she might need to find her way back.

For three nights she explored the caves while the pirates slept, always careful to return to the apple barrel before they awoke. On the final night, as she curled herself inside the cask, she began to fear that she might never again see the sky.

Some hours later she was abruptly woken by a whispering — a mournful sound as she later described it. Louder and louder it called, but the pirates slept on. Yet when they finally awoke, they let out terrible screams, the screams of grown men, fearless men, who now had terror in their cries.

"It will kill us all! It strangles us in our sleep. This monster, this devil of the deep."

Martha saw a tongue of lightning strike at the cave and then heard a huge thundering as a rock crashed down and the cave quickly filled with turbulent water. The barrel was sucked into a "whirling thing," as she described it. Down, down it went, and then up again, and the child was flung far from the island cave and there she bobbed in her apple barrel.

The breakers carried her tumbling to shore, and like a cracked nut, the barrel broke in two and the little girl could once again see sky, and watched as a star fell from the heavens.

Hours later she was found like a tiny mermaid asleep on the sand, her turquoise dress gathered up like a tail, her face, legs, and arms all dyed indigo by some mysterious pigment. The child told the story to those who would listen, of the pirates and the plunder, her mother and the rubies, the treasure caves, the whispering and the devil from the deep.

A search party went to find the Seahorse, some motivated by revenge, some by greed. But few boats could sail in those waters, and the ship, even if it had gone down where she claimed, had sunk far beyond human sight into the turbulent currents, and the jewels could not be retrieved. As for the hidden rubies and casket of gems, the caves the child spoke of simply did not exist, could not exist. Some brave souls searched, but no cave was ever found, and her talk of floating to the Sibling Islands on a raft was not possible with the currents in that region as furious as they were.

Martha was forgiven her ungodly lies because no one could doubt that she had been through a trauma so terrible, she could no longer speak the truth. Her mother dead, her inheritance lost. She never spoke one word more about those dark days of seafaring terror. And as for the story, it gradually became myth. The treasure, the Seahorse, the pirates? Perhaps the boat had just been hit by a terrible storm.

Ruby closed the book and sat back in her chair. She remained there for some time, quite still. She thought about Martha — her long, long-distant relative, her long-dead relative whose voice she almost thought she heard. *Believe me,* it seemed to say, *Listen, I tell the truth. I cannot lie.* Ruby opened her notebook and wrote:

QUESTION
Why would Martha lie?

ANSWER

So the search would continue for her lost mother? Because she could not bear to face the truth, that her mother was truly dead?

Possible of course.

But what if Martha was telling the truth?

What if her mother WAS carried off to join the pirate band?

What if the pirate caves did exist?

What if the *Seahorse* really did sink somewhere near the Sibling Islands, and for some reason the currents were still then too, like they were for my parents? Like they are right now?

And if it WAS the asteroid that calmed the waters for them, could the same one have passed by the earth all those years ago?

Ruby was well aware that asteroids can come back again and again, in very long orbits. Two hundred years didn't seem impossible. And Martha did talk about seeing a falling star as she lay on the shore. . . .

Then, of course, there was the matter of the whirling thing.

`A giant whirlpool?`

It was certainly possible.

`The cave?`

Perhaps the huge rock Martha heard crashing down covered the cave entrance so it could no longer be seen.

`A sea devil?`

Maybe the lightning had conjured the illusion of a sea monster by casting strange shadows on the cave walls.

`The whispering and mournful sounds?`

Just voices of woe and fear combining with the sound of sharp splitting rock as the cave collapsed and the water rushed in: no monster, no supernatural being, just weather and sea colliding.

The picture was getting less blurry. Ruby and Blacker's theory about ships being rerouted to keep them away from the Sibling Islands, the calmed currents . . . someone out there wanted something from the Siblings waters, and if Ruby Redfort could believe in the treasure of the *Seahorse,* then maybe she wasn't the only one.

Maybe, a mere two hundred years later, someone was trying to dive the wreck and secure its sunken bounty.

The only thing was how to prove it.

CHAPTER 29
A Schoolboy Error

WHEN RUBY GOT HOME, SHE WENT IN SEARCH OF HITCH: he was nowhere in the main house, so she guessed he must be downstairs in his apartment. She could hear him playing music — the clarinet, something he often did if he got more than a few moments to himself. He claimed it helped him think, but Ruby wondered if it didn't help him block out the noise of the day, the tricky thoughts that must buzz endlessly around that head of his. The music was probably his own form of white noise.

He didn't seem to hear her knock, but the door was ajar and Bug, who had followed her down, pushed his way in. Hitch continued to play until he noticed Ruby standing there in the doorway.

"Hey, kid, you not out riding the streets of Twinford fighting crime?"

"No, I've been at the library."

"How very civilized. Any new books I should be reading?"

"Maybe an old one," said Ruby.

"I've always enjoyed the classics. What's it about?"

"Pirates, treasure, sea monsters—that kinda stuff," she replied.

"Sounds gripping," said Hitch.

"Yeah, it was," said Ruby. "I'll tell you about it tomorrow."

"I look forward to it, kid. Oh, by the way, I got you the radio tapes, left them in your room."

"Thanks," said Ruby. "I'll go check them out."

She spent the rest of the night listening to the tapes, to the eerie music, the music that wasn't quite music. Eventually, the cassette clicked off and she fell asleep, her head resting on Bug, and for a couple of hours they both slept well.

The next morning Ruby felt terrible; she was suffering from lack of sleep and was kinda grouchy. The tiredness was building up in her and she was finding school a chore. All she really wanted to do was prove herself right: this Chime thing had to be more than it seemed, it had to be a code. It was the only way to make sense of it.

She was sitting in Mrs. Drisco's class listening to the noises in her earpiece. She had this neat little device, very discreet—a tiny tape player tucked into her satchel. In her exercise book she wrote the notes she was hearing. The tricky thing was that she kept having to stop and start the machine. This made a rather obvious clunking sound, a sound that did not escape the sharp ears of Mrs. Drisco.

Ruby felt a yank as the little speaker was pulled from her ear, and she looked up to see Mrs. Drisco's face level with hers, the teacher's eyebrows arched in an angry position.

"Can you explain yourself?" said Mrs. Drisco in a chilling whisper.

Ruby looked down at her satchel, and her alphabetic notes and excuses folder. She had a good one from Dr. Franton at the lice and flea clinic, asking her to please avoid all cheerleading activities or indeed anyone involved with cheerleading — but it wouldn't really work for this occasion since cheerleading was not the issue. And the note from the president was far too useful to be sacrificed merely to prevent a detention.

Ruby paused. "If you could give me a little time, Mrs. Drisco," she said. "I'm a little fuzzy today, so I might need a few minutes to come up with something good."

"That's it!" boomed Mrs. Drisco. "Principal Levine's office, NOW!"

Ruby sighed. She would take the punishment; she could do with a little quiet time. What did it matter if it involved sitting in a dreary classroom on her own? But what she had forgotten was that the tape player, and more importantly the tape, would be confiscated by Mrs. Bexenheath. A schoolboy error on Ruby's part.

Darn it, Ruby, you're off your game.

She would need to enlist the help of a couple of her friends. When Clancy came by the detention room (as she knew he would), she passed him a coded note under the door. He read the note, which told him all he needed to know, and immediately snapped into action.

Clancy knocked on Mrs. Bexenheath's door and began some complicated story about a water bubbler that wasn't bubbling in the lower hallway. He was halfway through this unnecessarily detailed explanation when Red Monroe knocked on the door, supposedly to tell Mrs. Bexenheath about a pigeon that was flapping around in the girls' locker room, but in fact she was actually there to "accidentally" knock the large piles of carefully sorted mail onto the floor.

While Mrs. Bexenheath was picking it up and Red was apologizing and Mrs. Bexenheath was struggling not to curse, Clancy Crew was opening the "confiscation cupboard" and retrieving the tape player.

He ran to the window and threw it down to Del, who sprinted around the back of the building and passed it to Mouse, who was standing balanced on Elliot's shoulders.

From there, Mouse managed to just about pass it up to the window of the room where Ruby was enjoying detention. A small hand reached out and took the tape player from Mouse and . . . mission accomplished.

Of course no one but Clancy knew what was on the tape. Mouse, Del, Elliot, and Red just assumed it was some music and that Ruby needed it to relieve the tedium of several hours of isolated study.

Ruby listened to the tape over and over. She worked hard and felt she was getting pretty close to cracking the code. She looked at her watch: forty-seven minutes before detention was over. Then she wrote her 3,000-word essay on why it was a good idea to pay attention in class — not an essay Mrs. Drisco was likely to enjoy.

When she was released, she went to meet Clancy at the Double Donut. He was moaning on about physics. "Mr. Endell just went on and on and on about **YKU 726**," he said, slumping down in his seat and resting his forehead on the table.

"You mean **YKK 672**," corrected Ruby.

"I mean he just went on and on about how super interested we should be because this only happens once in a blue moon."

Ruby shrugged. "Well, I guess he's right. It is kinda rare for a small part of the ocean to stop moving."

"Yeah," said Clancy. "It's interesting to mention this *once, twice,* even *thrice,* but not like sixty-seven times."

"Well, Mr. Endell is kinda obsessive," said Ruby. "Did he mention how often **YKK 672** happens to pass by the earth?"

"Did he mention it? Are you kidding? He didn't stop mentioning it! Once every two hundred years. That fact is now etched into my memory."

Ruby smiled. Her theory was correct.

"So what were *you* doing while Mr. Endell was boring me to death?" said Clancy.

"Well, I was writing an essay about paying attention to Mrs. Drisco," said Ruby.

"Yeah, but what were you ACTUALLY doing?"

"You remember how I was telling you about the Chime Melody interference?"

Clancy nodded.

"Well, what if it wasn't interference? What if someone was using music to deliver a message?"

"What kind of message?" said Clancy. He was staring at her, his eyes saucer-like.

"Like locations, information, instructions," said Ruby. "This someone is giving them all in code to someone else."

"You think these someones are the *pirates*?" Clancy looked puzzled.

"No," said Ruby. "I mean yes and no. The pirates don't strike me as capable of thinking up this kind of code or of deciphering it—not from what my mom said anyway. Those guys sounded kinda Neanderthal."

"So you're saying there's more than the pirates out there?"

"I'm saying there is more than likely someone who is kinda in with the pirates, but not part of their band. Someone super smart. Then there also must be someone else on the outside who's issuing the orders. One supersmart person sends out the code on the Chime Melody airways and one supersmart person working with the pirates deciphers it."

"So where have you got to? With the code I mean?" asked Clancy.

Ruby bit her lip. "That's the thing, I *haven't* got it yet. I'm just guessing at this point, and it's making me crazy."

Clancy patted her on the back. "You'll get there, Rube. No doubt about that."

"Yeah, but when?" She sighed. "Maybe only once it's all too late." She stood up and slung her satchel over her shoulder. "I better get going; got a lot to do."

"You can't go," said Clancy. "It's Friday night, we were gonna hang out, remember?"

"Clance, I got a job to do. It's kinda important, you know?"

"Yeah, for your information, I do actually! The job is more important than anything else, including your friends, including me. I got that, OK? Loud and clear!"

Ruby felt guilt wash over her, but rather than say the *right* thing, she said exactly the *wrong* thing. She regretted it as soon as she uttered the words and saw him flinch.

Clancy didn't reply. His face said it all, and Ruby just turned and left the diner, not once looking back.

By the time she made it home she had a horrible little voice jabbering in her ear, telling her what a crummy friend she was. She ignored it, and instead allowed the white noise of her busy brain to block it out. Up in her room, she turned on the mini cassette player and pulled on her headphones. The awful music played on and did nothing to ease her mind.

Then at about half past four that morning she got it.

1. She still holds her secret
2. She lies where the toes of the sisters meet
3. She won't be accessible for long—act swiftly

CHAPTER 30
The Toes of the Sisters

WHEN SHE FELT SURE SHE WAS RIGHT, when she was positive the code worked, that what she was putting together made sense, Ruby went down to find Hitch.

It was 5:05 a.m. on Saturday morning, and he was sitting in the kitchen drinking a cup of very dark coffee. He watched her as she placed the cassette player on the table. She pressed the play button, and out scritched the unharmonious sound.

When the piece was through, Ruby took out various pieces of paper, placing them in front of Hitch in order:

First the musical score.

Then the score marked with letters underneath the notes. Once he had taken in how it all worked, Hitch nodded, and Ruby laid more papers on the table, each one delivering another short instruction.

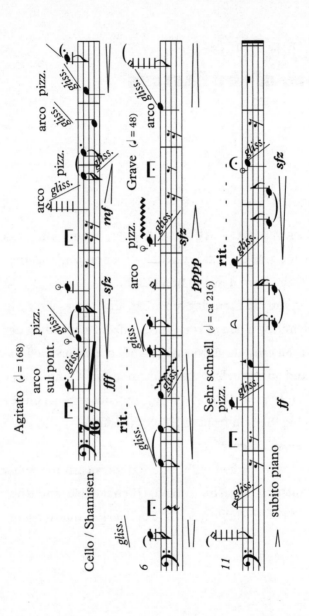

TO LEARN MORE ABOUT THE CHIME MELODY CODE AND HOW IT WORKS, *SEE PAGE 416.*

He looked at them for a long while, reading the messages over and over.

Finally, Hitch spoke.

"This *'she'* that they're talking about, got any ideas who it might be?"

"Uh-huh," Ruby replied.

Hitch looked up, his left eyebrow raised. "Go on," he said.

"I reckon *she's* a wreck, an old wreck," said Ruby.

"You better not be talking about me," called Mrs. Digby as she bustled through the room, bucket in hand — in one door and out the other.

"Never would!" Ruby shouted after her. They continued to talk, but with their voices hushed slightly: the housekeeper had sharp ears.

"The eighteenth-century wreck of the *Seahorse* to be precise," said Ruby. "I've been reading up about it, and I found an obscure account by some old guy named Featherstone that describes the night of the shipwreck as Martha Fairbank told it. She insisted the ship went down somewhere near the Sibling Islands."

"Even though every other account says it couldn't have?" said Hitch.

"Yes." Ruby nodded.

"OK," he said. "So tell me your theory."

"We start by assuming that the *Seahorse* did go down where Martha said it did," said Ruby. "**Where the toes of the sisters meet**—the toes of the sisters are the twenty small rocks sticking straight out of the sea a quarter mile from the islands; the wild currents make it difficult and dangerous to navigate around them."

"The toes of the sisters?" said Hitch.

"Lots of people used to call the Sibling Islands 'the sisters' in those days and the smaller rocks were called the toes. It's all because of that old legend about them."

"What old legend?" asked Hitch.

Ruby waved her hand impatiently. "I'll tell you some other time. It's not relevant to this. What I'm trying to say is that if the wreck sank somewhere in that channel between the rocks and the Sibling Islands, then this explains why the pirates are trying to keep boats out of the Sibling waters or anywhere too close to the islands. They block coast-guard signals and redirect cargo shipping way off course. If a pleasure boat comes by, they steal what they want and cut them adrift. It makes for good cover—makes it all seem random and about looting cash rather than premeditated and to do with two-hundred-year-old treasure."

"But why now?" said Hitch. "Why look for treasure that may not even be there, in a wreck that has been submerged for two hundred years?"

"Because now they can," said Ruby. "The currents are calm for the first time in living memory, so it's actually possible to dive the wreck."

"But this theory presupposes that the pirates knew this was going to happen, or made it happen somehow."

"Yes," said Ruby.

"They made it happen?" said Hitch. "This band of pirates knows how to quell the tides?"

"No, but they knew it would happen."

"How?"

"Because of something that happens once in a blue moon," said Ruby. "Something that happens every two hundred years."

"I'm listening," said Hitch.

"In her account, Martha Fairbank described a falling star and how the pirates floated to the island on a raft. They couldn't have done that unless the seas were still. The falling star was an asteroid. The same asteroid, the same falling star, that we're seeing now."

"**YKK** whatever-it-is?"

"**YKK 672**, yes. Well, that's what's stopping the currents. It has to do with gravity. Anyone who knew when it was coming back into orbit would know that they could swim the waters and dive the wreck then."

"OK," said Hitch. "But is it likely that these guys would know all this? Aren't they more brawn than brain? I can't see the thugs your mother described looking this stuff up in the local library."

"I agree," said Ruby, "which is why I think that guy my mom described—the nicely dressed fellow who was in with the pirates but not *like* the pirates—has to be the brains behind all this, or at least some of the brains behind all this."

Hitch nodded. "You have to wonder what a clean-cut guy was doing with a bunch of bandits."

"Another thing's still bugging me about all this," said Ruby. "That treasure might be worth finding, but if Martha was telling the truth, and I think she was, the priceless part of it, I mean the *really priceless part,* is not underwater at all; it's hidden in a cave inside one of the Sibling Islands. A cave lost under a rockslide. If this guy is so smart, then why doesn't he know that? I mean it's a lot of effort for some old gold and a few gems, right?"

"Maybe if we take a look at that wreck, we might find the answer," said Hitch. "You fancy taking a dip, kid?"

"When were you thinking?" said Ruby.

"Like the message said, we need to act swiftly. So how about just as soon as I can get hold of Kekoa?"

CHAPTER 31
A Seahorse and a Golden Bird

HITCH, RUBY, AND KEKOA TOOK A BOAT out to the Sibling waters. The two sister rocks rose dramatically out of the sea before them. It was easy to understand why sailors of days gone by had been superstitious about them. The rocks were beautiful but lonely, isolated there in restless seas—though today the water was tranquil.

They maneuvered the boat until they were between the two rocky outcrops once known as the "toes of the sisters."

"So what's the story with the rocks?" asked Hitch, peering at them through the haze of the morning light. "How did they come to be called the Sibling Islands, apart from the obvious I mean?"

Ruby listened closely as Kekoa explained: as one would expect, she knew a lot about the coasts and waters, but Ruby was impressed at how much she also knew about local history and mythology.

Ruby was familiar with this story from all her library research, but she liked the way Kekoa told it.

It was a melancholy tale of two sisters. Both had been flung overboard during a violent storm. Separated by the waves, they were then miraculously rescued by the tide, which carried them each to their own island. It was said that the girls climbed to the pinnacle of each rock and called to passing mariners. *"Help us,"* they cried, but their calls were muffled by the wind and sounded like whispers, and most did not hear them.

Those who did hear their calls mistook them for the voices of sirens, mermaids luring them onto the rocks. Sailors who followed sirens rarely lived to tell the tale, their bones smashed to pieces and their lifeless bodies dragged down to the depths of the indigo ocean. So the sisters were destined to call to each other across the turbulent channel forevermore.

Today, though, the islands looked far from tragic, glowing gold in the hazy morning light. Hitch scanned the horizon, but there were no other boats to be seen; they were alone as far as they could tell.

They waited for an hour or so, Hitch regularly scanning the radar for vessels that might prove sinister. To pass time more merrily he tuned in to the radio and an old-fashioned song spilled out. **"WELCOME TO CHIME MELODY,"** came the announcer's voice. ***"HERE FOR YOUR LISTENING PLEASURE."***

"It would seem your theory is correct, kid," said Hitch. "Chime is the only station you can receive in these waters, so I guess it's the old tunes or no tunes."

"I don't mind," said Ruby. "I kinda like the oldies."

Kekoa didn't say anything, but Ruby could tell she would rather have silence no matter what the radio was playing.

"So you find out anything more about the sea whisperings?" asked Ruby.

Kekoa shook her head. "No," she said. "Not yet."

"One of the kids on my swim team thought she heard it in Twinford Bay."

Kekoa looked up. "Really?" she said. "No one has heard it *there* before."

"Well, I wouldn't hold your breath," said Ruby. "Red's a very imaginative kid, if you know what I mean. She was prepared to believe it was mermaids."

Kekoa continued to stare at Ruby, but didn't say a word.

Hitch wouldn't allow anyone to dive until he had checked out everything he could check out. The coast seemed to be clear — nothing was beeping on the radar — and finally he said,

"Well, there don't seem to be any murderous pirates around, so I guess you're good to go."

The water was dead calm, the whirling currents and undertow gone for a while at least, but there was no way of knowing for exactly how long.

"Be careful, Ruby," said Kekoa. "This situation is not safe; these waters should not be so still, and might not be for much longer. These are dangerous seas."

If Ruby had interpreted the coded message correctly, then they were moored just above the wreck of the *Seahorse* where the toes of the sisters meet. The location seemed to fit with Martha Fairbank's description too. *"We sailed to the rock guarded by the golden bird."*

Hitch lined up the boat in such a way that indeed, from that angle, the pinnacle of the rock did look like a golden bird. As he did so, Ruby saw what looked like a blink of light flash from the smaller island. She squinted, staring ahead of her, but it didn't come again.

"What is it?" asked Hitch.

"I thought I saw something — a trick of the light I guess," said Ruby.

"You sure you're up for this, kid?" Hitch asked.

"Why wouldn't I be?" said Ruby.

"Diving for real is different from diving in training; you don't know what you're going to find down there."

"Isn't that the whole point?" said Ruby. "Oh, you think I might see a skeleton or two?" She gave him a mock-horrified look.

"I'm not so concerned about the already-dead; it's the live ones who can cause the grief. We don't know who's been down there recently or what they've been up to, so be careful and stay close to Kekoa. You hear me?"

"I hear you," said Ruby.

He tapped her hand where she clutched the boat's side. "I'll be right here, kid. And I can follow your movements on the radar."

She nodded, and the two Spectrum agents attached their breathing apparatuses and fell back into the water.

They saw it before long: a carcass of sorts, a ship's skeleton, covered in barnacles and seaweed, its wooden frame rotting into and blending with the very seabed. Amazing marine plants and coral had grown through it, around it, and within it, and this long-lost thing was now alive and crawling with sea creatures.

Ruby stayed close to Kekoa, who signaled them toward the less accessible part of the wreck, and they made their way inside a tangled mess of wood and seaweed. Ruby felt her way, her underwater flashlight illuminating small areas at a time, catching drifts of silt in its beam, flashes of silver as quick fish dodged and darted. Shy crabs scuttled sideways and bashful anemones drew in their tentacles as she passed. All manner of life had taken up residence here, undisturbed by the world above. It was unlikely that any of these creatures had ever seen a scuba-diving schoolgirl before.

She and Kekoa moved slowly around the old ship, where half-recognizable objects sat partially buried in the silt: something that could perhaps be a candlestick, a cup, something that might once have been a piece of furniture, but now was no more than a curiously shaped piece of wood, loomed out of the semidark.

They moved methodically and silently, swimming farther into the wreck, Ruby pointing the flashlight into the dark recesses of what was left of the ship. They looked for anything that might provide a clue that would in turn lead them to the pirates or whoever else might be after the sunken treasure.

They had been under for about forty-seven minutes when things went bad.

A loud noise, like the rumble of thunder, and Ruby turned to see Kekoa pinned under a huge wooden beam, part of the old ship finally succumbing to the sea. Kekoa was trapped, and blood was beginning to drift from her head into the water, creating a scarlet halo. But far worse was the leg wound. Ruby thought she could see bone. It didn't look good. She attempted to pull Kekoa free, but it was futile.

Kekoa was calm. Not the panicking kind, she signaled toward the surface — to Hitch — and Ruby nodded. She swam back the way they had come, through the maze of rotting wood and coral.

Then, as she turned a corner in the old corridor of the ship, she felt something glide past her legs, and she pulled back in surprise, dropping the flashlight. It hit something hard beneath her, flickered, and went out.

She was plunged into darkness, underwater, trapped inside a fragile wooden skeleton that might cave in at any moment, and with a limited air supply. Well, that was enough to bring on anyone's claustrophobia. Ruby was suddenly disorientated, unsure which way was out, and barely managing to contain her panic.

Nice going, Agent Redfort.

This was not meant to happen; the flashlight was Spectrum issue and should be robust enough to survive a knock. Ruby remembered her training and consciously slowed her heart rate and remained completely still until she felt calm, or at least calmer. **RULE 19: PANIC WILL FREEZE YOUR BRAIN.** Then she began to move forward. Now completely blind, she remembered what Kekoa had taught her, and methodically felt around her, feeling for a way through, a way out.

As she slid her hands over the inside walls of the ship, she felt something — a latch, a trapdoor, a porthole perhaps. She pushed and pushed, and finally it gave. Ruby was a petite girl, small enough to make it through a fairly tiny aperture, and she twisted and wriggled her way out of the watery prison.

She half swam, half clawed through a forest of seaweed and then out of the gloom ahead of her rose a horse's head (the old wooden figurehead of the ship) — a tiny fish darting in and out of its rotten eye. It stood there like a memorial or grave marker, which of course it was.

This *was* the wreck of the *Seahorse,* and where it rested many had died. Beyond the graveyard Ruby could see glimmers of light flickering — that meant a way out and up. She paused only when she saw something twinkle, something caught in the fronds of seaweed. She reached down and plucked it from where it lay. A stone, a cut stone, beautiful and of transparent yellow.

Ruby gripped the jewel in her palm and pushed on through the seaweed, drawn by a sound, a whispering, a calling, very distant but getting nearer. *Hitch? No, not Hitch.* She turned full circle in the water, but could see nothing but blue. Was this the mermaid sound that Red had heard? Or was it just the white noise of her panicking mind?

She started to make for the ocean surface. And then she caught her breath. Menacing gray shapes, like circling planes above her.

Sharks.

They were between her and the boat; they were between her and the boat and her and the rest of the ocean; they were everywhere, surrounding her, circling like some bullying mob.

But one of them wasn't circling; one of them was moving toward her.

So although it was true that Ruby Redfort had never been scared of sharks, not her whole entire life, that position was rapidly changing. Being surrounded by a whole batch of them (as Tilly Matthews would say) can do that to a person. Ruby opened her hand to grab for something, and as she did so, the yellow jewel slipped from her hand and fell through turquoise.

The retractable aluminum pole Ruby pulled from her belt did not do its job. She valiantly prodded it toward the gray menace, but it didn't make the impact she had hoped it would, and none of the sharks seemed even the slightest bit troubled. Despite what her dive master had told her, these guys were definitely interested. It was almost as if they'd been trained to show an interest, like they were guarding the location, making sure no one dallied too long.

Were they being controlled by someone? Guarding something? Like treasure? They must have smelled Kekoa's blood, she reasoned. But they didn't seem to head toward Kekoa. Rather, they just stayed in one area. That would be a smart way to guard treasure.

Treasure that was evidently no longer there. Just one small stone that could prove it ever existed, though even that had vanished. All these thoughts washed through Ruby's mind in split seconds as the predators closed in. The whispering was getting louder, much nearer, and the sharks were surrounding her. Bumping her. Knocking the breath from her.

She flailed one way, then the other, jabbing the stick, twisting, turning until she lost her grip on it and her only defense twirled away from her. She swiveled around and saw one of the creatures open its jaws to reveal those gums, those teeth.

CHAPTER 32
From the Jaws of Death

SOMETHING CRASHED INTO THE WATER, and white bubbles fizzed up to the surface. And just like that, the menacing gray shapes were gone.

Ruby was suspended in the deep blue ocean. She turned to check her back, and there behind her was Hitch. He was not in dive gear—there had not been time for that. He was treading water, a knife in his hand. He looked around for Kekoa and then made a gesture, pointing up, and Ruby followed him to the surface.

They clambered onto the small boat, both spluttering seawater, Ruby dizzy to be alive.

"Wh-what did you do?" she stammered from where she had collapsed on the deck.

"All *I* did was jump in the water," said Hitch. "Ruby, what happened to Kekoa?"

"I came to get you," wheezed Ruby. "She's trapped!"

"What do you mean, trapped?"

"Inside the wreck—something fell on her. She looks in bad shape."

Hitch turned the radar dial on his Spectrum watch, tuning in to Kekoa's signal. It wasn't there.

"Darn it," he said. "You're going to have to give me a pretty accurate description of Kekoa's location, kid."

Kekoa had taught Ruby well, and she described the place where they had entered the wreck and the direction they had swum through it. Finding Kekoa would be easy—getting her out would be the tricky part.

Hitch grabbed a rope and tool kit. He was already reaching a mask and air tank as Ruby described the cut to Kekoa's head and the leg wound and the fallen beam. Three minutes later and Ruby was alone. She looked out to sea, staring across to the Sibling Islands. She thought about the lost sisters, and as she thought of them, she saw that tiny glint of light flash once more on the smaller of the two rocks. Just for a second, and then it was gone. She stood stock-still and unblinking, waiting for it to reappear, but it didn't.

An agonizing nineteen minutes and five seconds passed before Hitch reappeared and deposited an injured Kekoa on the warm wood of the deck. She looked pale, and the blood continued to seep from her calf.

"It's not as bad as it looks," Hitch reassured her. But Ruby could see that it was. She grabbed the first-aid kit and handed it over. Hitch bound the leg wound as well as he could and then examined the cut to the head.

"Gotta stitch this," he said.

Kekoa nodded and didn't flinch once throughout the whole painful procedure.

"Kid, get the boat started. We need to make it to shore quick, and there's no chance of radioing for assistance out here — all signals are blocked."

Ruby got the engine started and began very slowly to steer the boat in the direction of Little Bay Beach. She had to move at a snail's pace because Hitch needed the boat steady.

As he worked, Hitch talked to Kekoa. "Those were *some* sharks down there. You shoulda seen them. They were more than curious."

"What was so special about them?" she replied weakly.

"There were a lot of them, and they were *interested*, not afraid."

"Perhaps someone's been feeding them," muttered Kekoa.

"I thought the exact same thing," said Ruby. "They were expecting something."

"If they were being fed, it would mean they're attracted to

divers rather than suspicious of them," said Kekoa, her voice barely audible now.

"Making them act like a security team . . ." said Hitch.

Kekoa almost nodded. "It would have that effect."

"So why did the sharks react badly to you?" said Ruby. "Why swim away when you appeared?"

"I don't think it had a whole lot to do with me," said Hitch. "Something spooked them. I glimpsed a movement in the water, but I couldn't make out what it was."

"You did? 'Cause you see, I heard something," said Ruby. "At least I think I did."

"What kind of something?" asked Hitch.

"Something that sounded familiar," said Ruby. "Something I think I once heard before."

"Like what?" said Hitch.

"Like a whispering," she replied.

"The same thing those other people heard?"

"I guess—maybe."

"But you didn't see anything?"

"No," said Ruby. "Just sharks."

When Hitch was done with his first aid, he took over steering from Ruby.

"Well, we better get out of here," he said. "While we still can."
He gunned the throttle, and the boat sliced through the water at
great speed. Once they made it to shore, Hitch radioed for Zuko.

"Agent down," he said. "We need her 'coptered out as soon as
possible." He gave Zuko their location, and seventeen minutes
later Kekoa was carried on board and they watched the chopper
buzz away, disappearing into a tiny fly-size dot.

"So you found nothing down there?" asked Hitch. "No
treasure, no sign of treasure?"

"I did find *something*," said Ruby.

"What?" said Hitch.

"I—I dropped it."

"Dropped what?" he asked.

"A yellow gem," she said.

"A gem? You're sure about that?"

"Yes," she said firmly. "I'm sure."

"But you're sure it was a gem, not just a piece of glass, a
shiny stone, something that caught the light?"

"You don't believe me?" she asked.

"Yes, kid, I believe you."

But it sounded like he wasn't sure, though maybe it didn't
matter one way or the other since it didn't change a thing. Apart
from that one tiny stone, the gems weren't there, and there was

nothing to prove they ever had been. Maybe the pirates never were looking for treasure. Maybe Ruby had just gotten caught up in Martha Lily Fairbank's imaginative world, a world that time had long since forgotten.

"So what are you going to tell LB?" said Ruby. "She's not gonna be too thrilled about Kekoa winding up in the hospital."

"I guess I'll just have to tell it to her straight." Hitch sighed. "When it comes to LB, there's no other way."

CHAPTER 33
Time for Some Answers

WHEN RUBY GOT DRESSED THAT MORNING, it hadn't occurred to her that she would wind up sitting in LB's office justifying her actions. If it had, she would have chosen a different T-shirt—this one read *excuse me while I barf.*

By the time they reached Spectrum, Ruby was unusually nervous, though Hitch was as cool as ever. He just headed straight to LB's office as if nothing was about to hit the fan. LB was talking on the telephone, and she waved for them to sit down. Whoever was on the other end of the line was getting quite a grilling.

"I don't want any more excuses—just make it happen," said LB, abruptly hanging up.

She looked at Ruby. "So, do you want to explain what occurred out there?"

Ruby opened her mouth, but she couldn't think of a thing to say.

Hitch came to her rescue. "As you know, the kid has been

listening to the Chime Melody tapes, and there's evidence that the interference is not interference but is actually coded communication, musical notes that can be translated into instructions."

"All right," said LB. "Show me."

Ruby took the file of papers from her satchel and laid the various communications on the desk. LB leaned forward, studying them.

"You see, Chime Melody is the only radio station you can clearly receive in the Sibling waters, so it makes sense that they would hijack *this* particular station," Ruby explained.

"I would agree," said LB. "The part I'm a little hazy about is what led you to believe that the 'she' they refer to in the messages was the wreck of the *Seahorse*?"

Ruby took a breath. "Well, that was kind of a hunch based on what I've been reading about in the city library. It just seemed to fit together that these pirates might be after the same treasure that the pirates were after two hundred years ago. I mean, it's super valuable."

"Super valuable?" LB evidently did not appreciate this description of treasure. "Well, *super valuable* it may be, but when all's said and done, you acted on a hunch, a hunch that left one of Sea Division's most *super valuable* agents out of action and me with a lot of explaining to do."

"But you see, I think someone got there first. I think they already found the treasure," said Ruby. "I found evidence of it, a gemstone that got left behind, dropped."

LB looked up. "You did? Where is it?"

Ruby bit her lip. "Well, that's the thing."

"The kid dropped it," said Hitch. "Not her fault."

"She dropped it?" said LB. She turned to Hitch. "So, Hitch, did you see this precious stone?"

Hitch shook his head. "No," he said, "I didn't."

"There were sharks," said Ruby. "A lot of sharks. And I sorta let go of it."

"You let go of the one piece of evidence that might make me believe this whole fairy tale?"

"It happened, OK? I'm sorry, but you might do the same if you were surrounded by a whole mob of sharks." Ruby was feeling the anger rise up in her. Sooner or later she was going to say something everyone would regret.

"The collective noun is a school or shoal, or if you must be dramatic, a shiver," said LB.

"Well, a mob is what it felt like to me," said Ruby, her voice loud and firm. She was on the very verge of telling LB where she might want to stick it. But fortunately, Hitch stepped in.

"Look, LB." His voice was calm and steady. "I wouldn't have

taken a risk like this if I hadn't thought there was something sound in the kid's thinking. Ruby's a smart kid; we all appreciate that. More importantly, I trust her instincts. Maybe these guys already plundered the wreck; maybe we were just too darned late."

"Acting on instincts is all very well. Acting on instincts without getting permission from your senior agent is reckless. Let me remind you both that you are not the ones who have to call up Agent Trent-Kobie at Sea Division and explain the actions of their renegade staff."

"I'll give you that," said Hitch. "But what if the kid had been right? What if the kid *is* right? Shouldn't we be trying to track these guys down?"

"Have you ever paused to consider why anyone would go to all this effort for something as corny as treasure? Is it really worth it?"

"No," said Ruby. "It isn't worth it."

LB turned to look at her, speechless. She waved for Ruby to continue.

"Either the mastermind behind this is a madman or the treasure is only a part of it. To my mind, there has to be something more."

"Now I'm interested," said LB. "Continue."

"I don't know," said Ruby. She didn't want to mention her theory to LB yet—that someone was after the rubies in a cave that a four-year-old girl had insisted was real exactly two hundred years ago. It would sound too crazy. Too "fairy tale," as LB had put it.

LB stared at her for the longest fifteen seconds ever recorded and then said, "Well, come back when you do." She picked up the phone, dialed a number, and launched right into a whole 'nother conversation.

Meeting over.

Hitch closed the door behind them. "Well, I think that went well, kid."

"She doesn't give a person a whole lot of slack, huh?" said Ruby.

"Never has, never will." He patted her on the back. "Come on, let's get out of here. You need to take some time off; you're growing dark circles around your eyes."

Ruby sighed. They had found nothing, but that didn't mean there had been nothing to find. Maybe, like Hitch said, they were just too darned late. Perhaps it was also too late to catch these particular sea bandits; perhaps they had found exactly what they wanted and were now miles and miles away....

Or perhaps not.

Wherever they were though, they had managed to find a pretty secret hiding place. There had been absolutely no sign of them today, neither below the sea nor above.

Ruby was right back at square one. And worse still, she'd managed to get Kekoa pretty badly injured and really annoy the powerful woman who ran the secret agency she worked for.

A great day's work, thought Ruby. *Nice going, Redfort.*

CHAPTER 34
Laugh All You Like, Sucker

THE HOUSE WAS QUIET. Ruby's parents were probably out at their tennis club, unaware that their daughter had almost been swallowed by a whole batch, shiver, or mob of murderous sharks.

It had been a sobering experience, and it made Ruby want to talk to one person above all. She dialed the number, but it went straight to the answering machine.

"Look, Clance, sorry for what I said, OK? Sorry for being a complete pain in the behind and a total duh brain. No excuses, just sorry. Call me." She replaced the receiver and went to change her clothes. Before she had made it four steps across the room, the telephone rang. She picked up the donut phone.

"Hey, Rube, you're forgiven. Wanna hang out?"

"Sure I do, Clance my old pal. What have you got in mind?"

It was Elliot's idea. Bike out to Far-West Beach and spend the night telling ghoulish stories under the stars. No one took a whole lot of persuading, but it was Elliot who was the true campfire kid. He liked nothing better than collecting driftwood and frying things out in the open.

Elliot, Mouse, Red, and Del were already there by the time Clancy and Ruby arrived. It had been a last-minute sort of plan, but like all the best last-minute plans it had come together easily. There was no danger of running out of supplies since Mrs. Digby had packed them off with way too many homemade burgers, ingredients for hot chocolate, marshmallows, and everything else that made an evening cookout satisfying.

It was a pretty perfect night for such a plan and once they had gotten themselves settled, they rolled out their sleeping bags and sat warming their hands by the fire's glow. Gradually, the talk moved from school to current Twinford events: the fleeing crabs, the dangerous dolphins, the confused sharks, and the sea strangler that had killed the fisherman. All of Twinford had read about it in the papers — it was big news.

"Who do you think he is?" asked Elliot.

"Or she," said Mouse.

"Yeah, that's right," agreed Del. "It could be a female strangler."

"How do you think she does it?" asked Red.

"Or he," added Clancy.

"I reckon she or he climbs aboard the boat while the victim

is looking the other way and takes the poor old fisherman by surprise," said Del.

"I don't think so," said Elliot, shaking his head. "It's just not realistic. The strangler's already in the boat—hiding under a tarp or nets or something."

"So what's the perpetrator's motive?" said Mouse, finally asking the question no one had gotten around to asking.

"He's a psychopath," said Clancy firmly.

"Or she's a psychopath," said Red.

"Did anyone ever think," said Ruby, the merest hint of drama in her voice. "Did anyone ever think that this he *or* she might be an *it*?"

Her words hung in the air. No one had thought this thought because it didn't really seem possible.

"What," said Clancy, "like you mean some kind of creature?"

"What kind of creature?" asked Del.

"I get it," said Mouse. "I see where you're coming from, like maybe this creature they talk about in the legends of Twinford."

"That kinda thing," said Ruby.

"Wow!" said Red. "You really mean there's an actual sea strangling-monster!"

A short grunting snort came from Elliot's nose, then silence. His face was contorted, his eyes shut tight. There was a twenty-second pause before Elliot Finch finally erupted into uncontrollable giggles, barely audible at first but gathering volume.

"You mean . . ." He was almost unable to string the words together as he gulped in air. "You mean you think . . . You think the strangler has to be some kinda . . ." He fell off the rock he was perched on. "Giant squid or humongous lobster or something? Oh boy, I think . . . I think I'm gonna pass out."

"Laugh all you like, sucker, but I don't see you getting in a boat and heading out to sea." Ruby had had a great deal of practice when it came to keeping a straight face around Elliot, but it wasn't easy. Elliot's giggles were very infectious, and sooner or later they would get you.

"I think Ruby is most probably right," said Red, trying hard not to succumb to the Elliot influence. She had great faith in Ruby: Ruby knew most things and was right about *a lot* of things. That said, Red *liked* to believe in monsters and ghosts, pixies even; she was what some would describe as fanciful, but others might describe as gullible. To her this was not far-fetched — she was quite prepared to believe in a monster squid or a humongous lobster. For this reason, she wasn't exactly helping Ruby's argument.

"Could you put a sock in it, bozo!" Ruby threw a burger bun

at Elliot. "I've been reading up on all this stuff at the city library, and it's all beginning to hook together. The Twinford treasure — I reckon that's true. I reckon the *Seahorse* went down exactly where Martha Fairbank said it did. So what if she was also telling the truth about the sea monster?"

"Wasn't she like four years old when that happened?" said Mouse.

"Yeah, but she was the smartest kid around — that's well documented. Besides, everything else she described is actually so."

"You're just saying that because she's your great-great-however-many-greats-grandmother," said Elliot.

"So who wants to go for a dip?" said Del, who was losing interest in the discussion. "I dare ya."

Elliot shook his head. "No way. You're not getting me in that water."

"How about you, Crew?" said Del, elbowing him in the ribs.

"You *are kidding,* I hope," replied Clancy.

None of the others volunteered either, so Del stood up. "OK, it looks like it's just me and old Bug here. Come on, boy."

The girl and the dog walked purposefully toward the sea; the moonlight was so bright that the ocean shone silver. Del started to wade in, but then something very curious happened. Bug did not follow. Bug never missed an opportunity to plunge into water of pretty much any kind. He loved to swim, but not tonight it seemed.

"Come on, fella!" called Del, but Bug stood there very still, a strange low growling coming from his throat. Del waded out farther and Bug became more agitated. He started to bark.

Ruby looked up at Bug and knew something was very wrong. She ran across the sand, hollering, "Del, get out of the water!"

Del stopped. "What? What is it?"

"I don't know, just get out!"

"Give me a break," said Del, moving forward again. She was up to her waist in water.

"Del!" hollered Ruby. "Quit arguing! Would you just listen *for once*?"

Del turned and shrugged. "OK, if you feel that strongly about it." And she began to stomp back out of the surf.

The fur on Bug's back relaxed, and he stopped barking. He ambled over to Del, licking the salt from her ankles.

"Cut it out, would ya?" said Del. "I have no idea what your problem is."

"Neither do I, but he sure is upset about something."

It turned out that Bug had done Del quite a favor—perhaps he had even saved her life, because the next morning after falling asleep on the beach they were woken by the screeching of seagulls. They were all tightly clustered together, making a sort of mound of birds, squawking and flapping. Elliot and Ruby climbed out of their sleeping bags and went to take a look.

"What is it?" called Mouse.

"You don't wanna know," shouted Elliot.

"Is it gruesome?" asked Clancy, scrambling to his feet.

"You could say that," called Ruby.

"How gruesome?" asked Red.

"You'll be glad you haven't had your breakfast," said Elliot.

"I have," said Del.

"Well, prepare to see it again," warned Ruby.

The four of them raced over to where Elliot and Ruby were standing.

As they approached, the gulls flew up in one screeching mass, and revealed the carcass of a killer whale.

CHAPTER 35
Connecting the Dots

THE AUTHORITIES WERE CALLED, OF COURSE, and various experts came down to look at the giant mammal dead on the sand. No one could offer an explanation as to what might have killed it other than it had been attacked by something huge.

Crushed and then drowned.

Ruby got home much later than she'd intended, and there was no sign of Hitch anywhere in the house. She looked out of the window — her mom and dad were sitting poolside, drinking fruit punch.

"Hey, honey," called her father. He was looking up, shielding his eyes from the sun. "You want to join us?"

"Ah, in a while maybe. I got some studying to do," said Ruby.

"Oh. By the way, Ruby," said her mother, "Elaine Lemon called earlier. She asked me if your skin condition had cleared up. I felt so terrible—as a mother I mean—I didn't know you had a problem with your skin."

"Oh," said Ruby, "didn't you?"

"No," said her mother. "What kind of skin condition? Elaine said it was contagious."

"No, it's fine," said Ruby.

"Contagious doesn't sound fine," said Sabina. Sabina believed that skin was the most important of all the body's organs. She was very fond of saying, *"Without it, you'd be all over the place."*

"Well, no need to worry anymore. My skin is all de-contagious again."

"Oh . . . good," said Sabina, unsure if the word *de-contagious* was a word or not.

"What subject you studying?" asked her father.

"Natural history," Ruby replied.

"That's a good subject," said Brant. "One of the best."

"I gotta go, Dad. Lots to read."

"That's our girl," called Brant.

"It sure is," said Sabina with a smile.

Her parents naturally put two and two together and figured that the studying must be schoolwork, but of course it wasn't. It was far more important than that.

❄ ❄ ❄

Ruby sat at her desk and took out her now very large piece of paper, several sheets stuck together with tape. The list of events and clues spiraled with some of the spirals connecting. She knew she was right about the treasure; she just knew it. Someone had gotten there first. The question now was where had these guys gone, what were they after next, and had they already found it?

Ruby glanced out of her window and noticed the stranger sitting on the wall on the opposite side of the street a couple of houses down. *What are you doing here?* He was wearing a hat and shades and by his feet was that same yellow carryall. From her vantage point she could make out a blurry blue shape printed on the yellow bag, a logo perhaps.

It was one thing to see him sitting outside the Full-O-Beans coffee shop and inside the Double Donut, not so strange to see him walking around town, but now he was in their street — waiting, but for what? Was he tailing her? Yes, had to be; this was no coincidence. *So what exactly do you want?* thought Ruby.

She would go and ask him, that's what she would do.

Right now.

She opened the hatch to the laundry chute and fed herself in headfirst. She shot through it in just a few seconds, landing on the lower ground floor on top of a bundle of sheets. She crawled through the hatch, ran out of the back door and through the gate into the alley. By the time she had sprinted into Cedarwood Drive, barely one minute later, the street was deserted.

The man was gone.

That evening Ruby caught up with Hitch over a glass of banana milk and a cheese sandwich.

"That milk you drink taste any good?" he asked.

"Wanna slurp?" offered Ruby.

"No, I don't think I'm ready for it yet."

"You don't know what you're missing, man," said Ruby. "So what are they saying over at Spectrum?"

"We have agents watching the Sibling waters, and yet nothing has been picked up: no strange whispers in the sea, no strangling, no pirate activity."

"Any more Chime communications?" asked Ruby.

"I was coming to that," replied Hitch. He took a brown envelope from his jacket. Ruby took a look — three cassette tapes, each one with a time scrawled on the label, each recorded that very day.

"So what do they say?" asked Ruby.

"Nothing," replied Hitch.

"What do you mean nothing?" said Ruby.

"It's just bursts of static, three of them — each one of exactly the same duration," replied Hitch. "We're guessing that all three recordings are the same piece of music, the same code. Looks like they had trouble broadcasting it — the code maker tried and failed to transmit the message three times. In the end, it seems he or she gave up, so we have nothing to go on."

Ruby picked up the envelope. "I'll take a listen anyhow," she said. "Just in case something got missed."

Hitch had been called out — he didn't say where — and so Ruby sat alone at the kitchen table listening to the static over and over on her tape machine, her headphones cushioning her ears and keeping all household sounds out. Reluctantly, she had to agree that Hitch was right: there was no message; some kind of error had prevented its transmission.

It was late in the evening, almost midnight, when her mother bustled into the kitchen. She and Brant had been entertaining the Pengroves, and they had just finished after-dinner drinks and were about to call it a night.

"Ruby, you're still up! You've got school tomorrow and circles around your eyes as big as pandas."

"Don't you mean circles as big as *a* panda's?"

"What?"

"Nothing," said Ruby.

"Teenagers need their sleep — you should know that. It's a fact of nature," asserted her mother. This was one of the few facts that Sabina was both certain of and correct about.

"OK," muttered Ruby. "I'll go to my room if it makes you so happy."

"That's exactly the attitude that comes from not having enough sleep," said Sabina.

"Yeah, yeah," replied Ruby.

"There it is again," said her mother.

"Ah, geez!" said Ruby. "I'm outta here."

In her dreams that night, Ruby found herself back in the deep, but this time "the thing" didn't appear in the indigo water. This time it only whispered to her — and the miniature diving man was not there at all.

She looked for the voice's owner, but all she saw was indigo. She felt something breathing right next to her — hot, moist breath, strong in odor, with a smell that was oddly familiar.

She woke up.

Two eyes were looking into hers, two piercing blue eyes. "Hey, Bug." She kissed him on the nose and he licked her on the cheek. "I get the impression you didn't brush your teeth this morning."

Relieved not to be drowning in the ocean, Ruby fumbled for her glasses and reached for the bedside light. She looked at her alarm clock — it was almost dawn, she might as well get up. She retrieved her notebook and sat down at her desk. She looked at the lists she had made, focusing on the one that was headed *Sea Sounds*.

There was something bothering Ruby. It had been niggling her since that first Spectrum briefing, but she couldn't quite catch it; it just fluttered back and forth in the corridors of her brain.

It was something to do with the people who had heard the whispering. She put her head on her desk: *teenagers need their sleep*. Her mother's words, her last muttered thought as she fell into oblivion. Words that seemed relevant somehow.

Minutes later, or so it seemed, something clunked down on the desktop, something that smelled good.

"Thought you could use an old-fashioned cup of tea — English style," said Mrs. Digby. Mrs. Digby was very proud of her English heritage, even though her ancestors had left England a couple of hundred years previously.

Ruby slowly lifted her head from the desk and looked at the mug sitting just to the right of her nose. She felt terrible; there was a candy wrapper stuck to her cheek and her barrette was digging into her scalp. She had been sleeping like that for almost two hours.

"Thanks, Mrs. Digby. I could certainly use it."

"I reckon so," said the housekeeper, looking her up and down. "What are you doing sleeping out of your bed?"

"Bad dreams," said Ruby.

"It'll be the cheese," said Mrs. Digby.

Ruby nodded, knowing that though this was not the reason, it wasn't worth getting into a discussion over. Mrs. Digby had her theories, and she stuck to them like glue.

"Hitch around?" Ruby asked.

"Gone somewhere," said Mrs. Digby. "And don't ask me where 'cause I don't know. Just saw his car was absent from the driveway early this morning."

Ruby checked her watch — it was early, but still she would have to cut school. She pulled on her clothes and grabbed her satchel.

As she rode her bike to Desolate Cove, the same thought went around and around Ruby's head: something to do with teenagers. But what? She hid her bike from view, crossed the pebble beach, and edged her way carefully around the cliff until she found the cove that the scuba-sub was hidden in. Would she be able to get it started?

How difficult can it be?

Pretty difficult, it turned out. Locating the key was no trouble at all. She used the rescue watch's magnetic metal detector to find it. Working out how to *use* the key was the near impossible thing.

An hour later and she had figured it out. The sub was not the easiest thing to *pilot* either, but once she got the hang of it, it *was* what you might call thrilling. She had paid close attention during that first trip with Hitch and seen the way he had gained entrance to the rock. She got in without a problem, navigated through the water tunnel, and parked, if scuba-subs *could* be parked.

These days Ruby didn't *need* to break into Spectrum, but she had no clearance for Sea Division, and she certainly didn't have permission to revisit the lecture theater by herself. So she snuck back in through the tiny internal window, situated six feet above the floor. Not easy to reach, but Ruby was an excellent tree climber, and this stood her in great stead for most vertical challenges.

By standing on the drinking fountain, she managed to haul herself up and through the opening without great difficulty. The window accessed the little booth where the projector and audio equipment were kept. The carousel containing the slides from last week's briefing was still sitting on the desk next to it. Ruby slotted the carousel in place, flicked the switch, and listened to the projector as the fan began to whir and the light beam caught the dust particles, which moved like plankton in and out of the darkness.

Ruby went through the slides slowly, pausing on each one, carefully studying them.

The swimming boy, Tommy Elson.

The smiling couple, Hallie Grier and Lyle Greene.

The surfer girl, Billie-May Vaughn.

The kid with the fishing rod, Danny Fink Junior.

Ruby wasn't sure about Hallie and Lyle, but the others were most definitely pretty young. She took out the slide of the smiling couple. There was a label at the bottom which read:

```
HALLIE GRIER, 18,
AND LYLE GREENE, 18,
FAR-WEST BAY.
```

That was the connection.

That was why she'd been thinking about her mother's words: it was to do with teenagers — kids.

Everyone who had heard the whispering was either a kid, or not yet quite an adult. This included Ruby herself, of course. She had read somewhere that kids and teenagers could hear sounds that adults couldn't — higher frequencies — *just like dogs.* As you got older, your ears became less sensitive, and these high tones started to fall out of reach.

What if the reason no one was taking these reports seriously was because no adult had heard the whispers? You had to be a kid to hear them.

So supposing the whispering was a fact, but could only be heard by kids, where was it coming from? Who or what was generating this sound? Red had heard it during the swimathon. Ruby herself had heard it when diving the wreck. Sailors of bygone times had heard it too, and sailors in those days were often boys, not yet grown men.

What was that thing Martha had said? A whispering sea devil? Could there really be such a creature?

Ruby headed out the way she came in — pushing herself backward through the tiny window — feeling around with her feet for the drinking fountain. It was higher up than she remembered, less stable too, and then she realized why; her feet were not resting on the fountain, they were resting on someone's shoulders.

Ruby's heart skipped.

Then . . .

"I'd recognize those sneakers anywhere," said a voice.

"Man! You nearly gave me a heart attack," hissed Ruby, peering down at Hitch.

HITCH: *You might well have a heart attack if Agent Trent-Kobie discovers you here. What do you think you're doing?*

RUBY: *Research. I needed to look at those slides again, the ones Kekoa presented last week.*

HITCH: *So why didn't you ask permission?*

RUBY: *In case they said no.*

HITCH: *That's not a good reason.*

RUBY: {Silence}

HITCH: *At the very least you could have asked* me.

RUBY: *You weren't around.*

HITCH: *I'm contactable, ever think of that?*

RUBY: *I couldn't be bothered.*

HITCH: *Am I hearing this?*

RUBY: *I mean, time was a factor.*

HITCH: *Well, it took you long enough to get the scuba-sub started.*

RUBY: *What? You followed me?*

HITCH: *Not exactly. I was looking for clues at Desolate Cove, then I saw you.*

RUBY: *So why didn't you help me get it started?*

HITCH: *I wanted to see if you could manage, and it turns out you can.*

RUBY: *So how did you get here?*

HITCH: *There's more than one scuba-sub.*

RUBY: *I guess there is.*

HITCH: *You find out what you needed to find out?*

RUBY: *Yeah.*

HITCH: *Then I would advise that we get out of here before you get in deep trouble.*

When both scuba-subs had reached the shores of Desolate Cove and both agents were walking back across the pebble beach, Hitch quizzed Ruby about her findings. She was about to fill him in when his watch flashed green.

"Got to take this," he said.

The voice coming through was LB's, and she did not sound happy. "I've been trying to locate you for the last forty-five minutes."

"Had to check something out at Sea Division," he replied.

"Well, you're needed in Spectrum. Something's come up."

"On my way. Over and out."

He turned to Ruby. "Sorry, kid, you're going to have to hold that thought. We'll catch up later, OK?"

Ruby shrugged. "Guess so," she said.

"Just hold that thought," he called as he strode across the iron-gray stones.

Ruby retrieved her bike and rode back to Twinford, all the while thinking, *Could there really be some kind of sea monster out there? Or am I beginning to lose it?*

To help answer both these questions (one preposterous, the other highly likely) she started heading for the place she knew would have most books on the subject — and then she had a better idea.

She turned her bike around.

CHAPTER 36
Stranger Things Have Happened at Sea

TWENTY MINUTES LATER, RUBY PULLED UP outside the Crew mansion. She knew how to disarm the security gate and was inside in a second. She then slipped around to the west side of the house and climbed up the vine to Clancy's bedroom.

It was a cinch. The house was built in the Parisian style and resembled a sort of mini chateau covered in creeper. She elegantly stepped from the vine into the room via the balcony window with musketeer-like ease.

"Hey, Rube, you didn't say you were coming over," said Clancy.

Ruby screeched in a most un-Ruby-Redfort-like way.

"Sorry, Rube, didn't mean to alarm you," said Clancy.

"You're skipping school *again*?"

"It's swim practice," explained Clancy. "Anyway, you're the one doing the breaking and entering."

"Yeah, sorry about that. But you're pushing your luck, my

friend. Two Mondays in a row, they're gonna cotton on sooner or later."

"Yeah, I know. That's why I'm lying low. Anyway, what's your excuse?"

"I want to take a look at your sea monster books," replied Ruby.

"You cut school for *that*? Kinda weird emergency if you ask me." But he simply shrugged and pointed to the giant stack of books next to his bed. "Be my guest." He seemed a little puzzled, but happy to oblige.

Ruby sat on the floor, flipping through page after page. What she was looking for were stories and legends that might relate back to accounts of a whispering sound, strange noises heard at sea.

She found many myths of sea monsters and strange creatures who would call to earthly folk: the Blue Men of the Minch who lived in underwater caves; the selkies, seal people who lived off Scotland and Iceland; mermaids calling sailors to join them under the waves; sea witches and pied pipers who lured children from the shores down to watery graves. Then there were the giants of the sea: the prehistoric monsters from the deep that dragged entire boatfuls of men to their deaths and devoured whole ships.

Most of the legends appeared to Ruby to be a way of explaining things that simple people couldn't understand, giving some reason for the random deaths in the cruel seas during harsh ages.

However, some of the tales seemed to have more substance, and told of sightings of strange and improbable beasts. The recurring theme of mysterious singers and whispered callings in particular appeared in various accounts connected to Twinford.

There was one tragic account of a cabin boy named Robin Farthingale who swore he could hear a woman calling to him in the fog, her mournful whispers, cries for rescue. He dove in and was never seen again.

There was the *Mary-Belle*, which was smashed to pieces on the Sibling cliffs after the youngest of the sailors steered the vessel off course, believing that there were mermaids whispering in the darkness, saying, *Help us, we beg you, help us.*

There were whispers in storms, urging crews to jump ship. Most of those who did so jumped to their graves, their drowned and battered bodies found much later, if at all, washed up onshore.

There were a few theories as to the cause of these eerie sounds. Most believed that far from being an actual creature, the whispering came from the ghosts of the lost sisters of the Sibling Islands calling for help. The less romantic said the sound was merely the sea pulling gravel along the ocean floor.

Others said it was the wind. But some claimed to have *seen* the sea whisperer, a giant and terrifying creature, bigger than any whale. A creature so strong that it could pull the burliest of fishermen from his boat and strangle six men at a time; some vowed eight.

After forty-six minutes of watching Ruby read, Clancy asked, "So what kind of sea monsters are you interested in?"

"The kind that attack sharks," said Ruby.

"Mythical ones, right?" asked Clancy hopefully.

"Uh-uh, real ones," said Ruby.

"A creature that attacks sharks?" exclaimed Clancy, and his arms started to flap.

"And killer whales," she added.

"Oh, brother!" said Clancy. This made him feel even worse: now there was something even bigger to fear, more dangerous than a shark, bigger than a killer whale.

"Clance, where are the *factual* marine-life books about the deep? The *deep* deep, I mean — about creatures that people aren't sure exist but think might?"

"They're in the closet," said Clancy. "Ever since this whole swimathon thing I haven't been able to look at them." He pulled a whole bunch of books out and slid them across the floor.

She went through each one; there was a lot to learn when it came to the deep, and she couldn't help reading facts out loud.

RUBY: *Did you know that we have only explored five percent of the ocean?*

CLANCY: *Yeah, I did actually.*

RUBY: *Did you know we know more about the surface of the moon than the bottom of the ocean bed?*

CLANCY: *Yeah, I know.*

RUBY: *Did you know that a new species is discovered every time we explore the depths of the ocean?*

CLANCY: *Actually between four and six new species. But yeah, I know.*

RUBY: *I didn't know you actually read all of this stuff.*

CLANCY: *What did you think I did with it?*

RUBY: *I don't know, look at the pictures and hide under your bed?*

CLANCY: *Yeah, funny, Rube. Excuse me while I die laughing.*

RUBY: *Hey, but really, Clance, how come you read all this stuff if you hate the ocean so much?*

CLANCY: *I don't hate the ocean, I just don't want to ever go in it. There's a difference.*

RUBY: *You know you're gonna have to get over this, you can't —*

She didn't finish her sentence. Her eyes had alighted upon something she recognized. A photograph that had fallen from the book, but didn't belong to it.

It was a half page torn from a magazine and tucked into the book. The picture was of a young man, the face a little out of focus, but it showed him smiling in a wet suit, standing against a blue Mediterranean Sea.

But it wasn't the man that Ruby recognized, it was the bag at his feet. Yellow with a blurred blue shape printed on the left side. She took her watch from her wrist and swiveled out the refocus magnifier and laid it over the blue. The blue became a logo, an animal — a dog? Something like a dog anyway. This bag was the same yellow bag she had seen the stranger carrying, but the man in the photo looked a good deal younger than the stranger, which made sense, because it looked like it had been taken a while ago.

In the photograph he had obviously just returned from a dive, and his boat was moored behind him. The name of the boat was partially obscured, though the last word could easily be read: *MARE*, the Italian word for sea. The middle word couldn't be seen because the smiling man stood in front of it and the other letters spelled *UPO*. Well, that didn't mean anything. UPO ___ MARE?

Unless of course the first letter of the word had been cropped by the photographer in which case it was likely to be an *L* . . . an *L* for *LUPO*, meaning "wolf."

LUPO DI MARE—the *Sea Wolf.*

The boat her father had dived from all those years ago in Italy. The boat that belonged to that marine biologist guy.

It was all adding up.

"What have you found?" asked Clancy, scooting over to where Ruby kneeled in a sea of books.

She pointed at the photograph. "This picture, where did you get it from?"

"Beats me." Clancy shrugged. "Most of these books are secondhand; I've never seen this picture before. What's the big deal about it?"

"This guy, I know who he is. Francesco something-or-other. I'm pretty sure my dad used to be part of his dive crew. In fact I'm sure of it. And I think he's been following me around too."

"You do?" said Clancy uncertainly.

"Look, can I use your phone?" Ruby had already picked up the receiver and was halfway through dialing.

"Be my guest," said Clancy, shrugging.

Ms. Blanche put her through right away. Ms. Blanche had no doubt her boss would want to speak to Ruby. Brant Redfort always took his daughter's calls.

"Dad, what was the name of that diver guy you worked for in Italy?"

"Fornetti," said her father. "Francesco Fornetti. Why are you asking?"

"You said he was a genius?"

"Oh, yes. He was a genius all right," replied her father.

"What happened to him? You mentioned he was laughed out of town. If he was such a genius, how come he was discredited?"

"He sort of lost it, was raving about a sea monster and crazy stuff. He even wrote a book about it."

"What was it called?" Ruby asked.

"I don't remember. All I know is he went AWOL after that. Some said he had sunstroke or maybe had swallowed too much saltwater; perhaps he was hallucinating."

"Did *you* believe him?" said Ruby.

"I didn't know what to think. I never exactly *knew* the fellow, not really. I just admired his work."

"But you spent time with him, right?" said Ruby.

"Only once after Italy. He happened to be in Twinford and we met while your mother and I were sailing around the coast. We were taking it easy because it was that crazy summer that your mom broke her arm and I dislocated my shoulder. Fornetti was free diving and joined us on our boat. Nice guy and . . . heroic too, but then I guess he just sorta went right off the rails."

Heroic: now that was a strange word to use.

"Look, sorry, honey. I'm due in a meeting any minute . . ."

"OK, but just tell me—did *I* meet him?" asked Ruby.

Her father hesitated. "Not really. Sorta. You were just a tiny kid." Ruby had the sense he was being cagey about something, which wasn't like him.

"How old was I exactly?" she asked.

"You were a baby, no more than a toddler. You wouldn't remember."

It was true, she didn't remember.

"So this Francesco Fornetti, would he recognize me if he saw me now?"

"No, how could he? Why are you asking?" said her father.

"Oh, you know, no reason," said Ruby.

"Shouldn't you be in school, by the way?" said her father.

"Yeah, you're right. Gotta go."

She hung up.

There were two certainties in Ruby's mind, and both of them worried her.

One: she was sure that Francesco Fornetti was following her.

Two: she was sure that her father was keeping something from her — something that might explain why.

Was this guy dangerous?

CHAPTER 37
A Cloud of Indigo

AFTER PROMISING THAT SHE ABSOLUTELY WOULD, on pain of death, call Clancy later, Ruby climbed back out of the third-story window and headed on down to the secondhand bookstore. It was named Penny Books after Ray Penny, the owner, but it had a sort of double meaning because a lot of the books were pretty cheap. It was one of those shops that was stuffed full of things that daylight would never see due to the sheer quantity of it all. Books stacked three deep one in front of another; books spread on rickety tables and piled in teetering towers on the floors of the narrow passages between the shelves.

Ruby started scanning the rows of paperbacks, hardbacks, and pamphlets, lost in a world of her own until she heard a raspy voice call.

"What are you looking for there?"

Ruby turned to see Ray standing at the counter, his broken glasses wedged on his nose. Ray knew Ruby pretty well and liked her a lot; she was one of his regulars, always in browsing, particularly the old graphic novels.

"I'm looking for a book by someone named Fornetti," she said. "Francesco Fornetti."

Ray scratched his cheek in a thoughtful sort of way.

"That name kinda rings a bell with me," he said. This wasn't surprising — Ray seemed to know most books; if you couldn't remember the title, he could usually identify it just by a description of the cover.

"Fact or fiction?" he asked.

"Fact, I guess," said Ruby.

"Subject?" asked Ray.

"Marine biology, the ocean," replied Ruby.

"Oh yeah. *That* guy, I know. So which book were you interested in?" asked Ray. "If I remember correctly, he wrote a whole lot."

"I guess the one I'm looking for he might have written around nine or ten years ago," said Ruby. "It probably would have been the last thing he had published," she added, thinking of what her dad had said about his reputation.

Ray nodded. "Can you just give me an hour or so? I need to search the back there." He pointed to the area at the rear of the shop, the area where the floor disappeared under a cascade of paper.

"Sure," said Ruby. "I'll go get a fruit shake from Cherry's. I'll be back."

Once she had paid for her beverage, she carried it across the road and sat on the low bench outside Penny's, enjoying the sun and making the drink last.

Nearly three hours and five fruit shakes later, Ray called out, "So I found your book. It's short, more of an essay really — it's called *The Sea Whisperer*. That's the one you wanted, right? Came out ten years ago. I made some calls — the guy hasn't written a word since *The Sea Whisperer* was published."

Ruby paid for the book: it was indeed a slim volume, a flimsy paperback; the dog-eared and torn cover was orange, and an image of a sinister black tentacle trailed across it.

Ruby returned to her bench and sat in the fading sun reading it, cover to cover, over and over.

The book made for more than merely *interesting* reading; it was gripping. The author described an encounter with a creature he identified as the Sea Whisperer, the very creature all the legends spoke of. He had met it quite by chance when sailing off the Twinford coast: it was a giant octopus, spanning fifty feet, by far the biggest he had ever recorded.

At the time, he had told no one about what he had seen. He

himself had found it hard to believe his eyes as he watched it pulse its way back down to the deep. He wanted evidence and became obsessed with the monster and spent every waking moment searching for it, and just six weeks later he was lucky enough to spot the octopus again. He had tracked it into waters north of the Sibling Islands. He had watched it attack huge prey — an eleven-foot shark.

Fornetti was busy taking pictures of the giant when it released a cloud of indigo into the water. He became disoriented, dropped the camera, and felt the creature pull the breathing apparatus from his mouth. Fornetti gulped in water and ink, stabbing at the creature with a knife — tiny by comparison with the monster's bulk. Perhaps the creature could not be bothered to fight this miniature man, perhaps it simply wasn't hungry, but Fornetti was lucky to live to tell the tale.

And tell the tale he did: in fact, he couldn't stop himself. He claimed that the ink he had swallowed acted as some sort of truth serum and so he blurted the story of the sea monster to everyone and anyone. He became the butt of every joke. No one took him seriously.

It wasn't this that Ruby found odd though. No: Ruby felt it strange that the diver's *first* encounter with the creature was described so sketchily. Why had he dived into the ocean in the first place? He mentioned something about being on a sailing trip. But why had he not bothered to put on his scuba gear?

However, despite the missing details and blurry facts, there was something about the passionate way the story was told that made Ruby believe every word of it.

So that's why this guy's been lurking around Twinford, she thought. *He's trying to find the Sea Whisperer and prove that he's not a crank.*

But why is he showing up every place I go? What have I got to do with any of this? Why would he be interested in following me?

CHAPTER 38
Just Static

WHEN RUBY WAS DONE READING, she stuffed the book into her satchel and rode back as fast as she could to Cedarwood Drive. She ran in to the house and called out to Hitch.

No reply.

She ran downstairs and knocked on his door, but he wasn't there. She tried contacting him via the rescue watch, but her signal was not answered. She walked slowly back upstairs. *Where was he?*

The sound of singing was coming from the living room. It was her mother's voice.

"Oh, my Ruby, your mother's jewel,
You lie there still as a tidal pool."

Ruby entered the room and saw her mom sitting on a chair rocking a sleepy baby; it was the neighbor's kid. Her mother smiled and said in a hushed voice, "Babysitting Archie. Elaine had to get her hair done; an emergency."

"A *hair* emergency?" said Ruby.

Sabina held her finger to her lips. "He's so cute. Wanna hold him?" she asked.

"Ah, not right now," said Ruby. "You seen Hitch?"

"Not all day," said her mother. Then she started up with the lullaby again. It was the one Sabina used to sing to Ruby when she was small.

"When the stars begin to fall,
You will hear the ocean call."

By the time Ruby had reached her room, the song had caught and was playing around and around in her head, and like a fly buzzing in a sealed room, she couldn't get rid of it. She had heard the song sung to her so many times when she was little that she knew it by heart even though she hadn't heard her mom sing it for many years. Around and around it went:

When you hear that whispered sound,
You will know that you are found.

A golden bird guards over you
My little gem, my words are true.

Ruby shook her head, as if it might be possible to shake the song out of her brain.

She needed to make contact with Hitch. She had to tell him about Fornetti's book. It had to be relevant, didn't it? This sea monster — it could be what had killed Agent Trilby; it could be what had scared the sharks. Something struck her: it was probably what her parents had seen too, when they were floating around the Sibling Islands. Hadn't they said that Pookie got covered in indigo ink?

Ruby was just about to try contacting Hitch again when she saw a message sitting there on her desk. It was a collection of musical notes, a piece of music. At the top of the page, written neatly in ink, was a message from Hitch:

Chime just broadcast one last unusual piece of music.
This is it.

Ruby quickly decoded it and saw that the musical notes read:

I will meet you at Far-West Point in the caves of Horseshoe Bay;
wait there for my arrival. Stay put until I come.
There will be no further messages.

Underneath, Hitch had written:

See you when things are all tied up. Sit tight till then.

Ruby sat back in her chair. So that was where Hitch was. The case was wrapped up. Spectrum had gone to arrest the pirates and whoever was on their way to meet them, the mastermind behind the whole operation. She breathed out a long sigh, but not one of satisfaction: something was still bugging her.

She looked at the spider map, working her way through each incident, each clue.

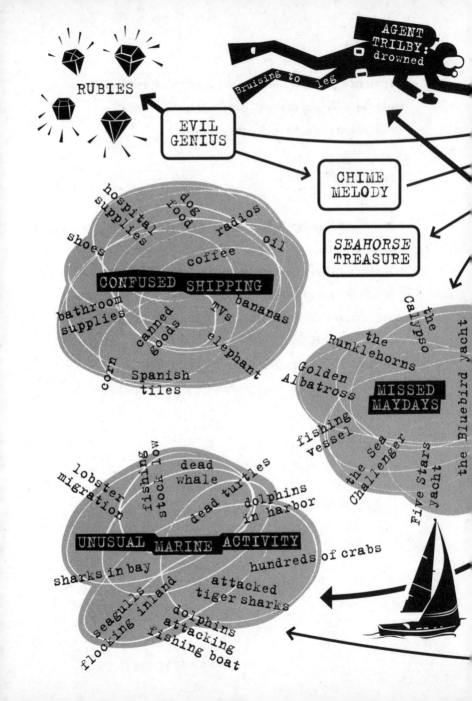

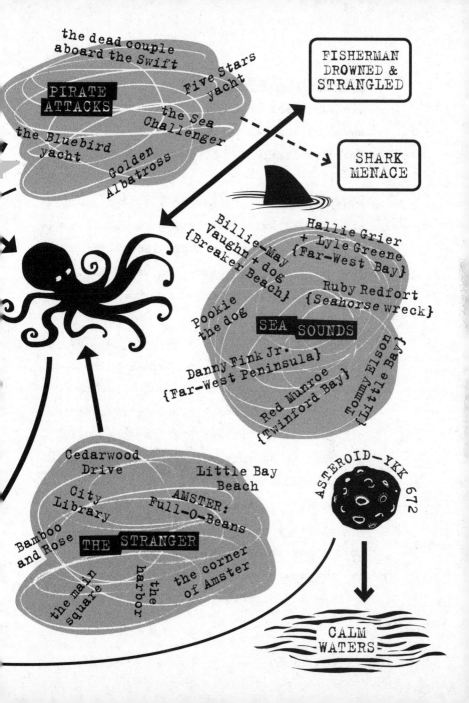

THE WHISPERED SOUNDS came from the giant sea creature, the creature that had bothered the dolphins, killed the sharks, the killer whale, and most likely the diver and the fisherman.

THE STRANGER was Francesco Fornetti, marine expert, who wanted to keep a low profile due to events that had seen him ridiculed; he had put two and two together and was tracking the sea creature—presumably to prove a point.

THE PIRATES wanted the treasure from the *Seahorse* and their radio transmissions had kept boats out of the Sibling waters by blocking Maydays and by sending cargo ships off course. A cleverer guy than they were knew how to do this, and it was this guy who was in charge of the whole operation, issuing orders in code transmitted via radio. One of the pirate crew was capable of code-cracking, more brain than brawn. The pirates were able to dive the wreck and retrieve the treasure because the currents had calmed.

THE CURRENTS had calmed because of the
asteroid. This change to the seas had in
turn changed the behavior of the marine life:
crabs, gulls, fish, etc.

She exhaled a deep breath. Basically, it all added up. Made
perfect sense, all neat and tidy. Well, almost—there were a few
unanswered questions, a few loose ends. Problem was, Ruby
didn't like loose ends.

THIS FORNETTI FELLOW, why is he trailing me?
If he's a good guy, then why doesn't he just
come right out and say what's on his mind?

THIS EVIL GENIUS, this so-called mastermind,
would he really be satisfied with the *Seahorse*
treasure? Was that really enough? Once
everyone had taken a cut, it wouldn't amount
to much.

AND THAT LAST CHIME CODE, what was he doing
relaying such a very obvious message? Yes, it
was coded, but once deciphered, it was hardly

cryptic. All the previous communications had
been pretty tough to understand, so why was
this one so simple? And why go silent for so
long after Kekoa and Ruby dived the wreck?

IS THERE SOMETHING I'VE MISSED?

Ruby picked up her satchel and dug out the three tapes Hitch
had given her of the strange static that had been heard on Chime
Melody. Maybe she had overlooked something. She slotted two
of them into the stereo's double cassette player, the third she
clicked into the portable cassette machine on the floor. Then
she played each one in turn. She listened, concentrating hard,
using all her powers.

Nothing. No underlying voices, no secret message, no code
whatsoever. *OK*, she thought. *The static is just static.*

She couldn't concentrate properly, that darned lullaby was
going around and around on a loop, occupying her brain:

Oh, my Ruby, your mother's jewel,
You lie there still as a tidal pool.
When the stars begin to fall,
You will hear the ocean call.

When you hear that whispered sound,
You will know that you are found.
A golden bird guards over you.
My little gem, my words are true.

Ruby gave in to it, letting the lullaby wash through her; it was calming somehow. She even began to sing it out loud. She had never thought too much about the words. You don't when you're a newborn baby; they are just sounds sung to soothe, and as you get older, like nursery rhymes, you don't question them. It's all about the rhythm and not the meaning.

Finally, she came out of her trance: she needed to talk things through with someone, someone who would listen.

She plucked the receiver from the squirrel in the tux and dialed Clancy's number.

"Hey," he said. "You're there."

"How'd ya know it was me?" said Ruby.

"Rube, it's kinda late. Who else is it likely to be?" said Clancy.

"You wanna get over here?" It was a demand rather than a question.

"When?"

"Like now, bozo." She returned the receiver to the rodent and pressed the call button on the rescue watch. It should reach

Hitch immediately — but it didn't. She pressed again, this time contacting Buzz.

"I need to speak to Hitch," she said.

"He's not contactable," came the reply.

"Blacker then."

"Not contactable."

"LB?"

Buzz inhaled, but Ruby got there first.

"Don't tell me — not contactable?"

"Correct," said Buzz. "Can I assist you with anything else?"

"No," said Ruby. "You've been super, just super."

She lay back on the beanbag. Spectrum seemed satisfied with how things had turned out, so why wasn't she? *Couldn't this whole case simply be about a few gems and some gold coins?* Was she overcomplicating things by insisting that there was more to it?

Unable to let it go, she turned the tape machine back on, switching from one to the other, around and around, but it was still all static, just static . . . until she heard another sound, a loud tapping, coming from the window.

Ruby looked up. It was Clancy. She got up and released the catch on the sill, and the huge glass pane swung open. He pushed himself through — arms first — and ended up sprawled on the floor. Not very dignified.

"That's no way to come in through a window," said Ruby.

"Sorta lost my balance," said Clancy, rubbing his knee. "So what's on your mind?"

"A few things actually," said Ruby. "There's this first thing that doesn't make sense."

"Hit me with it," said Clancy, flopping down on the beanbag.

"Why would someone go to all the trouble of devising a super-smart code, which even when translated is super cryptic, and then just when they're almost home free, they blow it by being unnecessarily obvious? Why would they do that?"

"Human nature," said Clancy. "Criminals' remorse, they want to get caught. It's like in *Crazy Cops*, Detective Despo always says that criminals want to confess. They can't help themselves."

"I don't think that's it, Clance. We're not talking about some accidental murder here, or some heat-of-the-moment crime. This plan was thought through in triplicate; this plan is about locating something and stealing it. This gang wants to get away with it. Why wouldn't they? But maybe someone else doesn't want them to; perhaps the mastermind of this plan wants them to get caught."

"What do you mean by that?" said Clancy, trying to wrestle himself out of the beanbag, but his arms were restricted so he resembled a beetle flailing on its back. "You saying the mastermind criminal mighta set up the rest of the gang?"

"Yeah, I guess that's exactly what I'm thinking. But then I'm thinking, why?"

"Revenge?" suggested Clancy.

"Then why not take the treasure too? Getting the pirates caught means losing the booty — makes no sense. There has to be something bigger, far more valuable, that this top guy wants. He must know we're onto him, watching the waters, so he's using the little guys as a distraction; if you like, they're the bait, the sprats, and this guy is fishing for sharks."

Inevitably though, Clancy only registered the word *shark* and immediately looked panicked.

Ruby rolled her eyes. "It's an expression, dummy. What I mean is, this guy is most likely looking for the *real* treasure."

"Meaning what?" Clancy was scrunching his brow.

"Meaning the Fairbank rubies," said Ruby.

"But I thought that was just some legend," said Clancy. "No one really believes they actually exist."

"I do," said Ruby. "Martha Fairbank said they were left in that cave, and I believe her."

"Why?" said Clancy.

"Because," said Ruby, "she couldn't tell a lie."

"Why not? Little kids often come up with crazy ideas. Take my sister Amy — she thinks a pixie lives up the chimney."

"You're missing the point, Clance. Martha couldn't tell a lie because she had ingested a truth serum."

"Now *you're* talking crazy, Rube. Martha was born in the eighteenth century, and correct me if I'm wrong, but I don't think she would have just happened to swallow a truth serum."

"Well, that's where you are wrong, my friend; that's exactly what happened, just like it happened to Pookie, the Gruemeisters' dog, and possibly to Francesco Fornetti, the famous marine biologist."

Clancy was staring at her in disbelief.

"Quit with the face, would you, Clance?"

"I'll quit with the face if you explain what the Sam Hill you're going on about."

"OK," said Ruby. "You've heard of the Sea Whisperer?"

"Of course," said Clancy.

"So what I'm saying is this creature actually exists, not a devil but a giant octopus."

"What?" said Clancy. "A giant what did you say?"

"Octopus," said Ruby. "The sea devil, the creature Martha Lily Fairbank heard those pirates shrieking about, not the same actual octopus obviously, but the same one Red heard, the same one I heard, and all those other kids and possibly the same one that Francesco Fornetti *saw* ten years ago."

"Octopuses only live for a maximum of four to five years," said Clancy. He was sure on this point.

"Yeah, but this octopus isn't like others. It's bigger for a start. Most giant octopuses have a thirty-foot span, but this one, according to Fornetti, is more like fifty feet wide."

"Geez," said Clancy. "You saying a giant octopus has been terrorizing the sharks?"

"And strangling unfortunate fishermen," said Ruby. "Remember the guy found strangled in his boat?"

Clancy nodded.

"The octopus did it," said Ruby.

"Huh?" said Clancy.

"There's this seafarers' legend about the Sea Whisperer," said Ruby. " *'They say it can lure a child to a watery grave, that it can strangle the breath from the strongest man. . . .'* "

Clancy chimed in.

" *'Some say it can persuade a stranger to tell his darkest secret.'* "

"You know it?" asked Ruby,

"Yeah, I know it," said Clancy. "It's mentioned in one of the myths of the ocean books I got."

"Of course, why am I surprised? I am speaking to the boy who knows everything about the ocean, but never dips a toe in it.

Anyway," said Ruby, "the Sea Whisperer must have pulled the fisherman out of his boat, dragged him underwater, strangled him, and then dumped him back."

"Why didn't it eat him?" said Clancy.

"I don't know, Clance. I'm not sure what makes a giant octopus tick, but it killed that diver by dragging him under until he ran out of air. *'It can strangle the breath from the strongest man.'* The strange marks on his ankle were from where the tentacle — or rather octopus arm — grabbed him. Also, the legend says, *'They say it can lure a child to a watery grave.'* Well, that's true too, in part anyway. It makes this sound, you see, like a siren calling out for help. Only the young can hear it, and if they follow the sound, they end up drowned or in its clutches."

Clancy wasn't feeling so good. This was meant to be fiction, just a legend.

But Ruby hadn't finished. " *'Some say it can persuade a stranger to tell his darkest secret.'* There's a truth serum in its ink; if you swallow it, even a little, it will make you talk and talk, and for a while every word will be the truth. Francesco Fornetti experienced it for himself."

"OK, so let's say you've convinced me, and I'm not saying you have, but just say for argument's sake that the sea monster is real, the rubies exist, the arch villain wants the rubies, the rubies are in a cave. And this villain has sent Spectrum off chasing the pirates to get everyone out of the way."

"Uh-huh," said Ruby.

"So how did he know Spectrum had broken the Chime Melody code?" asked Clancy.

Ruby frowned. She thought about the question for a couple of minutes and then replied. "Because he saw us that day when we were diving the *Seahorse* wreck."

"How do you know?" said Clancy.

"Because I *saw* him, at least I saw a flash of light, his binoculars catching the sun maybe. He was watching us that day. He saw me and Hitch and Kekoa turn up. He must have known we'd cracked the Chime code, otherwise why would we be there in that exact spot? He must have been standing there on the island; he must have found a way into the caves."

"OK," said Clancy. "If all that's true, then where's the cave?"

"That's a question, and a good one." Ruby sighed. "That part I haven't figured out. Somewhere in the smaller of the two Sibling Islands. But if Martha was right, it was most likely covered by a landslide — that's why no one ever found it."

"So you don't have any way of proving your theory?"

"Not yet," said Ruby, exhaling heavily.

Neither of them said a thing, not for several minutes.

The silence or near silence was broken by Clancy suddenly becoming aware of the static tape playing in the background. "What are you listening to, by the way? It sounds like white noise. It's pretty boring, and it's giving me toothache."

He reached over from his reclined position to switch off the tape, but instead clicked play on the second cassette. Two static sounds played one on top of the other, making an eerie sort of noise. "Oops," he said. "Even worse." He reached for the off switch, but fell backward into the beanbag, his hand landing on the portable player to his left and triggering the play button on that machine.

Now all three static sounds were hissing at once, but it wasn't static Ruby and Clancy could hear anymore — it was jumbled words.

They looked at each other, utterly speechless.

CHAPTER 39
Your Mother's Jewel

RUBY REWOUND EACH CASSETTE TO THE VERY BEGINNING, then she held her fingers over the two play buttons on the double cassette player. Clancy held his finger over the play button of the portable player. When Ruby gave the nod, they both pushed all three buttons at once, and then Ruby and Clancy sat there in amazement, listening to the clear voice that the three simultaneously playing static tapes had magically turned into.

A golden bird sits above the tidal pool where the Sea Whisperer lurks. Look up and you will find your reward. I don't need to count on your loyalty, just remember you cannot tell a lie.

The three static messages weren't three different messages, they were just one. Played together, the sounds layered on top of one another to form words.

All of a sudden Ruby sat bolt upright, realizing something else too. The lullaby that for so many years had sent her to her dreams had now woken her up. The words — not just empty sounds but a message.

A golden bird guards over you . . .

Without explanation she raced downstairs and flung open the door to the living room.

"Ruby!" her mother hissed. "I've just gotten him to sleep!"

Ruby tried to whisper, but her heart was pounding. "I just have to know, where did that lullaby come from? Did *you* make it up?"

Sabina looked surprised. "Oh no — it was handed down from my mother."

"And where did she get it from?" said Ruby.

"From *her* mother," replied Sabina. "It dates right back to your great-great-great-grandmother Martha Lily Fairbank. *She's* the one who made it up. I just changed the word *rubies* to Ruby!"

Ruby stood there in the doorway, stunned by this revelation. All these years the location of the Fairbank rubies was singing in their ears, just waiting for someone to really listen.

When the stars begin to fall,
You will hear the ocean call.

In other words, when the asteroid comes, the currents fall still, and it's possible to get to the cave.

When you hear that whispered sound,
You will know that you are found.

A reference to the Sea Whisperer, which according to the criminal mastermind's static code message, lived in the tidal pool below where the rubies were hidden.

A golden bird guards over you.
My little gem, my words are true.

In other words, the cave should be just below the bird shape on the rock of the smaller Sibling Island.

Ruby was breathing hard, and her mother was looking at her anxiously.

"Honey, you OK?"

Ruby nodded, turned, and closed the door. She stumbled back

upstairs. Clancy by now was on his feet and his arms were flapping uncontrollably. "What is it?" he asked. "What's going on?"

"I gotta talk to Spectrum."

Ruby radioed through to the only agent she could think might actually still be at HQ.

"Froghorn," she said, trying to catch her breath. "Listen, this is real important."

"Look, little girl, the grown-ups are busy right now. Try calling back tomorrow."

"Yeah, well, they wouldn't be busy if it wasn't for me."

"Rather full of ourselves, aren't we?"

"Look, Froghorn, I'm trying very hard here not to call you a potato head, so could you help me out with that by not behaving like a potato head? I need to get some important information to Hitch, and unfortunately, I gotta talk to you to do this."

"They're out of range," came the reply. "You should know that. All radio transmission is dead. Besides," he said unhelpfully, "they are a little bit too busy catching pirates to chat to schoolgirls. I —"

Ruby clicked off before she felt compelled to go over there and sock him on the nose.

She walked to her closet and pulled out a huge carryall bag

that was already stuffed full of something bulky. She opened it, checked inside, and zipped it back up.

"What are you doing?" asked Clancy.

"What does it look like?" said Ruby. She was pulling on her hooded sweatshirt and scanning the room for her boots. "I'm going out."

"But it's eleven thirty at night," said Clancy.

"Eleven twenty-eight, I think you'll find," said Ruby, checking that the rescue watch was secured around her wrist — it still kept coming loose.

"Darn this strap," she cursed. She grabbed the limpet lights and rummaged around for the sea-sting antidote, finally finding it in her desk drawer. She threaded it though an elastic hairband and pulled it onto her right wrist. She didn't have time to fiddle with clipping it to a zipper right now — she was in way too big a hurry.

"Now, where's that breathing buckle?" she said, looking around.

"This it?" said Clancy, picking the silver buckle — still attached to a belt — from a heap of discarded clothes.

"Yeah, that's it."

"OK," said Clancy. "Just where are you thinking of going at eleven twenty-eight at night?"

"Don't you mean where are *we* going?" said Ruby, slinging the carryall over her shoulder. It was heavy.

"*I'm* not going *any*where," said Clancy.

Ruby shrugged. "So I'll go on my own."

"Are you crazy? You can't go on your own, wherever you're going."

"So come with me," she called as she climbed out of the window.

"Oh, brother!" grumbled Clancy as he scrambled to his feet. "Sometimes I really hate you, Rube — you know that?"

CHAPTER 40
Looking for Trouble

CLANCY AND RUBY WERE WALKING down the harbor road: it was dark, and though a few of the bars were still open for business, on the whole it was pretty quiet.

"What's in the bag?" asked Clancy.

"You'll see."

"So apart from trouble, what exactly are you looking for?"

"Rubies," replied Ruby.

"What, you're gonna rob Keller's jewelry store?" said Clancy in a rather sarcastic tone.

"Ha-ha, funny," said Ruby flatly. "I might bust a gut laughing."

Clancy stopped walking. "Don't tell me you're going alone on this. Man, are you totally out of your mind? You don't even know if the rubies actually exist, and if they do, then they're most likely in the hands of a psychopath."

"So?" replied Ruby.

"So you just get a kick out of doing stupid things?" said Clancy.

"As a matter of fact, I think I would be pretty stupid not to."

"Really? How'd ya figure that?" Clancy was standing with his hands on his hips; he looked somehow comical when he was all indignant, like an angry teapot.

"Look, Clance, what you gotta see is that there's a pretty villainous guy, in fact at least two of them, who seem to think there's something to this legend. Now, what you gotta ask yourself is why?"

"'Cause they know something we don't know? Is that what you're trying to suggest?" said Clancy. "Have you not considered that these guys are as crazyfied as all those other folk who believe in the Twinford treasure?"

"I have considered that, Clancy. Yes, I have," replied Ruby calmly. "But even if these 'bad' fellows are mistaken about the gems and gold, even if there is no treasure to find, it doesn't change the fact that these bad guys will be there in the caves looking for it and, correct me if I'm wrong, but I believe *we* are looking for bad guys."

"*You* are looking for bad guys," corrected Clancy.

"OK, *I* am looking for bad guys, and if I locate the treasure caves, I'll find them."

Clancy frowned. "Have you considered just how bad these bad guys might be?"

"I have; as a matter of fact, I have a feeling I know one of them quite well."

Clancy shivered. "You're not thinking of a certain someone are you? Italian shoes, beady eyes, slow, agonizing deaths?" His voice sounded thin.

Ruby nodded.

Neither of them wanted to actually say his name, but they were both thinking of him. Count von Viscount: a man so deadly that once caught in his clutches, few ever escaped. In fact, only two: Bradley Baker and Ruby Redfort. And Ruby hoped that she'd never lay eyes on him again.

"Why are you so sure?" said Clancy.

"A couple of things," replied Ruby. "First, all that drama of the pirates and the old-fashioned-looking pirate ship — like from some old B movie. It's the Count's style: theatrical, cinematic."

"OK," said Clancy, "but that doesn't make it him."

"No," agreed Ruby, "but that last message, the static one, it was like an order the way it said, *I don't need to* count *on your loyalty, just remember you cannot tell a lie.* I think it's a message *to* the Count, not *from* him, warning him to be careful. Don't double-cross me because I can make you drink the truth serum so you cannot tell a lie."

It made perfect sense, and as a result, Clancy wasn't feeling so good. Just a few weeks ago the Count had almost succeeded in burying Ruby alive under several tons of sand. When that didn't work out for him, he'd given permission for one of his cohorts to cut her throat. And Clancy wasn't forgetting his own narrow escape from extinction by the hand (or rather diamond revolver) of Nine Lives Capaldi, the Count's most deadly assassin. Though at least now she was all out of lives.

"So will you come with me?" asked Ruby.

"Uh-uh, no way." Clancy was sure on this point. "You're not getting me in a little sailboat hunting for a crazy murderer, and that's final."

"But it isn't a sailboat," assured Ruby.

"It isn't?" said Clancy.

"No," said Ruby. "It's what they call a dinghy."

"What!" spluttered Clancy. "You have to be kidding! No way. Not now, not ever."

"Oh, come on, Clance. Live a little," said Ruby in her best Ruby Redfort persuader voice.

"Yeah, well, that's what I want to do, and that's why I absolutely am not coming. You're not using me as fish food."

They walked out to the farthest part of the harbor, past a man who was settling in for a night sleeping rough on a wooden bench. He was busily securing his bag of possessions underneath the seat and took no interest in the kids who should be all tucked up in bed by now.

The two of them walked and argued. Ruby the persuader, Clancy the resister.

After fifteen minutes and forty-seven seconds Ruby had broken him down, and Clancy found himself stepping into the little yellow dinghy that was sandwiched between fishing boats.

"Don't expect me to get out of this boat until it's time to step back onto dry land," was all that he asked.

"Sure." Ruby was checking the scuba equipment stored in the dinghy. "I reckon I can promise that 'cause I *think* my dad mended the holes," she said casually.

"What!" said Clancy, desperately attempting to scramble back out.

"I'm fooling with you, Clance. This is a Spectrum dinghy; it travels faster than you can imagine and is pretty tough. D'ya wanna turn your humor switch up a notch?"

"Ha-ha," said Clancy — no hint of a smile. He peered into the bag. "By the way, why have you brought two wet suits and two pairs of flippers?"

"Thought you might enjoy a dip, check out the scenery."

"Ha-ha," said Clancy again.

They used the paddles until they made it out of the harbor, bickering the whole way, and then Ruby pulled the engine cord and their voices were drowned out by the buzz of the motor. The little vessel headed out to sea. The man on the harbor bench looked up for a minute or two and watched until the dinghy became a speck on the horizon and finally disappeared completely from view. He yawned, sat up, and rummaged for something in the yellow bag he was using for a pillow. He took from it a leather scabbard, unclasped it, and pulled out a jagged knife.

"Now where do you think you're going, Ruby Redfort?" he muttered.

CHAPTER 41
Swimming Blind

RUBY HAD TURNED OFF THE ENGINE, and the little boat was bobbing about on the dark water, the moon partly obscured by slow-moving clouds, most of the stars faint or invisible. It was not a pretty night; there was something menacing about it, and the sea not as calm as it had been two days previously.

"Why have we stopped here?" Clancy was looking around him; the Sibling Islands were still a way off.

"We don't want anyone to hear us coming, *do* we?" Ruby was tackling her wet suit, not the easiest of things to get into while bobbing in an unstable craft. While she wrestled with the suit, she talked. "I'll swim out there. It's not so far."

She looked out at the silhouette of the smaller island. The unmistakable shape of the bird was just ahead of her. If the lullaby was right, the cave entrance was just beneath. Ruby didn't expect to see the cave mouth — according to Martha's account, it had probably been covered by a rockslide. But Martha had *also* said that the pool in the cave had turned into a whirlpool when the currents started up again, had sucked her down and spat her out in the sea outside.

And an underwater exit was also an underwater entrance. So Ruby was pretty sure there was a way in.

Clancy grimaced. Ruby knew what he was thinking, and she couldn't help thinking it too, but she had to do this so she would just make herself believe it was going to be OK. **RULE 12: ADJUST YOUR THINKING AND YOUR CHANCES IMPROVE.**

"Sea monsters aren't all bad, Clance. I mean, they're just going about their sea-monster business, same as you."

"Well, not quite," said Clancy. "'Cause I don't go about eating people who accidentally cross my path."

"It's not their fault if they mistake us for lunch."

This little pep talk wasn't helping Clancy one bit. "I'm still not going in, Rube."

"OK, but it means you're gonna have to wait here on your own—in the boat—on your own," said Ruby. "In the boat—alone."

Clancy didn't take the bait. "Fine," he said.

"OK," said Ruby. "If you're staying here, then stay here. Don't go taking off with the boat or anything, OK?"

"Of course I won't," assured Clancy. "Why would I do that?"

"I don't know. You might get chicken or something and make for the shore."

Clancy folded his arms. "I told you I will be here and I will."

Ruby zipped up her wet suit and put on her mask. "So you're sure about this?"

"You bet," said Clancy.

Sitting on the edge of the dinghy, she said, "This is your last chance . . ."

"Good," said Clancy.

Ruby let herself fall backward and disappeared under the surface of the water. Clancy stared in after her, but all he could see was dark water and all he could hear was the thwack of the waves against the side of the boat.

Ruby swam through coral reefs that towered up like castle turrets, fish darting past her, the more confident ones following at her side. As she swam, she dropped the phosphorescent limpet lights, which told her where she had come from and would lead her neatly back to the boat — they should last a few hours at least.

What was she looking for? She didn't actually have any firm idea, a sort of vague one maybe, but no coordinates, only the rock's golden bird to navigate by, and when she surfaced, she found it was too dark to make that out. She would just have to trust her instincts.

Clancy bit his nails. He wasn't feeling so good. It wasn't seasickness. Clancy didn't suffer from seasickness; he had good sea legs. What Clancy was suffering from was more akin to anxiety sickness, but right at that moment he couldn't tell the difference; all he knew was that he was feeling pretty queasy and it had a lot to do with being on the ocean. The best way to treat seasickness was to get into the water, but there was no way Clancy was going to do that.

Which, as it turned out, was just as well.

Ruby found herself in a forest of slick seaweed. She swam blindly, pushing her way through, and then quite suddenly she banged her hand on a sheer wall of rock. She had reached the smaller of the Sibling Islands, the one known to sailors as Little Sister. If Martha was right about what she had seen, then this was the island where the treasure was hidden. The cliff face rose up high out of the water all the way to the bird, and seemed to sink down many miles below the surface.

Ruby stopped and pointed her flashlight, casting light up and down, methodically looking for a fissure in the rock's surface, an entrance, but there didn't seem to be one. She realized she wasn't exactly where she hoped she'd be; the current was beginning to return and must have gently carried her a little to the east. She was going to have to work her way around. She looked back at the trail of Hansel and Gretel lights she had dropped in her wake. They twinkled in the dark, inviting her to swim back to Clancy — beckoning her home.

At first Clancy thought the boat had somehow hit a rock. The bump to the underside of the vessel nearly knocked him off his feet. He steadied himself; his legs felt very weak, and he sat down heavily in the center of the dinghy. Maybe it was nothing, just his mind playing tricks on him. Sailors said being alone at sea could make you half crazy, maybe that was what was happening to him. He began to think about Ruby — it seemed like she'd been gone an awful long time. How much air did she say she had?

Ruby had been searching for some time now, way longer than she had expected, and her oxygen was getting low. She checked her tank: she had just about enough to get all the way back to the boat, *nearly* anyway.

＊ ＊ ＊

A huge jolt catapulted Clancy from his musing, and he had to snatch quickly at the dinghy's ropes or he would have been flung into the dark water. His breathing was so loud he could hear nothing else. His head was hanging over the side of the boat and he was staring down into the depths.

And that's when he saw it.

CHAPTER 42
Whatever Happened to Plan B?

CLANCY WAS CROUCHING OVER THE ENGINE, the ignition cord in his hand. He paused, not because he didn't have every intention of pulling it, but because he didn't know which direction to go in.

Ruby had told him to stay put. But that was not really an option anymore. The only choice he had was the direction he took. Ruby had been pretty clear that the boat should not be taken too much nearer to the caves because you never know who might hear the motor or spot the dinghy. Clancy would have considered rowing, but that option (in the form of the oars) had been devoured by the thing in the water.

He would head for shore, he would get help, he could alert people. Yeah, that's what he would do. It was the heroic solution, surely?

He pulled the cord five times before the engine began to whir and then, as he was about to speed off in the direction of dry land, a horrible thought occurred to him. What if Ruby was on her way back to him? What if she was left in the middle of the deep dark sea with no boat, no air, and nothing but the thing for company?

Oh, dear. Life can force some terrible decisions. It was a shame Clancy and Ruby had not followed one of her most important rules: **RULE 36: ALWAYS COME UP WITH PLAN B BEFORE YOU HAVE EMBARKED ON PLAN A.**

Ruby was also wishing she had come up with a plan B. Her air was just about out and she was going to have to either give up on finding the underwater entrance or risk drowning. The Sibling Islands were not the sort of islands one could clamber onto — they were, for the most part, sheer rock cliffs with very little in the way of foot- and handholds, so clambering out of the water was a near impossibility. But she couldn't give up looking; there had to be an entrance somewhere. She would chance it; she felt lucky.

Darn it, Ruby!

Clancy knew what he had to do, and he was not happy about it.

He switched off the engine and slowly, very reluctantly, reached for the scuba gear. He listened out. The thing had gone quiet — maybe the noise of the engine had upset it. Maybe he could stay put. Sure, it was getting a bit wet in the boat, but he could bail out the water and just wait it out for Ruby.

But maybe not.

Thud.

The boat sprang another small leak. Spectrum dinghy it might be, but it could not withstand the battering of a two-ton sea beast. There was another terrible jolt, and Clancy hung on for dear life. The thing had not gone; in fact, now there seemed to be two things, two very different things, fighting with each other. The second a whole lot more terrifying than the first, a giant beast with massive tentacles. But if he was to make it out alive, then this was the very distraction he needed. If he was quick, he could escape the boat while the things tried to kill each other instead of him.

As he grappled with the wet suit, he muttered to himself, thinking about all the times he had been told to forget his ocean fears. How people were always telling him how unlikely it was that he would be attacked by a sea creature.

The probability is really small. You have much more chance of being run down by a truck or drowning in your own tub.

He mimicked their patronizing voices. Boy, would he tell them a thing or two when he made it home . . . if he made it home.

The way Clancy saw it, he didn't *have* to go in the ocean; his family had a pool. The other point was he could be careful when he crossed the road, he could be careful when he was in the tub, but it didn't matter how careful he was in the ocean off Twinford, he might still get devoured. Who knew what was swimming about in the waters off Twinford Bay Beach?

Well, he did. He'd just seen it. And it had terrified him.

All this he muttered to himself as he pulled on the wet suit. He checked the oxygen tank just as he had seen Ruby do, and that's when he discovered that it was all out of air. He stood up in the boat and yelled at the sky and then yelled at the sea, and when he was done yelling, he picked up Ruby's belt and in a fury started thwacking it against the redundant oxygen tank. *I'm going to die*, he cursed to himself.

As luck would have it, Ruby *was* lucky. She ducked down under the waves one final time to search the underwater cliff face for a tunnel in the rock that might lead her inside the island.

And there it suddenly was, a passageway.

Kekoa was a good teacher, and Ruby had listened hard. It couldn't be the main entrance to the island, not the one the pirates had used all those years ago — this entrance would be a squeeze for a grown man, and as for supplies and the like, not a chance. The snag was there was no way the oxygen tank was going to fit through this tiny opening, but of course she did have the breathing buckle. She reached for it, and that's when Ruby discovered that no, she did not have the breathing buckle because she had left it attached to her jeans belt, and that was lying on the floor of the boat.

Nice going, Agent Redfort.

She could hold her breath for one minute and one second, but was that long enough to make it through a water-filled tunnel? Did she really want to find out? Not like this she didn't, but she would push her luck; it seemed the only thing to do—she was tired after so much swimming, and she honestly wasn't sure if she would be able to make it back to the dinghy.

Ruby breathed her very last bubble of air from her tank before letting it sink to the bottom of the ocean. She pushed her way in; it was pretty dark and very small. As she moved forward, the thought occurred to her that this underwater tunnel might not actually lead anywhere. But Ruby could feel a stream of cold water rushing past her from deeper inside the rock. Fresh water, she guessed, from some source within the island. It gave her hope that her tunnel was leading somewhere: whether it was leading somewhere big enough to crawl through was another matter.

Not ideal, not for anyone, but particularly not for someone who suffered from claustrophobia, the kind where just the thought of being trapped made you want to tear your way out of your own skin. She was beginning to feel waves of panic sweeping through her. If there was one thing Ruby Redfort loathed, it was small dark spaces, spaces with limited oxygen, and in this case, spaces with no oxygen and possibly no way out. **RULE 21: DON'T THINK BACK; DON'T THINK AHEAD; JUST THINK NOW.**

Ruby focused on slowing her heartbeat and propelling herself forward by pushing against the narrow rock walls. All the way, she heard Mrs. Digby speaking to her. *"Stop fussing, child. We don't have all day."*

Finally, after what seemed like twenty minutes but was in fact only forty-five seconds, she surfaced. Gulping in dank air, she took stock of her surroundings.

She was in a cathedral-like cave, filled with sound, the acoustics such that the lapping of water, the drips, the splashes created a piece of strange and melancholy music. There was no pool in the cave, save for a small puddle on the rock floor, so this obviously wasn't the chamber where Martha had seen the pirates hide the rubies, nor could it be the cave where the Sea Whisperer lurked and where the whirlpool had appeared. OK, so she wasn't quite where she wanted to be, but she was alive and she was in. Ruby wasn't about to give herself a hard time for winding up slightly off course — the point was, she was breathing.

A million glowworms illuminated the stalactites. It was beautiful, eerie, and no doubt dangerous. Ruby quickly pulled off her fins and mask and stuffed them into her bag; she would take these with her. Her dive booties sort of protected her feet from the broken shells that covered the surface of the grotto floor. She climbed nimbly through the cave, picking her way through the elaborate rock formations. She moved quickly until she was faced with a choice: left or right?

She chose right. From here she was careful to mark the rock surface as she went with an X, nothing too visible, just enough to notice if you were looking for it.

Very soon the slope became rough rocky steps, in some places narrow and very slippery. But as she made her way farther up, the air got drier and the path became easier to climb. The passage felt more like a corridor, caves to either side like chambers. Ruby's adrenaline levels were just beginning to drop and her heart to calm when she heard a familiar sound, the sound of footsteps coming toward her.

**Hitch had been
on surveillance for
more than an
hour. . . .**

His binoculars were trained on Horseshoe Bay, but though he could see the pirate ship waiting in the deserted cove, there was no sign of a rendezvous. It looked like whoever was joining them tonight was in some sort of fix. Something must have happened; something had gone wrong with the plan.

CHAPTER 43
A Stitch in Time

THERE WAS SOMETHING ABOUT THE CLICK-CLACKING of the shoes on stone that reminded Ruby of something she had struggled hard to forget. Not that she ever would.

It was the very particular sound of handmade, leather-soled Italian shoes.

The first time she had heard them, the wearer had been making his way down the stone corridor of the Twinford City Museum. Back then she'd had ample time to ponder who the shoes might belong to — this time she knew all too well.

Sometimes there is something about *getting it right* that gives you no comfort; this tends to happen when the thing you are right about is so bad that you wish it were dead and buried five hundred feet beneath the ground.

This was how Ruby felt as the familiar sound approached. She held her breath, only releasing it when the click-clacking had passed her hiding place and traveled some way down the corridor.

She waited until she could be sure the Count had turned the corner, was out of earshot, couldn't possibly hear the breathing of a girl crouching behind a rock.

But then the footsteps came to an abrupt stop.

There was a pause.

A few seconds passed and then slowly and steadily the sound changed direction, the click-clack footsteps got louder, nearer, and then stopped. Ruby held her breath.

Did he see her? She didn't dare look up.

"Oh, my. Is that little Ruby Redfort?"

Ruby looked up at him — at his elegant nose and chiseled features, his silver-gray hair perfectly combed, his trim silhouette clothed in a fine black gabardine suit. She looked at his black polished shoes, his sharp white teeth, and then into his cold dark eyes. He seemed at first surprised and then almost delighted by her sudden appearance. Ruby, however, felt nothing but doomed. The last thing she felt she needed was a face-to-face meeting with the man they called the Count.

"You look well." Ruby tried to sound casual, as if this evil genius was the very person she had been hoping to run into. "The sea air suits you. Have you been taking time off?"

"Oh, you know how it is," replied the Count. "I'm all work and no play."

"I'm sorry to hear that," said Ruby.

The Count smiled. "No, no, don't be," he said. "I get so much pleasure from my business pursuits I find I really don't crave time away from the metaphorical desk. I am fortunate to enjoy my work; not everyone does, you know."

"Yes, lucky old you. Did you stumble into your line of business, or did you always plan on being a psychopath?"

"The work sort of found me," said the Count, shrugging.

"Oh, that's nice," said Ruby.

"There are worse things you can do." The Count smiled.

"Worse than being a cold-blooded killer?" pondered Ruby. "Maybe, but I think the hours of a maniac are too long for my liking — must eat into your social life."

"What social life?" Again the Count smiled. "So how do you plan to fill *your* time?" he asked.

"I don't know. There are so many options — gas-station attendant, tap-dance instructor, rocket scientist, dog walker — I reckon I'll just wait until I grow up, see which career finds me," said Ruby.

The Count fixed her with his cold shark's eyes, and then he gently sighed, flashing his sharp white teeth. "Ah yes, the eternal question of what to do *if* one should grow up."

Ruby gulped. She didn't like the use of this tiny word *if*;

it put a very different skew on things. Her mind was beginning to race — what was she doing talking when she needed to run? He was hypnotizing her; her feet were rooted to the ground.

The Count waved his arms in theatrical apology. "You find me at an inconvenient time; all my help left this afternoon."

"You mean the pirates?" said Ruby. "The ones you betrayed?"

"I'm not sure that is the word I would use, but yes."

"What happened to honor among thieves?" asked Ruby.

"Honor," spat the Count. "They didn't earn honor; such stupidity. They had their uses, but I find working with idiots so tedious." He calmed down a little and said, "I knew you must have cracked my rather skillful code when I saw you diving the wreck of the *Seahorse*, so I threw Spectrum a bone and directed them to that merry band of fools. They deserve each other."

"But in doing so you had to set up one of your own men, sacrifice your own code breaker," said Ruby. She was referring to the guy her mother had described, the sophisticated one who looked more like a college professor than a pirate.

"Sacrifices, sacrifices. It's all part of the job," sighed the Count.

LB might be a tough boss to please, but right now Ruby was glad she wasn't on Count von Viscount's team.

"Now, look at me! Here I am not even thinking to invite

you in. Oh, but then of course you've already had a good snoop, haven't you?" His smile faded.

"I didn't realize this was a *private* cave," said Ruby.

"Finders keepers," said the Count.

"Well, I apologize," she said. *Run,* she thought. *Run.*

"No harm done," he said. "Not yet anyway."

Jeepers! Here we go, thought Ruby. "Well, sounds like we're both busy people, so I better shake a leg." *Yes, run, Ruby, run!* she told herself. *Just run!*

But it was too late.

As she turned to flee, a powerful hand grabbed her from behind and pulled her right arm into a painful twist, enough to make her eyes water and her voice cry out.

"I'll see you in two ticks, when Mr. Darling has you all settled in nice and secure."

That didn't sound good.

"They'll miss me, you know. They're expecting me back. They'll send a search party — a big one."

The Count shook his head and tutted. "Liar, liar, pants on fire."

"That's how little *you* know," protested Ruby. "I radioed in this second, on my watch. There'll be hundreds of them looking, hundreds."

"Oh, what . . . this watch?" said the Count, pulling it from his pocket and dangling it in front of her face.

Ruby's heart sank. The broken clasp. Not only had she let go of the one thing that might have saved her life, but she had also neatly tipped off the Count as to her whereabouts. That's why he had retraced his steps. That's why he had found her. **RULE 7: NEVER FORGET THE LITTLE THINGS — IT'S THE LITTLE THINGS THAT WILL LEAD PEOPLE TO NOTICE THE BIG THINGS,** or as Mrs. Digby would no doubt say, "A *stitch in time saves you a whole lot of bother later on.*"

Ruby exhaled heavily, resigned to her fate, which she supposed was not a happy one. Mr. Darling did not look like a nice man.

And as it turned out, she was right about that.

**In a hospital room at
Twinford City General . . .**

Agent Kekoa was sitting in bed reading a little orange paperback book. It was a slim volume with an illustration of a black tentacle wrapping around the cover. She had been using her convalescing time to maximum effect, reading anything and everything that might relate to the *Seahorse*, Martha Fairbank, the legend of the rubies, and the myth of the Sea Whisperer. This trail had led her in the same direction as Ruby had taken — to Francesco Fornetti and his little orange book.

The book, ordered by express mail, had arrived that afternoon while Kekoa was sleeping. Now it was late evening and she was awake, wide awake. Assuming this Fornetti guy wasn't a total nut job, she now knew what was out there swimming around in the deep dark ocean. She now knew that the Sea Whisperer was no fantasy; it was horribly real. She needed to warn Spectrum; she needed to warn them to stay out of the water.

She placed the volume on her nightstand and pressed a button on her watch: the signal to Hitch went unanswered. Likewise Blacker. She tried Ruby — same thing.

Finally, she called another number: Froghorn answered this time, but the conversation did not go well and ended abruptly. With great effort, Kekoa hauled herself out of bed, hobbled to the door, and checked the corridor.

Empty: it was way past midnight.

She limped back to the bed, opened the locker, and pulled out her clothes. It took her more than ten minutes to pull on her jeans over her cast. Once she was dressed, she grabbed the crutches that rested next to the visitor's chair, opened the door, and began making her way slowly down the hospital corridor.

No one noticed her leave.

CHAPTER 44
Playing for Time

RUBY REDFORT WAS MARCHED DOWN SOME STONE STEPS carved right out of the tough Sibling rock. The steps became slippery as they traveled farther into the cave, and there was a danger that she might lose her footing and fall, but maybe that was a better end than the one Count von Viscount had prepared for her.

Ruby thought she could hear the ocean, the waves crashing against the cliff, but that couldn't be so because the sea had still been relatively calm. She pictured the little dinghy, Clancy waiting patiently for her return, so near and yet so far.

Then they arrived at the place Mr. Darling was taking her to.

It was pretty much as she feared: a natural pool, deep and dark and filled with seawater. A plank of wood was sticking out across the water. She presumed this must be for balancing on — and no doubt falling off. There would be some kind of tunnel under the water, which would allow hungry carnivores to swim into the pool. Ruby had seen it a thousand times before, in thrillers and less than thrilling shows — everybody had.

Mr. Darling took a knife from his pocket and walked slowly toward her. He was a huge man, silent and mean. He grabbed her by the throat; she struggled.

"Hold still," he said. "Or lose a limb." And he ran the knife up the left sleeve of her wet suit, hacking it off to expose most of her arm. He repeated the action to the right side and then sliced the suit's legs off at the knees. He drew not one drop of blood; he was very precise, very skilled with a knife.

Before long the Count reappeared. He was carrying a black leather case and had his coat over his arm. He looked like he might be preparing to leave.

Ruby tried very hard not to show her fear. "Are people still doing this?" she said. "It's a bit of a cliché, isn't it? Being eaten alive by sharks?"

"Sharks?" spluttered the Count. "My dear Ms. Redfort, how uncreative you must believe me." He laughed. "No, no, not sharks." This notion seemed to have really tickled him. "At least not at first."

"What do you mean, not at first?" said Ruby.

"All in good time, Ms. Redfort. All in good time," assured the Count.

Ruby needed to think on her toes and fast, or she would have no toes left to worry about. If she could just think of something, some means of escape, stall for time.

"So how long have you been residing here?" she said, the merest tremble in her voice. "Looks like you're really settled, got everything just the way you like it — what with the torture pool and all."

"Oh, you're mistaken! This isn't a torture pool. I've been doing some research for a client of mine, and discovered this wonderful species, you see. Could revolutionize my industry," he said.

"I'm super pleased to hear that," said Ruby.

Ruby was putting on the best show of her life: outwardly calm, inwardly her brain bounced ideas like a pinball machine.

RULE 44: WHEN IN A TIGHT SPOT, BUY YOURSELF SOME TIME: ONE MINUTE COULD CHANGE YOUR FATE.

"You could say I've been searching for this place for most of my life," said the Count. "A distant relative of mine told me about this island when I was just a slip of a boy. He mentioned how pirates occasionally used the Sibling caves to store . . . well, things that were not, strictly speaking, technically their own. It was a particularly good place to wait things out while the storm blew over, if you understand my meaning."

"Yeah, I don't suppose you're referring to the weather here."

"No. Apparently, the townsfolk were constantly baying for blood; not very forgiving people these Twinfordites, revenge constantly on their minds."

"Yes, that does seem petty," said Ruby. "I mean, what's the big deal about a few thousand gold coins and the odd sack of gems? You'd think they could get over themselves."

"*Wouldn't* you?" agreed the Count.

"I expect that they objected to all the cutthroats and the general murder bit more than anything," continued Ruby. "You bump off someone's husband and that's it, they'll never let it go."

"Yes, people can be so sentimental." The Count nodded. "Sentiment won't get one anywhere, not in this world of ours. I mean, take your situation: all those Happy Holiday cards you've sent over the years to your 'pals' and where are these so-called loyal friends?" He looked around him theatrically. "Nowhere." He made a sad face. "So you will have to die all by yourself."

"Would you mind," said Ruby earnestly, "if we did that thing where you explain how you came to find this place and exactly what you're looking for? It would give me something to think about while I endure whatever it is I'm about to endure."

"Oh, you mean that marvelous tradition of the villain explaining himself to the victim because he can't resist bragging about his cunning and guile?"

"Yes, that," said Ruby.

"Why of course, Ms. Redfort. It would be my pleasure."

He puffed himself up and began his monologue. Ruby, it had to be said, was only half listening, her brain being occupied with the more immediate concern of dodging death. So far nothing was coming to mind.

"Like you," the Count was saying, "I know the importance of stories, particularly those other people ignore. It was a child who led me to these caves; others discounted his story, but not me. Always pay attention to even the youngest voice; it can be a terrible error not to."

Ruby couldn't help thinking of Froghorn: a case in point.

"I, of course, learned to value the younger mind when I first encountered Spectrum's very first child agent, Bradley Baker. He nearly brought about my demise, but in the end I won out. I have to admit he was the brightest child who ever lived."

"So I've heard," said Ruby, yawning.

"Oh, I'm sure you're very clever too." The Count smiled.

Ruby smiled back; she wasn't feeling so clever right now, but she was thinking hard. *So at least you still have the antidote; if there are stinging things, you'll survive. If there are chomping things, you're in big trouble.*

The Count was getting into his stride. "Anyway, to cut an

ancient story short, one pirate survived that night along with little Miss Fairbank. But unfortunately for him, he was bitten by the Sea Whisperer, and though he washed up on the sand still breathing, he died soon after." The Count raised his arm dramatically. "But not before he had confessed everything to a small boy who was collecting crabs on the shore. The fellow couldn't help it, you see; the truth serum made him. He told the boy of the monster, the rubies, and the cave."

"And who was the boy?" asked Ruby, now gripped by this tale, quite forgetting to concentrate on her escape.

"My great-great-grandfather," he replied, fixing her with his cold, cold eyes. "So you see, you're not the only one with family ties to this place. And of course I knew that asteroid **YKK 672** would be passing close by again, providing me with still waters in which to work."

"Of course," said Ruby.

"Now hand me the trinket," said the Count.

"What?" bluffed Ruby.

"That tiny one attached to the band around your wrist. It must be for something — surely it's not simply decoration." He cocked his head to one side and smiled.

Ruby looked up at him, puzzled.

"Always check for life-saving gadgets," said the Count. "This looks like something that isn't just part of your costume; this looks like it might have some higher function."

Very slowly she pulled the band from her wrist and handed it to him. She didn't have a whole lot of choice.

The Count examined it carefully and smiled. "What irony," he said, and let it fall to the floor. With some pleasure he stamped his beautiful Italian shoe down on top of it, and Ruby heard the glass vial inside the canister smash into a thousand pieces.

Then he turned to the unhappy-looking Mr. Darling, who seemed like he might be in a hurry to get started; his fingers were twitching.

"So let's get on with it," said the Count with a flourish. "Time to release the *little* darlings."

If not sharks, then what? thought Ruby. *What could be worse than sharks?*

Mr. Darling was untying her hands. *Why? Why would he do that?*

"So take a long walk off a short plank!" said Mr. Darling, shoving her in the direction of the high board that extended across the pool. Ruby moved very reluctantly, very slowly, pausing to look down, but she could see nothing but water.

"All the way!" bellowed Mr. Darling.

As she edged forward, the plank got less stable and began

to bend alarmingly. Ruby was small and she weighed very little, but even her slight body was too much.

"I said all the way!"

Ruby was perched at the very end now, her toes gripping on for dear life. She felt like a cartoon character but without the laugh track. Mr. Darling started to jump up and down, gently at first and then with more vigor, and the board began to bounce. It would have looked very amusing to the ignorant bystander, this pudgy, sweating man jumping for all he was worth, this miniature girl balancing like a gymnast.

But not so amusing if you knew that the man had murder on his mind.

Ruby began to wobble. She tried to move with it the way one might if jumping up and down on a diving board. She kept her balance for almost two whole minutes and then suddenly she felt herself slip and a split second later the cold salt water whooshed past her ears.

Her head emerged and she gasped for air, treading water and frantically looking about her, but there was nothing to see, nothing at all.

And then she felt the most tiny of tiny stings.

**Hitch looked up and was
surprised to see Agent Kekoa
struggling aboard the
Spectrum vessel. . . .**

He moved quickly and silently toward her. It had to be more than important, her reason for being there. She was sweating and looked to be in some pain.

"What is it?" he asked.

"Ruby," she whispered. "Where is she?"

"At home," said Hitch.

"I don't think so," replied Kekoa. "I tried to make contact, but her signal is down. She must be somewhere in Sibling waters, out of radio range."

"But why?" asked Hitch. "The action's happening here." He indicated the pirate ship. "Why would she head off somewhere else?"

"There's something bigger going down," said Kekoa. "Much bigger, and Ruby must have worked out what."

"You sure about this?" asked Hitch.

"I called into Spectrum, got Froghorn; apparently, she was trying to make contact with you and, evidently, Froghorn didn't take her seriously."

"That dumb schmuck. Why didn't he send someone to tell me?" Hitch was already putting a plan together; he would have to put someone else in command here and then he had better move like the wind if he stood any chance of getting to Ruby before someone else did.

"By the way," said Kekoa, "the currents are returning. We have around an hour."

"An hour before what?" said Hitch.

"An hour before it's too late."

CHAPTER 45
You Can Count on Me

IT DIDN'T HURT EXACTLY, but it made her finger feel odd, sort of numb.

How strange.

After the men left, the cave was plunged into darkness, and Ruby found herself suspended in blackness, utter and total blackness . . . except . . . *What was that? What were they?* Floating in front of her were beautiful iridescent umbrellas. They seemed to be hovering in space, but of course they were not; they were in the water with her, all around her, under her, beside her, drifting past her. Dragging their lazy tentacles as they gently twirled by.

Now and again she felt a small shock like a tiny jolt of electricity. She went to close her fingers but couldn't. She tried to wiggle her fingers, but they didn't move. Her brain was no longer in control of her hand. She was slowly being paralyzed.

These were jellyfish, glow-in-the-dark, beautiful parasol

jellyfish. Their sting was by no means fatal, not even life-threatening; you could be stung a hundred times, two hundred times at least, and recover. The sting caused temporary paralysis, not a problem if you lost the use of a leg or an arm for a while, but what if you lost the use of *both* legs, *both* arms? What then?

Ruby realized she would know the answer before long. And she understood why the Count had sniggered at the irony of it as he destroyed her anti-sting serum.

Only her right leg seemed to be functioning in any useful way, but she was tiring, her body was failing her, and drowning would soon be her fate. The one thing that could have saved her was trickling through the cracks of the rock floor.

A voice came out of the darkness.

"Alas, I am afraid myself and Mr. Darling must leave you; so much to do before we retrieve the rubies and return home. I'm sure you understand, do forgive me. Although . . ." He paused. "You won't be completely alone. In just a few minutes our hungry friends will be joining you; it's feeding time, you see, and they follow a very strict routine. Farewell, Ms. Redfort."

"I knew it!" shouted Ruby valiantly. "Sharks, so corny — every evil genius uses sharks."

"Corny they might be, Ms. Redfort," the Count called back. "But they are *very* effective."

She heard the footsteps retreat, the elegant ones and the heavy ones, as the two men exited the drowning cave. She thought of her mother and subconsciously began to hum the lullaby, Martha Fairbank's song. It echoed eerily around the chamber, floating through the island passages. A sad tune and a soon to be forgotten one, never more to be passed down from mother to child.

Like Ruby herself, it would soon be lost.

She took her last breath as her legs and arms finally became inert. Her face dipped beneath the surface, and she was aware that there was just one minute, one second before she either began to drown or was eaten alive. The following spiraling thoughts twirled through her mind.

Why had she told Clancy not to go back to shore? At least she would have some chance of being rescued. Maybe he would have had the sense to call the coast guard, the sheriff, Mrs. Digby, anyone. But then no, Clancy would never have made it, he was certain to get lost; it was just as well not to have even the hope of a chance, she couldn't count on him. Sure, he was a good friend, but he was useless in an emergency. *I mean, take this situation for example. What good would he be even if he was here?* He would never come anywhere near the water; she would be eaten alive before he would even think of coming to her aid. Yes, all in all it was just as well he wasn't here. At least she could wriggle off this mortal coil without him yacking at her all the time.

Ruby was so busy trying to distract herself from the inevitable that she hadn't noticed that something strange was happening. She was rising above the glowing things — she was floating in space. No, wait a minute, the glowing things were sinking. The part of her right foot that could still feel was now touching the bottom of the pool, the water no longer above her nose.

The water level was lowering.

She looked up and saw a shimmery figure standing by the pool. Someone small. It wasn't Mr. Darling. No — it looked like, sort of like a boy.

Clancy?

It couldn't be . . .

But it was.

Ruby tried to smile, but her face was sort of numb. "I thought you were meant to be scared of sharks," she mumbled.

"And I thought you were meant to be some kinda secret agent," he replied.

CHAPTER 46
M Is for Martha

CLANCY HELD OUT HIS HAND, AND GRABBED RUBY'S. He pulled her up and half out of the pool just as one gray swimming beast pushed its way through the opening. It came directly at her, aiming for her legs, which still trailed in what remained of the water.

"No you don't, buster!" Clancy hissed as he heaved with all his might, pulling the deadweight that was Ruby free of the water and far from the pool's edge.

The shark snapped its jaws and swam away.

"You look a bit pale, Ruby. You OK?"

"I guess I've been better. How did you find me?"

"I heard you singing. Can you run?"

"I'm not sure I can *stagger!*" croaked Ruby.

"Can you crawl at least?"

"Doesn't crawling involve the use of at least two limbs?" Ruby was spread flat on the floor.

"Could you crawl if I told you that the Count might be making his way back down here and could find us at any minute?"

Ruby's eyes widened. "I can run," she said.

But this was certainly an exaggeration. She couldn't actually stand without falling over, and Clancy found himself half carrying, half dragging her and her bag along the cave passages. He wanted to put as much space between them and the drowning pool as he could manage, which was not easy. For though Ruby was not what anyone could call heavy, and though Clancy was remarkably strong considering his build, it was awkward to carry someone who had no ability to hold on.

Several times he nearly dropped her, and she was accumulating bruises that fortunately for now she could not feel.

Finally, they stumbled into a huge cave that had passages peeling off in several directions. Clancy picked a route and staggered, with Ruby on his back, up some roughly cut steps that led to a cramped cave . . . and a dead end.

For now it felt safe though. At least no one would be passing this way. Clancy set Ruby on the ground like a sack of vegetables and then slumped down next to her.

"Boy! Am I glad to see you," said Clancy. "I wouldn't want to be in this place alone."

"Oh, it's not so bad if you don't mind jellyfish and murderers for company," replied Ruby, her speech slurred, her face still half paralyzed. "What happened?" she wheezed. "Suddenly fancy a little dip?"

"Ah, just missing your good conversation," said Clancy.

"That all?" said Ruby. "Because I'm not feeling particularly blabby right now."

"Well also, something there in the ocean wanted me out of the boat, and I didn't like the way things were headed. I thought it might be safer in here with the madman and his large assistant-in-madness."

"Well, I'm glad you managed to work out the scuba gear."

"I didn't," said Clancy. "The tank was empty."

"You just didn't know how to work it," said Ruby.

"I turned it to the right like you did," Clancy snapped.

"But did you push the valve down first?" she asked.

"No," said Clancy.

"Well, there you go," said Ruby. "The tank was full."

"Oh," said Clancy.

"So how did you get here?" Ruby slurred.

"With this." Clancy held up the breathing buckle. "I found it in the boat where you left it. Some agent you are."

"Well, you should be grateful; it saved your life," said Ruby.

"Don't you mean yours?" said Clancy.

"OK, so I'm grateful. But now what?"

"Well, I was kinda counting on you for the escape plan. I believe you are the secret agent here," said Clancy.

The movement in Ruby's neck was coming back, and her left arm was tingling. She wiggled her fingers: her hand was working. Her legs, though, were still useless. She looked around her.

"Clance, do you have a flashlight on you? It should be attached to your dive belt."

"This?" he said.

"Yeah," said Ruby. "Shine it around a bit."

As he moved the beam across the surface of the rock, Ruby began to make out markings scratched in the cave wall.

What are they?

"*M*," said Ruby.

"What?" said Clancy. "What do you mean, *M*?"

"Martha," whispered Ruby. "She was here. She told the physician how she scratched her initial into the rock when she was exploring the caves while the pirates slept."

"Why?" said Clancy.

"So she wouldn't get lost, duh brain." They stared at the carving; it was amazing to see that two-hundred-year-old letter clearly etched into the wall.

"Are you feeling brave?" said Ruby.

"Depends. Are you asking me to go back in the water?" replied Clancy.

"No," said Ruby. "At least not right now."

"Then I'm feeling brave," said Clancy. "Not happy, exactly, but definitely brave."

"Good," she said. "Because we need to follow the trail of Martha's initials until we reach the cave where the sea monster lurks."

"Right," muttered Clancy. "Why is it I feel like I'm in ancient Greece? Would you quit saying 'sea monster' and 'lurks'? It's putting me on edge."

"OK, the cave where the 'octopus' 'hangs out' is the place where the 'goodies' got stashed," hissed Ruby. "I just wanted to warn you that this octopus is more of a 'monster' than the usual cephalopod."

"I know that," said Clancy. "I think I saw it from the boat. And I have to say it makes me feel a tad cowardly."

"So let's go," said Ruby. "Before you start blubbering."

"I could leave you here, you know," said Clancy. "You should be careful—you're the one with Jell-O legs."

"Actually, I believe my legs are coming back to me. I might even be able to run if the situation demands."

"Great!" said Clancy. "That's OK then, we're bound to make it outta here in one piece!"

"Quit with the sarcasm, Clance."

They made their way back down the steps and followed the etched initials until they reached a place where the letters went off in either direction.

"So which route should we take?" Ruby pondered.

She turned right and they walked on, stopping every few yards so she could examine the letters. As she followed them, they seemed to get less careful, more hurried. Ruby guessed that these were made later as Martha traveled farther from the relative safety of the apple barrel, a sign that perhaps she felt she needed to be quick now, get back while there was still time.

"I think it's the other way," Ruby said, abruptly turning around.

It turned out that her instinct was exactly right, because barely twenty minutes later Clancy and Ruby found themselves in a huge cave illuminated by the pinkish glow of the rising sun. It shone through the cave opening and cast a silver light on the dark water that lapped in a deep-looking tidal pool.

"This is the cave," said Ruby to herself. A perfect hideout, until the rockslide had closed it up. Though it wasn't closed any more: the Count's pirate band must have worked hard to clear the rocks, for now it was exactly as Martha had described it, a sheltered cove. You could sail right in and be hidden from view.

"Smells bad," said Clancy, holding his nose. He looked around him. Stacked at one end was a whole load of supplies and equipment. The bad guys had been busy. "So how does your mom's lullaby go again?"

Ruby sang:

"Oh, my rubies, your mother's jewel,
You lie there still as a tidal pool."

Clancy peered into the pool. "Well, I don't think they're in here, and if they are, then I don't think we're gonna find them."

"They aren't in it, they're above it," said Ruby. "Martha said that the pirates placed the casket on the very highest ledge, the most difficult to reach."

"Not very practical," said Clancy.

"On the contrary, my friend, a very practical solution if one of your 'colleagues' gets greedy in the night and tries to double-cross the rest of your pirate band."

As the sun continued to rise, some adventurous rays crept farther into the cave, and the interior began to glow gold.

"It has to be that ledge there," said Ruby, pointing at a perilous crag of rock that jutted high from the cave's wall. "It's the highest and most difficult to reach."

"But, Rube, don't you think the Count will have already taken it by now?" suggested Clancy. "I mean, why would he leave it?"

"Because it's safe," explained Ruby. "It's been there for nearly two hundred years and no one's found it. My guess is that the Count decided to leave it there until he'd dispensed with the pirates; he didn't want them getting their thieving hands on the real treasure." She was pretty confident about this and was already beginning to scale the cave wall. It wasn't an easy climb, and Clancy stood underneath her, flapping his arms and telling her she was most likely going to fall.

She scrambled onto the ledge, wriggling forward on her stomach. She was sweating, and it wasn't just to do with the effort of it. Time was a factor, and time was getting scarce.

As she sat there catching her breath, Ruby scanned the rock wall and there, almost invisible, lodged in a small crevice, was a decorative casket of oak, reinforced with ornate iron bands.

Very carefully, she lifted it from its hiding place, undid the catch, and slowly, slowly, creaked the lid open.

So that's what all the fuss is about. She held her breath for seven or eight seconds before lifting Eliza Fairbank's rubies from the treasure chest.

My, were they beautiful. Ruby held them in front of her, and they sparkled even in the semi-darkness.

"So did you find anything?" hissed Clancy.

"Yeah, I found something all right," said Ruby.

"Well, could you get yourself back down here before someone finds *us*!"

"OK, OK," muttered Ruby. She threaded the ruby necklace through the back of her dive belt and stuffed the casket into her bag. It was awkward and difficult to manage the climb with the bulky bag; she glanced down at the drop below.

"Do you think you can catch this?" she hissed.

"No problem," said Clancy. He caught the bag without trouble, and Ruby began to edge her way over the perilous ledge, feeling around for a foothold.

"Get on with it," urged Clancy. "You need to be quick."

But as bad luck would have it, it was already too late.

"I hear something," she whispered.

Clancy looked up at her queryingly.

It was whistling.

Clancy's eyes widened.

Ruby's heart skipped a beat.

The tune was familiar. It had been sung by her mother and her mother's mother, and her mother before that, notes that echoed right back to Martha Lily Fairbank herself: the lullaby of the rubies.

CHAPTER 47
Where's an Apple Barrel When You Need One?

THERE WAS NO TIME TO HIDE, no apple barrel here, just time to imagine the end.

Clancy squeezed himself behind a rock. If he stood on one leg, he was almost out of view. He closed his eyes in a hopeless attempt to disappear. Ruby balanced there, both hands clinging to that ancient ledge, her feet not quite securely positioned on the slippery wall. Silently she begged the sun to stop rising, for the cave to remain in semi-darkness.

The footsteps echoed around the walls and there he was, this shadow of a man. This Count, this conjurer of fear who could make even a battle-hardened warrior tremble. He looked around and saw nothing . . . but he felt something; something was not right. Breathing. He was sure something was breathing, maybe two things. And then a drip. It came from above. The smallest of droplets from Ruby's still wet hair, just enough to make him look up.

He seemed almost pleased. "Ms. Redfort, not *dead*? Once again you surprise me. You really are quite the Houdini. Don't tell me you escaped all on your own?"

Ruby said nothing, but her eyes told the truth; the slightest glance in the direction of one slender rock was enough to betray her friend.

The Count set down his attaché case, and then very slowly walked toward the rock. He stepped to one side, he stooped, and there he saw the wobbling left foot of Clancy Crew.

"And your little helper . . . why, it's Master Crew! We met at the museum function — isn't that so?" He said this with a wave of his hand as if remembering some pleasant and perfectly happy occasion. As if this was not the *same* occasion when he had attempted to steal a priceless jade Buddha and in the process almost succeeded in murdering Clancy's dearest friend.

The Count pulled a silver flashlight from his pocket and shone it up so that he might see Ruby better. The light bounced off the rock, and behind Ruby there was a sparkling reflection, like a mirrorball flickering across the ceiling of the cave. Ruby saw his puzzled expression and then understanding.

"The rubies," he said. "How fitting that you, Ruby Redfort, heir to the Fairbank fortune, should retrieve them." He beckoned her down. "I was planning to use a ladder, but you have saved me the trouble." When she reached the cave's floor, he held out his hand. Ruby, without drama, without words, took the ruby necklace from her dive belt and handed it to the Count.

He examined the rubies carefully, reverently. "Flawless," he uttered, turning them over and over in his elegant hands. "Exquisite beyond words." His long, perfectly manicured fingers glided across each stone. Clancy and Ruby stared on; the Count was no longer aware of their presence, so wrapped up was he in the rubies' beauty.

The spell was broken by Clancy's sneeze.

"Damp, isn't it?" commented the Count. "I detest the damp; it does so penetrate one's bones." He smiled. "Could you be so kind as to pass me the casket? Surely you don't expect me to think that this necklace is all there is. I believe the other jewels must be in that bag young Master Crew is holding."

Clancy looked at Ruby as if to ask, *"What now?"*

Ruby looked back at him, her eyes intense. "Listen to me," she urged. "Do as he says." She was tapping her foot nervously for she could see the bulky shadow of Mr. Darling lurking in the passageway.

"Very wise, Ms. Redfort," said the Count.

Clancy lifted the casket from the bag. The threat of Mr. Darling became all too obvious as he lumbered into the cave.

"Listen," repeated Ruby.

Clancy hesitated, because suddenly he realized that with the tapping of her foot came another message, a message Clancy Crew heard loud and clear:

- .... .-. --- .-- / - .... . --

Clancy held the casket in front of him as if about to hand it across and then all of a sudden he threw the contents high in the air just as Ruby had told him to, causing a glittering cloud of exquisite jewel-drops to rain down into the waters below. The Count froze for exactly one second, just time enough for Ruby to snatch Eliza Fairbank's necklace from his loosened grip.

Mr. Darling lunged forward, stumbled on the Count's attaché case, and in so doing knocked Ruby off her tiny feet so she was flung high into the air and down into the tidal pool.

She resurfaced, her face ashen as she lunged out, trying to grab at the pool's edge, but to Clancy's horror she suddenly vanished beneath the water.

The Count watched as, in the blink of an eye, both Ruby and rubies disappeared from his reach. "Gone, gone forever to the deep!" he cried. He spun around to face Mr. Darling. "You incompetent fool!" he bellowed.

Mr. Darling, realizing his terrible error and fearing his master's wrath, stepped backward, a step too far, and with an almighty splash crashed into the water. He flailed around spluttering, trying to reach out for help. But help didn't come.

He gasped a last lungful of air before the ocean took him.

"Unfortunate," said the Count in a chilly tone. "Dear Mr. Darling's not much of a swimmer. I fear that will be the last we'll see of him, and no doubt *her* too." He spat out the word her. "Take your last breath, Ruby Redfort."

"Ruby won't drown!" shouted Clancy. "You're wrong about that!"

The Count smiled, his head cocked to one side, looking for all the world like a kindly uncle.

"Ordinarily, I would agree with you, Master Crew. But that octopus doesn't take prisoners."

Perhaps for a split, split second Clancy's blood stopped still in his veins; he had forgotten a giant octopus lurked there in the tidal pool.

. . . it can strangle the breath from the strongest man.

Ruby didn't stand a chance.

"Could I trouble you to pass my case? Oh, and just a warning, I wouldn't do anything stupid this time. I *will* kill you; make no bones about it."

Trembling more than a little, Clancy carefully passed the case over; it smelled of highly polished leather and a strange scent he couldn't identify. The Count unclasped and examined the contents, and his face fell.

"All broken?" he whispered. "Every one?" And then quite suddenly his face relaxed and he lifted out a small glass flask of dark liquid. He inspected it carefully and breathed a sigh of great relief. "One survived," he said. "And one is enough." He placed the flask gently back in the case. "The rubies were mere trinkets, but the main prize is saved." He picked up the bag. "Farewell, Master Crew. I do hope we shall meet again."

Clancy was stunned. "You're *not* going to *kill* me?" He didn't mean to say it, it just came out.

The Count smirked; this evidently rather tickled him. "I don't as a *rule* murder children, not unless they become particularly irksome. One a day will keep my temper at bay. And as you have witnessed"—he gestured toward the pool—"I've reached my daily quota, so I believe this *is* your lucky Tuesday."

He turned to leave, paused, and said, "Also it is so much more dramatic, don't you think, to leave one soul alive. If you should ever make it back to shore, which I somehow doubt, then perhaps you would be kind enough to pass on a message; tell LB 'the truth is safe with me.' She'll understand." He clapped his hands. "Now, hurry, hurry. There's no time to lose. The hours tick on, and the asteroid moves farther away, too far to exert any gravitational pull."

"What?" said Clancy. "What does that mean?"

"Ah," said the Count, his voice tripping lightly. "It means if you don't move quickly, you're going to die."

Clancy glanced down at the rising water. It was beginning to hiss and fizz.

He turned back to the Count, but the Count had gone, and in his place the rescue watch lay. A bitter joke. For what use was a watch when what you really needed was an apple barrel?

Not a Dream

The sea was cold; its chill ate into her very bones. But the temperature was not her immediate worry: a twenty-foot tentacle was.

She felt a sharp jolt, and it coiled around her. It was strong, it was crushing, and it was determined. Together the thing and Ruby traveled downward; turquoise became blue and blue became indigo and beyond that was a place without color.

Ruby held her breath and felt the pressure build inside her lungs.

She was drowning.

She had felt the sensation before. She had met the *thing* before: the dream was not a dream, it was a memory; she realized that now. She'd encountered this monster before, long, long ago.

The thing was an octopus so huge and so powerful she wondered how her three-year-old self had ever escaped it. Why had it let go its grip that day? This time she knew it would not; this time she knew it would drag her to the place where all the other children dwelled at the very bottom of the ocean; silently resting on the cold seabed.

Clancy counted the milliseconds. Ruby could hold her breath for 61,000 of them, he knew that very well. Sixty-one whole seconds, but not a second more. He watched as the numbers pulsed on his digital watch, tenths of seconds growing into whole seconds. Time so nearly up. In a fit of frustration, he picked up the rescue watch and tossed it at the cave wall; what use were all these life-saving gadgets if the one thing you needed was air? If only he could throw Ruby some of that, then she might have a chance.

And then he remembered — he could.

Ruby raised her gaze one last time. *Say good-bye to your world,* she told herself, and as she did so, she saw a little silver fish swimming down to escort her away to the underworld. It twinkled in the gloom, and she looked at it as it moved closer and closer and became not a fish but a buckle.

A breathing buckle.

Clancy's aim had been lucky, and the little device traveled straight to her. She reached out and felt it in her hand, clutching her fingers around it, bringing it to her mouth, and then she breathed.

Not that breathing was to be her salvation: she was still in the grip of a strangling sea monster. It curled her toward it, bringing her close to its strange and ancient face, drawing her to its razor-sharp beak. She looked into its eyes, but could see no flicker of mercy. She turned her face away from it and found herself looking into the dead eyes of Mr. Darling, his body squeezed lifeless by one of the monster's massive arms.

She twisted around, struggling now, fighting for her life, and suddenly out of the gloom came a tiny blue figure, growing larger with every heartbeat.

The figure was a diver — a man she thought she recognized. The man from her dreams. He latched on to the creature's great limbs, pulling and stabbing with a tiny weapon; a miniature diver fighting a sea giant with a tiny dagger.

What chance did he stand?

But a chance was all he needed: his knife struck lucky and the octopus released its orange-tentacled grip, spilling ink as it did so, and Ruby began to rise away from the beast, back through indigo, through blue, through turquoise, and to air.

She felt hands grabbing, pulling her free of the sea. She felt rock grazing her face. She tasted salt in her mouth and smelled dank, acrid air.

She heard a sound so muffled she could not identify it as a voice, and then through the blur she saw eyes she knew well.

She looked up.

"Clancy," she said, "did anyone ever tell you that you're the coolest boy alive?"

CHAPTER 48
The Truth Is Indigo

ARE YOU QUITE ALL RIGHT IN THE HEAD, RUBE?" Clancy looked concerned.

"I'm just telling you you're cool, Clance. Is there a law against telling someone they're cool?"

"No," said Clancy warily. "It's just it isn't like you to come out with a compliment like that—for no reason I mean."

"You think I don't pay compliments?" said Ruby.

"I think you swallowed a lot of seawater down there, Rube."

"*Sometimes* you can be a total bozo," she said. "But when you pull it together, you really are super cool."

"OK, Rube, maybe you should sit down. I'm getting worried here. How did you get away from that octopus?" he asked.

"A tiny man saved me, a miniature diver." This wasn't entirely inaccurate; against the colossal size of the octopus he had indeed appeared minuscule. But Clancy was not to know this, and now he was beginning to worry that perhaps Ruby had held her breath after all. Held it a minute too long. Holding your breath was considered a highly dangerous activity, he knew that.

"You threw me the buckle," she said, her words singsongy and happy. "Smartest kid I ever knew."

Clancy was relieved. OK, so maybe she was just in shock. That would explain things.

"Ruby, you know you're all blue?" he said. He looked at her hard, and it all began to dawn on him. Not only was she covered in indigo, but she had probably also swallowed some of the stuff too — drunk on indigo might be the best way to describe her state. He remembered what Ruby had told him about the ink of the giant octopus, the serum. She was blabbing the truth.

"Where did that Count go?" she asked.

"He sort of vaporized," said Clancy. "Not literally, but he suddenly wasn't there."

"He does that," said Ruby. "Though I'm real surprised he didn't kill you."

"Thanks for being so honest."

"I can't help it," said Ruby. "I swallowed the ink; I can't tell a lie."

"So I can ask you anything and you'll answer me truthfully?"

"Yes." She beamed.

"So what next?"

"We have to get out of here fast or we'll drown."

"What? You're kidding?"

"Can't kid, Clance."

"But why are we gonna drown?" Clancy was flapping.

"The currents are returning. I felt it. The asteroid is getting too far away."

"That's what the Count said." Clancy was beginning to panic.

"Any minute now, a giant whirlpool will swirl up and drag us down to the unexplored deep." The serum had the unfortunate side effect of making the speaker sound happy and relaxed, which was annoying for the person listening, especially when the news wasn't good. "It happened to my great-great-great-grandmother Martha." Ruby was smiling. "But she was lucky enough to climb inside an apple barrel."

"OK," said Clancy, trying to keep upbeat. "So we get a bit scratched, grazed even, but we'll live."

"No, I don't think so, Clance. You see, Martha's barrel would have contained air, and you need air to breathe while you're held under by the current, and to be honest even then you might suffocate. I mean, who knows how long we'll be under?"

Clancy looked around desperately. "You see an apple barrel anywhere?"

"No," said Ruby.

"Don't you have any ideas?" said Clancy.

"Too bad we don't have the rescue watch; it might have some device that could have saved us," said Ruby.

"But we do!" said Clancy, his voice bright again. "We do, the Count returned it."

"So where is it?" said Ruby.

"I threw it at the wall," said Clancy, pointing toward the furthest corner of the cave.

"You what? What kind of bozo are you?" She ran to look. "Darn it, Clance!" That part of the cave was filled with supplies, equipment, and demolition tools all left by the pirates. She picked her way through the rocks and rubble.

"Can you see it?" called an anxious Clancy.

"No," replied Ruby.

"It might have landed in something," said Clancy. "It sounded like it dropped inside a container of some sort."

Ruby looked up from her crouching position to see a large blue plastic cylinder; its lid lay on the ground next to it. Not an apple barrel exactly, but something that might do just as well. She peered inside; it was empty but for Bradley Baker's watch.

"You're a genius, Clance; we might just make it outta here after all."

Without further discussion the two of them worked to pull

the container out of the debris. The roar of the water was getting stronger, and as Ruby and Clancy climbed into the makeshift barrel, they were aware of the whirling water bubbling over the edge of the rock floor. They fumbled with the lid.

"Quick, duh brain! We don't have time for this."

"*Quick* yourself, buster!"

Finally, they lined it up right and twisted it in place, which was lucky for them because one second later there was an almighty crashing as several tons of water forced their way into the cave, and a half second later the barrel was lifted high into the air before being sucked down, down, down into the eye of the whirling thing.

"You know we still stand a very good chance of dying!" shouted Ruby merrily.

CHAPTER 49
The Truth Will Come Out

THE MAKESHIFT CRAFT WAS SUCKED DOWN into the whirling ocean current, tossed and tumbled by the returning Sibling tide. It seemed to spin and rise and sink and spin, over and over. They might have been underwater for several hours, days even, or just ten minutes, they really couldn't tell, but it felt like a very long time.

Finally, the pressure forced the barrel up and out, and they surfaced somewhere to the east of Little Sister rock. Not that Ruby and Clancy were aware of that—for all they knew they could be in the Atlantic or the Dead Sea. The only thing they were sure of was that they were bobbing on the water, a little bruised, very shaken, and slightly queasy.

"Am I still alive?" moaned Clancy.

"Yeah, but you look awful. You've turned a funny color."

"It's the barrel, bozo," said Clancy. "It's making us look blue. Although you already are blue."

Ruby inspected her arms. "I guess I am kinda blue."

"I hope that ink comes off," said Clancy, "or your parents are gonna be asking some pretty tricky questions. You do look weird."

"Yeah, well, you're not exactly looking picture-perfect there," said Ruby. "Kinda ugly actually."

"Thanks a whole bunch," muttered Clancy. "Speaking of ugly, what happened to Mr. Darling?"

Ruby wrapped her fingers around her throat. "Squeezed to death."

Clancy shivered. "I guess that octopus got his tentacles on him."

"Arms," corrected Ruby. "They're called arms."

"You've been calling them tentacles," Clancy pointed out. "I heard you say tentacles."

"Yeah, but they're called arms—technically they're arms."

"Could you quit being so pedantic?" said Clancy.

"I can't help it. I swallowed the truth serum, I gotta say what's on my mind."

"You always say what's on your mind. What's the difference?"

"Listen!" hissed Ruby. "Do you hear that?"

"The Sea Whisperer?" Clancy sounded alarmed.

"It's a boat, buster!" snapped Ruby.

Then they heard voices. Two of them.

"Do you think it's the pirates?" whispered Clancy. Their container wasn't spacious enough to flap in, but Clancy's arms were thinking about it.

"Do I look like I have X-ray vision?" said Ruby.

"Well, you certainly look weird," replied Clancy.

There wasn't a whole lot they could do, so they just sat there while they felt the barrel being tugged toward the boat and the boat's occupants struggling with the lid.

They breathed in fresh air and looked up at two puzzled faces.

"Kid, what are you doing in there?" said a familiar voice.

"Just holding my breath," replied Ruby, staring up at Hitch. She switched her gaze to the other face and was surprised to see Kekoa. "Hey, how come you're out and about? I thought you were in the hospital nearly dying?"

"I figured you'd be somewhere you shouldn't be," said Kekoa.

"You figured I'd be in a barrel?" said Ruby.

"No," said Kekoa flatly. "But I tried to call you and your signal was off, so I figured you'd gotten yourself somewhere you shouldn't be. Listening isn't your strongest attribute."

"I'll say," said Hitch. He leaned in and pulled out first Clancy and then Ruby. "Kekoa dragged herself out of her hospital bed and came to find me. She guessed where you'd be, kid."

"But how?" said Ruby.

"I did some reading while I was convalescing." Kekoa held up a copy of the orange book, *The Sea Whisperer.* "Not a myth after all. The monster, the wreck, the cave, the treasure, it all began to sound like it could be true."

Ruby's eyes took in the familiar cover and then they focused beyond the book on a man who was standing a little distance behind Agent Kekoa. He was clad in a blue wet suit that had a rip at the shoulder. His face was lined and brown from too many days in the scorching sun.

"Francesco Fornetti?" asked Ruby.

He smiled just barely — he looked all out of energy. "*Buon giorno,* Ruby Redfort."

She looked at him hard. "It *was* you down there!" she said.

He nodded.

"I read that book of yours," she continued. "It was interesting. I thought it was going to be pretty bad, you know, what with the professional ridicule and all, but I was actually impressed."

"You speak the truth," laughed Fornetti.

"It must have been hard knowing you were right about something when everyone else thought you were a looney tune," said Ruby. "A madman, a complete ding —"

Clancy clamped a hand over her mouth.

"Sorry, Mr. Fornetti. She's drunk a little too much ink and

doesn't know how to keep her mouth shut. But thanks for saving her life."

"Ah, no problem," said the diver. "It was my pleasure."

"Yeah, that's right," said Ruby, freeing herself from Clancy's grip. "I owe you one."

Francesco Fornetti raised his thumb and forefinger. "Two," he croaked.

"How'd ya mean, two?" said Ruby.

"You owe me two. I saved your life twice. Once before, many, many years ago," he said.

"That was you?" said Ruby. "You're the one who rescues me in my dream, my dream that's not a dream?"

He nodded again. "I was sitting on the deck with your parents. You fell into the ocean, on purpose I think; the sea called to you. Your mother had a broken arm, and your father had dislocated his shoulder, but he went to save you anyway, and got caught somehow in the anchor chain. So I dived in and there I saw this incredible cephalopod, this octopus bigger than any octopus I had seen in all my long days, what they call the Sea Whisperer. It had grabbed you. I fought it and to my amazement it let you go. Why, I don't know. It was a magnificent creature, and one I never expected to see a second time, let alone a third."

"But why did my mom and dad never tell me?" Ruby found it hard to believe that anyone could keep such a story from her.

"I never told your parents about the Sea Whisperer. It was enough, for them, the terror of their daughter so close to drowning in their beloved ocean. I didn't want to mention a sea monster on top of that." He shrugged. "So I never breathed a word."

All those dreams, thought Ruby. *Not dreams at all.*

Clancy looked at them both. He was excited, his whole face bright. "But this is great," he said to Francesco Fornetti, his arms flapping. "The octopus is real, and you can prove it! You can tell everyone. Now they'll see that you're not a nutcase after all. I mean, not a complete crazy."

"No, no," said Francesco, holding up a weathered hand. "That must remain a secret barely even whispered among friends. A creature from the ancient deep deserves to be left in peace. It's enough I saw her again." He looked at Ruby. "That *you* saw her again." He clearly meant what he said, and there was no point arguing. The Sea Whisperer was a secret that should be held tightly.

And so Ruby just nodded.

CHAPTER 50
Hard to Explain

WHILE HITCH RETURNED KEKOA to her hospital bed, and Francesco Fornetti went back to his boat to rest and dream, Clancy and Ruby returned to Cedarwood Drive. It was around midday by now, and they were hoping to sneak back into the house unnoticed so they could scrub the blue from Ruby's skin and hide out until the truth serum wore off. Clancy thought this might be a good idea, or things could get very complicated; this was not the time for straight answers.

Regrettably, though, this is not what happened. They were halfway up the eucalyptus when they heard a voice shout, "Ruby, Clancy, what are you doing out of school?"

Clancy and Ruby looked down at the three faces looking up. The Redforts were standing there, drinks in hand, and behind them Mrs. Digby was holding a tray of exotic-looking nibbles. Sabina was shielding her eyes from the sun.

"Get down here right now," she ordered.

Reluctantly, they climbed back down.

Sabina had her hands on her hips and was launching into what would have been a rather long rant.

"Look at your wet suit—it's in absolute tatters. Can't you take care of anything? Is that the one your father and I . . . why are you wearing a wetsuit? Why are . . ." She stopped midsentence, for she had noticed something very strange: Ruby was not looking the right color.

Brant spilled his drink down his shirt front, and Mrs. Digby said a word considered unsuitable for polite company.

Clancy was right: it *was* going to be tricky to explain the blue to Ruby's folks. Her face was indigo-colored and so were her hands, her arms, and her legs.

"Heavens, child!" scolded Mrs. Digby. "What in tarnation have you been doing? You look like a giant blueberry."

"It's octopus ink," said Ruby.

"What?" said her father.

Clancy kicked her hard on the shin.

"I got pulled under by this giant cephalopod," said Ruby. "It nearly strangled me to death, but then I got rescued by Francesco Fornetti, and Clance and me climbed into a barrel and—"

"Rube!" said Clancy firmly. "I'm sorry, Mr. Redfort. I think the sun got to her."

"Call Dr. Makeland," said Sabina.

"But what were you doing?" asked her father.

"Looking for the Fairbank rubies," said Ruby merrily. "The Count tried to kill me with jellyfish, but you know what? I found them anyway, and then he tried to kill me with an octopus."

"The child's raving," said Mrs. Digby.

"No, better call Dr. Grenveld," said Sabina. "She's good with heads."

Ruby reached into the small dive bag that was attached to her dive belt and pulled out the most exquisite rubies that Sabina or indeed anyone there had ever seen.

"The child has robbed Keller's jeweler's!" squealed Mrs. Digby.

"Well, I'll be darned," said Brant.

"Oh, my!" said Sabina. "However did you come by those?"

Clancy held his breath.

"Like I said," replied Ruby. "I found them!"

A Real Emergency

IT WAS TUESDAY, and Ruby was looking forward to an evening watching *Crazy Cops* and stuffing popcorn into her mouth. Her folks were going out to a cocktail party, and Mrs. Digby was joining her fellow poker players in East Twinford; Hitch, who had come up with a plausible explanation for the recent wild events, was in his apartment listening to music. Dr. Grenveld had ordered that Ruby be kept at home for a few days just to make sure that the sunstroke had not caused any lasting damage, and so here she was home alone on a Tuesday night.

She scratched the husky behind the ears. "I guess it's just you and me, Bug old friend." Just what she needed, a bit of downtime.

As soon as everyone had left the house, Ruby padded over to the refrigerator and poured herself a glass of banana milk, piled a plate high with cookies, and set the popcorn popper popping. The telephone in the kitchen rang.

"Twinford lost property department, how may we assist you?"

"What?" came the reply. Ruby recognized Mrs. Lemon's panicky voice. Mrs. Lemon was a very panicky sort of person.

"Oh, hi, Elaine. It's Ruby."

"Is your mother in?" she asked.

"Uh-uh," said Ruby.

"Your father then?" Elaine Lemon's voice rose slightly.

"Uh-uh," said Ruby.

"Mrs. Digby, she must be there?" Elaine was sounding like she had swallowed helium.

"Gone to poker," said Ruby, munching on a cookie.

"But you're there?" said Elaine.

"I guess I am," said Ruby.

Ruby failed to recognize the relief in Mrs. Lemon's voice and didn't register what was coming.

"Is your skin OK these days?" Mrs. Lemon asked.

"Fine, Elaine. Thanks for inquiring." Ruby had forgotten about her earlier lie, and in doing so had forgotten one of her rules: **RULE 32: TELL ONE LIE AND GET READY TO TELL A WHOLE LOT MORE.**

"Thank goodness," said Mrs. Lemon. "I need you to take care of Archie. I've got this emergency thing."

"Ah, the thing is, Elaine . . . I mean, I'm not so great with babies. I'm not really qualified, you know — not for the whole baby thing."

"Oh, you don't need to be! You babysit other kids, right?"

"Yeah, but not actual babies. I mean I don't really get them, and they don't get me." Ruby was floundering.

"Oh, you'll love Archie — he's a dear, no trouble at all. And it *is* an emergency."

"An emergency? A real emergency?" asked Ruby.

"Oh, yes. It's an emergency all right."

"Darn it!" hissed Ruby under her breath. What could she do? "OK, I guess, if it's an emergency."

Elaine Lemon was standing on the front doorstep approximately two and a half minutes later.

"So what's the deal?" said Ruby as Archie was bundled toward her.

"Bethany Mule is having a swimwear sale and I didn't want to miss it."

"That's it?" said Ruby. "That's the whole big emergency?"

But before there was a chance for Ruby to deposit Archie back in his mother's arms, Elaine Lemon was running down the steps, jumping into her car, and backing out of the drive.

"Oh, brother!" cursed Ruby.

She called Clancy, but he said he couldn't make it; his dad

was expecting his family to be all present and correct at some ambassadorial party. Del was at a basketball game, Mouse was with her cousins, Red had twisted her ankle and couldn't even hobble, and Elliot was not answering the phone. She called down to Hitch, but his reply came back, "You're on your own, kid."

Oh well, how hard can babysitting a baby be? thought Ruby.

She switched on the TV and Archie smiled. He waved his arms as the theme tune to *Crazy Cops* played. *No sweat,* thought Ruby.

Detective Despo walked into the frame and Archie started to howl.

Ruby ignored him.

Detective Despo was running down an alley pursuing a suspect.

Archie howled like he was fit to burst.

Detective Despo froze, the muzzle of a gun pressed to the back of his head.

Archie puked.

Turned out babysitting a baby was *hard*.

The green light on the rescue watch flashed and bleeped. Archie howled louder.

Ruby pressed the receive button on the watch.

"Redfort?" came a gravelly voice.

It was LB.

LB: *What are you doing, strangling a cat?*

RUBY: *Babysitting.*

LB: *I didn't peg you as the mushy type.*

RUBY: *I'm not, believe me.*

LB: *So we need you to come in for a debriefing.*

RUBY: *I know but I'm a little tied up with this babysitting deal right now.*

LB: *What, now you're suddenly a Girl Scout?*

RUBY: *What do you suggest I do, dump the baby?*

LB: *Improvise, isn't that what Girl Scouts are good at?*

RUBY: *I wouldn't know. I never joined.*

LB: *Shame, so what exactly do you know?*

RUBY: *The Count is working for someone else. He wasn't only after the rubies, he was there for something else.*

LB: *How do you know?*

RUBY: *The Count said, "Tell LB the truth is safe with me."*

LB: *He said that to you?*

Ruby paused: she was going to have to tell a lie, a white lie, because of course the Count had told Clancy, not her, and this was not a time for telling the truth.

"Yes," she said.

LB was quiet for a moment, and then she seemed to register Archie's howling and said, "Redfort, put that baby on the phone."

Ruby held the receiver to Archie's ear, and in a matter of seconds the baby stopped howling and peace was restored to the Redfort home.

Ruby took the phone. "What did you say to him?"

"Something I learned in Girl Scouts," said LB. "Too bad you never joined."

THINGS I KNOW:
....

That the Count took a vial of the truth serum.
That he is working for someone bigger than him.

THINGS I DON'T KNOW:
....

Who he is working for.
What he is planning to do with the serum.
What LB said to that baby.

Ruby Redfort

WHAT RUBY AND CLANCY SAID IN MUSIC CLASS

RUBY:

```
-.-. .-.. .- -. -.-. -.-- --..-- /
-.-. .... .. .-.. .-.. / --- ..- - /
-- .- -. .-.-.- / -.-- --- ..- / .-.. --- --- -.- /
.-.. .. -.- . / -.-- --- ..- .----. .-. . /
.- -... --- ..- - / - --- / -.. .. .
```

CLANCY, CHILL OUT MAN. YOU LOOK LIKE YOU'RE ABOUT TO DIE

CLANCY:

```
- .... .- - .----. ... / -.-. ..- --.. /
.. / .- -- / .- -... --- ..- - /
- --- / -.. .. . --..-- / - .... .. ... /
... .- - ..- .-. -.. .- -.-- /
-- --- .-. -. .. -. --.
```

THAT'S CUZ I'M ABOUT TO DIE, THIS SATURDAY MORNING

RUBY:

- .... . .-. . / .- .-. . / -. --- /

... .- .-. -.- ... / .. -. /

- .-- .. -. ..-. --- .-. -.. / -... .- -.--

THERE ARE NO SHARKS IN TWINFORD BAY

CLANCY:

.--. .-. --- ...- . / .. -

PROVE IT

RUBY:

--. . . . --.. --..-- / - .... . -.-- /

-.-. .- .-.. .-.. /

- .... / -- ..- ... .. -.-. . ..--..

GEEZ, THEY CALL THIS MUSIC?

A note on the Chime Melody musical code,

with help from Dr. Thomas Gardner, music consultant

This is how Ruby cracks the code:

She first decides to ignore the synthetic music in the background, which she assumes is designed as a distraction, and to concentrate on the melodic fragments laid over it.

She starts with the principle that each note in the strange music must represent a letter.

But the question is, what notation was used to create the music? Even though Ruby thinks it's unlikely, she starts by trying the Northern European note naming convention of A, B, C, D, E, F, G, H (where H is actually B and B is actually B flat). But this doesn't get her anywhere. Nor does the twelve-tone system, or any of the other scale systems, such as Japanese, Indian, or Arabic (though since the Chime Melody music is very definitely in equal temperament she realizes this is a long shot).

Once those more esoteric options are ruled out, Ruby tries the English and American system of seven notes — A, B, C, D, E, F, G — and finally starts to get somewhere.

The first thing she realizes is that there are no flats or sharps used in the melody: there are only the seven plain notes: A, B, C, D, E, F, and G. This means that the person setting the code had to come up with a way to use only seven notes to represent all twenty-six letters of the alphabet.

Eventually she realizes that the way they have done this is to apply effects to the notes that tell the decoder to shift the letters forward. She notes down all sorts of details that she notices — crescendos, articulations, speed changes — but works out that these are all red herrings. What DOES turn out to be important is the glissando that she can hear.

She quickly discovers that if a note is played with an upward glissando, it shifts the corresponding letter forward by seven places. Thus the musical note A, played with an upward glissando, becomes the letter H instead of A, and the musical note G, with an upward glissando, becomes the letter N.

Similarly, a downward glissando shifts the corresponding letter forward by fourteen places. The musical note A, played with a downward glissando, becomes the letter O.

Finally, the letters V to Z are represented by the notes A to D, played with a tremolo (though these letters don't appear in the example code).

The best way to understand this is to look at this table:

Letter	Played as is	Note with glissando up	Note with glissando down	Note with tremolo
A	A			
B	B			
C	C			
D	D			
E	E			
F	F			
G	G			
H		A		
I		B		
J		C		
K		D		
L		E		
M		F		
N		G		
O			A	
P			B	
Q			C	
R			D	
S			E	
T			F	
U			G	
V				A
W				B
X				C
Y				D
Z				E

A note on
Count von Viscount's
static code
by Marcus du Sautoy,
super-geek consultant

One of the most common codes used across the planet is binary,
or digital, code. It is not a secret code, but is a powerful way to
store and communicate information. Pictures, music, movies,
the sound of a voice, in fact everything that is sent across the
Internet is changed into a stream of zeros and ones.

Take a black-and-white picture. To see how to change the
picture into zeros and ones, first you need to pixelate the picture.
You draw a square grid over the picture, then you color a square
black if the majority of the image in the square is black, and color
the square white if it's mostly white. Each colored square is called
a pixel. The combination of the pixels produces a rough version of
the picture. The finer the square grid, the better the representation
of the picture. The pixelated picture can then be changed into code.
The black squares are represented by zeros and the white squares

by ones. Then 001110101000 ... is code for: color the first two pixels in the grid black, the next three white, then black, and so on.

More complicated versions of this process can change a color picture, a movie, music, or even a voice into zeros and ones.

Now, if you want to make a picture or a message secret, there is a clever way to hide the message if it is made up of zeros and ones. You can take a pixelated black-and-white picture and pull it apart into two separate black-and-white pictures in such a way that the two separate images look like a random mess. But when you print them on transparent sheets and put one on top of the other, the original picture appears as if by magic.

To change the picture into the two random images: first, take the square grid for the original picture and divide each square into four smaller squares. In the encrypted pictures, these two-by-two squares have two squares colored white and two squares colored black. If you check, there are six different ways you can color a two-by-two grid where half the squares are white and the other half are black.

The first encrypted picture just consists of a genuinely random selection of these two-by-two black-and-white blocks. To create the second encrypted picture, you need to look at the original picture. Place the random picture over the top. Take each two-by-two block in the random picture you've created.

Above: How to combine the original picture and the first encrypted picture to form the second encrypted picture

Hold up to the light . . .

If that block sits over a white square in the original image, then the two-by-two block in the same position in the second encrypted picture is chosen to be the *same* two-by-two block. If it's over a black square, then make the corresponding two-by-two block in the second encrypted picture the *opposite* of the one in the random picture (where black and white squares are swapped over).

The second encrypted picture you've created looks as random as the first. But now when you place the two pictures on top of each other something magic happens. The original picture seems to appear out of the combination of the two random images.

Hold this page and the next page with the pointing finger up to the light and look at the random-seeming picture at left. Line up the rectangular images on both pages, and the light shining through the pictures should reveal a message. Do you see it?

Now, how does this work?

The combination of a two-by-two grid in the first random picture with the *opposite* two-by-two grid in the second picture creates one big black pixel. If the two-by-two grids are the same, then although the combination doesn't create a completely white pixel, nevertheless it is white enough that looking at the combined picture, your eyes see the same combination of black and white pixels that made up the unencrypted picture.

In the book, Ruby encounters a similar code using sound when the three static tapes combine to form the sound of a voice. This code would have been built using pictures too, in a very similar way to what has just been described. This is how the Count's static code was created:

If, instead of a picture, you take a recording of a voice, you can translate that using binary code into a sequence of zeros and ones. Then translate *that* into a black-and-white picture. Then apply the same process as above to pull it apart into two random pictures consisting of

Hold up to the light . . .

black-and-white pixels. Translate these two random pictures back into zeros and ones. If you now translate this into sound again, the two messages sound like random static noise. But play them together and, like the two pictures combining, you will hear a message appearing from the static.

Clancy and Ruby stumbled on a version of this code. The secret message had been pulled apart into three random static tracks that sounded like white noise, but which, when combined, revealed a message to Count von Viscount that led Ruby and Clancy to the rubies.

Marcus du Sautoy

A note on Arvo Pärt

ARVO PÄRT, BORN IN 1935 IN ESTONIA, is a real and much-celebrated classical composer, predominantly of sacred music. He is known for working in a minimalist generative style, using his mathematically-based compositional technique, *tintinnabuli*.

In addition, Pärt has been known to encode messages into his music, as Ruby knows very well. In his *Cantus in Memoriam Benjamin Britten*, for example, the word BACH (simply rendered by the notes B, A, C, and H) is played as a repeated motif by the string orchestra as a hidden tribute to the composer Johann Sebastian Bach.

Acknowledgments

Thank you to Rachel Folder; without her I would have been in quite a muddle. She did very well to untangle a tangled plot and generally push me into picking up my pen when I didn't feel like it. To Thomas Gardner for composing (and explaining) the Chime Melody code on very, very short notice. To Marcus du Sautoy for inspired code ideas and general brilliance. To David Mackintosh for exquisite design. Thank you to A. D. for inspiration. To Lucy Mackay for pointing out flaws in the nicest possible way. To Lucy Vanderbilt for being authentically American and helping make Ruby appear that way. To my editor Nick Lake for being calm as well as clever. Last, huge thanks to my publisher Ann-Janine Murtagh for, as usual, being wise, supportive, and a pleasure to work with.

Hey, Buster!

How many times can Ruby Redfort defeat the villains threatening Twinford?

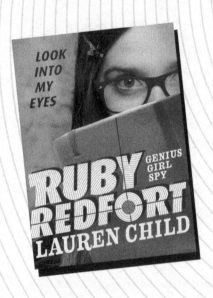

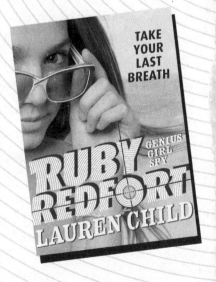

LAUREN CHILD, the U.K. Children's Laureate, first introduced the character of Ruby Redfort in her three award-winning, best-selling CLARICE BEAN novels. Since then she has been inundated with letters from fans asking for RUBY REDFORT books. Those letters worked, because this is number two in the six-book series.

Lauren is also the creator of the CHARLIE AND LOLA books, as well as associate producer on the TV show of the same name. Her books have won many prizes, including the Smarties Prize (four times), the Kate Greenaway Medal, and the Red House Children's Book Award.

The RUBY REDFORT series features codes and puzzles created with the help of super-geek consultant Marcus du Sautoy, Simonyi Professor for the Public Understanding of Science at Oxford University and all-around genius.

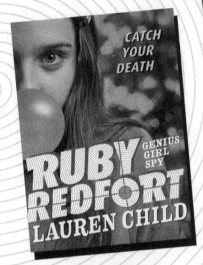

FEEL THE FEAR

GENIUS GIRL SPY

RUBY REDFORT

LAUREN CHILD

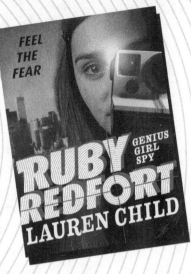

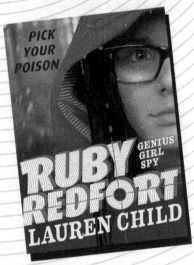

CATCH YOUR DEATH

RUBY REDFORT

GENIUS GIRL SPY

LAUREN CHILD

PICK YOUR POISON

RUBY REDFORT

GENIUS GIRL SPY

LAUREN CHILD

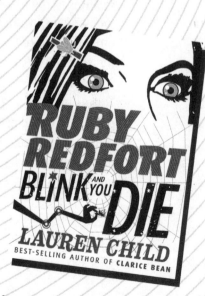

RUBY REDFORT

BLINK AND YOU DIE

LAUREN CHILD

BEST-SELLING AUTHOR OF CLARICE BEAN